Out in the Cold

Out in the Cold

A Western Double

Levi Johnson Mountain Man Scout

Book Eight

Ash Lingam

Out in the Cold
Paperback Edition

Wolfpack Publishing
1707 E. Diana Street
Tampa, Florida 33610

www.wolfpackpublishing.com

Paperback ISBN 979-8-89567-571-7
Ebook ISBN 979-8-89567-570-0

Contents

Out In The Cold

Rocky Mountain Fever

Out in the Cold

Out In The Cold

Levi Johnson Mountain Man Scout 15

This novel is dedicated to my son, Dr. Chaska Carlos Walton.
He couldn't have made me a prouder father.

"Two things are infinite: the universe and human stupidity; and I'm not so sure about the universe."

Albert Einstein

The Squabble

Snow came down, slanting like rays of light, sparkling in the sun, nearly frozen. It appeared in such quantities, nobody could remember a harder snowfall —at least for the people living in the compound. Rusty Steel and Angus McFarlin had decided to strike out two weeks prior for parts only known to them. With the young men marrying, the testosterone levels were high in all the males, and the two elders dared anyone treat them special due to their ages. Both were too proud for their own good.

Even Angus, who had sworn off trapping the year before, signed up for yet another challenge. They seemed determined to prove they could still do anything the young men could and even better. Their target was the best quality cold-water beaver they had ever seen with a plushness nearly unknown by then, ten years later. Where they were going, the water was freezing, and although it had been a decade prior, they had trapped the best beaver they had ever seen in this secret spot they had discovered.

It was so far off the beaten path that few humans neared, and none ever stayed. It was too high in the mountains, so the risks were greater than ever, but the prize far outweighed the danger. Especially as they were out to prove themselves to their apprentices and maybe even to themselves, it was a while since they took on the high altitudes and dangerous elements of the Rocky Mountain winters and Mother Nature. Now, they had decided to do just that.

Levi Johnson and Will Forrester headed off for the last hunt before the brutal winter set in. They already had sufficient supplies, but an extra reserve always helped. This also gave them a few days away from their new lives as husbands before the weather locked them down. It seemed to happen before they knew it—suddenly, they found themselves wed for better or for worse. Now, they would have a chance to exchange opinions on married life. They headed north of the big Crow stronghold a half day's ride above the compound and beyond that a few more days.

Back at the warm and comfortable cabins, Virgil, Dennis, and Joseph sat wrapped in bearskin coats and raccoon hats as they smoked ceramic pipes on Rusty's porch and sipped on glasses of whiskey. They were ensuring they got all the time possible outdoors before being confined to the cabins when a series of blizzards and then January and February weather set in.

This time was set aside for the impossible weather, for staying indoors and curing the newly trapped pelts they had accumulated over the fall and winter. The only ventures outdoors would be grabbing a couple of arms full of firewood, gathering snow for water, or going to the outhouses.

That summer, as they had renovated the last cabin at the northern edge of the compound to accommodate the new couples, they dug out a small cellar under Rusty's cabin. A heavy timber door with a thick lock led down the clay steps to the storeroom. Javelin hams, sides of elk, and deer hung from hooks in the ceiling. Garlic, Indian corn, and chili peppers, among other dried food, accompanied the meat.

The cabin's front door swung open with a bang, and both women stormed out. Betty cocked her leg and perched her fist on her hip. Dahteste was behind her, but she wrapped her fingers around the handle of her knife as her eyes shot daggers at the surprised mountain men.

They were all three taken aback, and Marshal Walker grumbled, "What in the world has gotten into you two? Y'all look to be fightin' mad."

"The last time I looked, your house had a porch, too, Mister Dennis Breed," Betty Crockett Forrester growled. "Don't expect to spend the day here, leaving a mess for us to clean up. Look at the floor; it's covered in tobacco ashes, and yesterday, you left your dirty glasses on the table. I'm not here to do a wife's job for a man who's not my husband, nor is Dahteste. The porch's edge isn't three feet away, so you'd think you could reach over to empty your pipes. Plus, we decided we wanted some time without the presence of men. Sometimes males can be a nuisance."

"Well, pardon me for living," Joseph retorted. "You're awful sassy, ain't cha? And who made you the boss of Rusty's cabin while he and Angus are gone? I figure we can sit where we danged well, please, and you can't do nothin' about it."

Of course, such bold talk from a guest at the compound wasn't looked on lightly. Dennis was instantly on his feet, but on the way, his eyes shot daggers at the marshal.

"Girls, please, don't listen to that fool. He has no say-so whatsoever here at our home. Of course, we can use my porch. We just came here out of habit. Get a broom, Virgil, and let's sweep things up. I apologize for being a burden. I'm afraid I never even thought. Mind you, I know that's no excuse." Then he turned on the marshal and said, "Now, unless you want to sleep outside tonight, you better move your behind over to my porch. It has the exact same view. Tonight, you can clean up after us for making all this trouble for Levi and Will's wives. If Rusty was here, he'd be at cha with a hammer. He don't take kindly to guests sassing off."

"Ah, come on, I didn't mean it like that," Joseph replied. "It just came out the wrong way. We didn't make that much of a mess anyway."

"You have a habit of doin' that," Virgil said. "You know, lettin' your words come out the wrong way."

They stepped off the porch, and Dennis pulled off his fur cap, doubled his arm across his waist, and bowed formally.

"I do hope you ladies will accept our apology," Mountain Dennis said.

"And please don't tell Levi and Rusty," Virgil added, "or even the captain. If not, there will be trouble for sure. They're all sticklers on manners in the presence of women. Levi said his mother told him to treat ladies just like he treated her—with the utmost respect. And without women, none of us would be here at all. I doubt you wanna spend the winter in the Crow camp even if they'd have ya, after you mouthed off to Dahteste. She's a war chief, ya know, and one of Hachta's favorites."

"Next, you'll be scratchin' at the snow, tryin' to uncover bugs and worms," Joseph retorted. "You're already clucking like a hen."

Deep footprints in the snow followed the men to the next cabin, where they took their places under the roof. This time, they all had their eyes on Rusty's place. Both women glared at them, then they turned and walked inside, slamming the door behind them. The bang echoed across the mountains and back.

Betty and Dahteste's eyes locked. They were full of laughter. They slapped their hands over their mouths to stifle the chuckles, which became gut-wrenching fits of hilarity. They knew the men in the other cabin were close enough to hear, but just the same, they couldn't stop. Tears streamed down their faces as they rolled on the floor before the fire. Flames danced in their pupils as their eyes crinkled.

Finally, Betty caught her breath and said, "Joseph sure is a sassy sort, ain't he? I thought Dennis was gonna shoot him then and there. He's right, too. Levi said Rusty is as serious as the plague when it comes to manners. Rusty doesn't tolerate poorly behaved men—or women, either."

"Nor do we." Dahteste smiled. "I'll make some coffee and bacon, and you can make the biscuits. Yours come out better than mine."

Sunlight spilled into the cabin from the front window. Particles of dust danced in the rays of light. The smell of fried eggs, bacon, biscuits, and coffee filled the room. The girls gobbled down their meals like they hadn't eaten for days. The little rebellion had gotten their dander up, making them vibrate with energy, eventually leaving them spent, especially after all that laughing. Both held their sides where they had a stitch. Even while shoveling food into their mouths, the odd snicker escaped them, spraying food onto the table, which just made them laugh more.

Once their pie pans were empty, Betty got a mischievous look in those sky-blue peepers of hers, and her mouth curled at the edges. She uncorked the whiskey bottle Dennis forgot on the table and poured a dose into each cup.

Mrs. Forrester giggled, shrugged her shoulders, and asked, "Who's gonna ever know? Do you even drink?"

Dahteste shook her head and said, "Chief Hachta says it is forbidden for the members of his tribe to drink White men's spirits. He says the fiery liquid captures your soul and never lets you go."

"That's for people who drink too much and do so every day." Betty laughed some more. "Anyway, today we're here all alone in our compound. Whatever we do, only you and I will know." Her grin grew so wide that Dahteste could see her tonsils.

The Crow woman put the tin cup to her nose and whiffed, instantly wrinkling her nose and frowning. "I don't know about this."

"Come on, don't be a chicken." Betty chuckled. "The worst that can happen is we get groggy and fall asleep. If the men notice, we can say we had a siesta."

"Do you really think they will be back here to bother us today?" Dahteste guffawed.

The Crow woman took a sip of the labeled whiskey and made a face like she just sucked on a lemon. Then came the fiery feeling as the alcohol burned its way down her throat. Surprise showed on Dahteste's face, and a fit of giggles captured Betty, and she couldn't stop.

At first, Dahteste pushed her glass away like she didn't want anymore. She kept smacking her lips, trying to get the bad taste out. But after a few minutes passed, that fuzzy feeling hit her like a kiss of fresh air. She smiled as she heard a strange buzzing sound between her ears, and she felt warm all over despite the cold. Betty came out with a fresh pot of coffee, and again, she put a splash into each cup. After a second thought, she added another.

"I've hardly drunk at all in the past," Betty admitted. "The Crockett family are strict Baptist and not the kind to drink. There's more than one kind of Baptist, though."

"Is a Baptist the same thing as a Christian?" Dahteste asked.

"Of course we are." Betty laughed at her ignorance. "Didn't Levi teach you anything about White people and our religions?"

"Levi spends most of his time learning how to live in the wilderness and not lose his life," Dahteste replied. "Not like your captain, who believes he has to save the world."

Now, both women sipped at their harsh liquor unconsciously, and little by little, they became utterly inebriated. They drank far more than they had ever intended. Somehow, they now looked at an empty bottle, and their heads spun around and around.

Betty's eyes were locked in cages of hot wires, red-rimmed. You could almost see the smoke come out of her ears. Somehow, she was offended by Dahteste's remark about her husband, but she couldn't remember exactly what that was.

Dahteste never even saw it coming when Betty drew back her fist and stepped into the punch. It hit her square in the jaw, making a loud crack. Blood sprayed, and her knees buckled, then her eyes rolled. She blinked repeatedly as she sat up. The Crow woman held her jaw in her hand and wiggled until it popped.

When they came busting through the front window, they sounded like two wildcats in a life-and-death struggle. Tiny glass squares fell on them like rain and crunched under their hands and feet as they struggled. The White and Red women rolled across the porch, knocking over tables and chairs. A shiny brass spittoon rolled across the floor, slinging a fine spray of brown spit. Finally, they hit the snow with a thud. Dahteste managed to get on Betty's back and pushed her face deep into the icy crystals. Blood ran from the corner of the Indian's mouth and down her cheek, dripping into the white powder.

Footsteps came running, rushing to the women, but they were oblivious to their surroundings. They were totally focused on inflicting pain on their opponent. Marshal Walker manhandled the six-foot-tall Betty, but it took both Virgil and Dennis to subdue the small-framed woman war chief. She kicked, bit, and spat like a lioness.

"Why, they smell like a brewery," Virgil said, surprised. "I do believe they're both as drunk as skunks."

"What were you two fighting about?" Marshal Walker asked. He knew how to sound like an authority, especially with people who had too much liquor.

"I don't rightly know," Betty replied as she rubbed a knot on her head the size of an egg.

"I don't remember either," Dahteste said just before she dropped on all fours and upchucked her breakfast. She wobbled for a moment, then fell onto her side.

As soon as Betty smelled the vomit, she joined in involuntarily. Her body responded all on its own. Both women lay in the snow, purging themselves of the liquid poison. Finally, they were too sick to fight.

Hell Froze Over

As soon as the aging Rusty Steel saw the ring around the moon, he knew it was a bad sign—a 22-degree halo stood twenty thousand feet above his head. Earlier that day, he had noticed the high cirrus clouds, which had given him pause. The silver globe stood just over the horizon and seemed so big it dwarfed the mountains before it. He turned his eyes toward the heavens, and his face reflected a pearly glow. It was already too cold for this time of year, but in the Rocky Mountains, the weather changed with a hint of a breeze from the wrong direction.

Now, they were afraid that a full-blown blizzard was on its way. As veteran mountain men, he and Angus McFarlin knew they had to find someplace safe to shelter, or they would freeze like the icicles hanging from the limbs of trees.

Heavy snowshoes left tracks like two snails as they descended, even visible in the moonlight. Their breaths disappeared before their faces, and sweat dripped off their noses with every step. Two sleds full of first-quality pelts followed the trappers. They trudged forward with the straps over their chests and shoulders as they pulled like old mules.

Of course, horses were out of the question in so much snow. They would be lost instantly in the deep drifts. That was why Rusty designed these sleds more like luges—extra-long to distribute the weight evenly. The three six-inch-wide wooden runners ensured they didn't sink in the powder.

Their shirts stuck to their backs despite the moon replacing the sun, and the temperatures began to tumble. Their hearts hammered in their ears, but they knew they couldn't stop. Now, they were racing against the clock.

"How ya holdin' up there, old pard?" Rusty asked. "I could swear there were two caves just over there, but I don't see any sign. Still, I know I ain't lost. I've never got lost in my life."

"Do you remember who you're talkin' to?" Angus smiled, despite the weather. "I can't see so good by the moon's light, but I'd say the entrances to those caves got buried in the snow. I reckon we've got eight or ten feet of white powder under us right now."

"That makes sense." Rusty groaned. "I don't know of another place to weather the storm, and I doubt it's gonna take too long to hit. Maybe as early as tomorrow afternoon."

"These sleds ain't helpin' us go any faster, either," Angus replied. "If it gets too bad, we might have to cut our losses and run. The two of us on foot are about as fast as anybody around these parts, local Indians included. The way it is, we're takin' four times as long dragging a hundred pounds each."

"Don't even let that little worm work its way into your tiny, weak mind," Rusty growled. "We came up here for those pelts, and I'll be danged if I'm gonna go back home without 'em. Come hell or high water, I swear I will not leave a single fur behind, and you know I don't take an oath lightly."

A thunderclap and a rush of cold wind set the pines gnashing. Angus' snow-drenched hat brim fell to his shoulders. Rusty had his raccoon cap pulled snugly over his ears. Rifles were slung over their shoulders, adding to the weight, and another lay on each sled. Angus carried two flintlock pistols in his belt, and Steel had four pushed into his pants. The problem wasn't something they could shoot, stab, or wrestle, though. It was a force beyond all others, that which the Native Americans called the Great Mother.

Later that night, when they were too cold and tired to carry on, they stopped for a few hours of sleep. They dug out long holes the size of their bodies on the leeward side of their sleds. This protected them from the icy wind that would come that night. Still, it would be nothing when compared to what they expected the following day. They were probably looking at a total whiteout.

Despite the situation, both men fell into a deep slumber in minutes. Each had a pistol in his fist and a rifle on either side. They knew this may still be land claimed by the Blackfeet Nation, so they planned to sleep a few hours and carry on their way. They didn't have time to stop anymore anyway, and even then, they knew they could never beat the storm. All they could do was hope they spotted a shelter where they could weather out the blizzard.

They rose with the first sparkles like diamonds on the blanket of snow, which rolled brightly for miles. The sun came alive with the color of steel, and they stepped into the freezing cold wind. Still, pockets of shadows lingered with the sun as it still lay low on the horizon.

Rusty stopped dead in his tracks, holding out his arm to stop Angus beside him. McFarlin looked questioningly. Steel squatted and inspected tracks crossing their path. As the bass drums boomed in their chests, they were sure the tracks were those of Indians but had no idea which tribe. Ten years before, the Blackfeet Indians had run them off the creeks and streams. That was why they forged deeper until they found the significant Crow stronghold and their future mountain home. Was it just about to happen again?

Rusty looked up and asked, "Do you reckon there're Blackfeet huntin' White men in this weather?"

Angus shook his head in wonder. "I didn't think even Blackfeet Indians were that tough, but it looks like I'm wrong, don't it?"

"I see two sets of tracks, and they're travelin' light," Rusty panted. "There're no dog tracks, so they don't have sleds either. Yeah, I reckon they're warrior braves. Now, all we gotta do is confirm which tribe they're from and act accordingly."

"The way things have been goin', it might even be Comanche," Angus moaned.

"Nobody's seen the Comanche past Yellowstone Valley, and that's already a trot. But they're spread from Oklahoma and Kansas to Texas, and some of 'em make their way to the valley with raiding parties. All those buggers like to do is fight."

"And they're danged good at it, too," Rusty replied. "Even Levi and Will had their share of trouble with the Comanche, and it's the same with most other tribes. Sometimes they get along with the Apache, Wichita, and some say they're making a peace treaty with the Southern Cheyenne and Arapaho right now."

"Yeah, well, let's see how long that lasts," Angus grouched. "They're a vengeful and suspicious lot, so they easily fly off the handle."

Their ears perked up, and they heard something to their left. Pistols instantly appeared in white-knuckled fists. It sounded like footsteps on soft snow. The frosted cover crunched under feet.

Little by little, the Indians unexpectedly emerged from the almost-dark stillness from somewhere deep in the shadows made by the slanting sun—there wasn't even a breeze. Both mountain men gasped and squeezed their pistol grips harder. Sweat ran down their arms, over their clenched fists, and down the barrels, finally making little holes in the snow. When the truth settled in, Rusty's eyes spread.

"Sho'daache Kahee," Hachta said, touching his heart with a clenched fist.

"Howdy to you too, Chief," Rusty replied, smiling in relief. "I thought there were some Blackfeet out here. Last time we were here, we got run off by the tribe."

"That was over a hundred moons ago, my old friend," Hachta replied. "Sho'daache Kahee, McFarlin. You must already know my oldest medicine man, Whisper."

"Yeah, I know him, all right. Sho'daache Kahee to you too, Chief Hachta." Unlike Rusty, he proffered his hand. "I thought you would be wiser than us and be back spending the winter with Pine Needle in my camp. I can see what you're doing, but don't you think it's the wrong time of year?"

"Not for the cold-water beaver, it ain't." Rusty grinned. "I ain't seen finer pelts for years."

"You know my medicine man, Whisper, don't cha, Angus?" Hachta asked. "You must have run into each other back in camp."

"Chief. Whisper." Angus nodded, but he stared at the ground rather than look into the shaman's eyes. It wasn't that he was afraid of him or of *anyone,* for that matter. He just didn't like the man because Whisper thought he was God's gift from Heaven and wasn't even a Christian.

Angus finally looked up and did a slow burn as his eyes shot daggers at the medicine man, and he scowled. This made Whisper frown and glower back with icy eyes.

"Yes, the White man who sometimes likes to play like he's a Crow Indian, which is, of course, nonsense," Whisper scolded.

"That's it, not another word of Crow," Angus spat. "If you're gonna speak badly of me, at least you can do it in my own language where I can defend myself better. Not with a smart-alecky sort like you."

The medicine man's voice was like daggers to his ears. Angus already knew him from the winters he spent with his Crow wife, Pine Needle, in the stronghold. He never hid his hate for White men or anyone who didn't believe his tales about spirits and visions. Still, he was known across the Crow Nation as a respected shaman, but McFarlin wasn't having any of it.

He wasn't bamboozled by his charm and spooky stories about miracles and ghosts.

"You're not much better, are you?" Whisper said to Rusty. "At least you didn't marry a war chief like your apprentice, Levi Johnson. What she saw in him is a mystery to me. You like to play Crow Indians, but you're not one of us and never will be."

The agitation needle slammed into the red when the shaman bold face insulted Rusty Steel.

"You sure are a sassy sort, ain't cha, fool? Do you let dogs like this off their leashes, Chief?" Rusty turned to Hachta and said, "I'd have this mouthy sort chained to a post." The chief laughed.

Whisper looked at his chief for support but didn't get what he expected.

"Don't look at me," the chief spat with a piercing look. "You're the reason we're out here in the first place. And never be mistaken—Rusty Steel is my blood brother, so for me, he is a Crow Indian. It would serve you well to remember that because you are not my blood. You work for me, even though most times you think you're above everybody. I think you're getting stupid in your old age. Maybe you should listen to what the White man has to say. Call it an outside opinion of something that's beginning to smell bad."

"There's a little evil in everybody," Angus said. "Ya just got to have it drawn out of ya by an agent like a snake."

"Envy and rivalry." Chief Hachta snickered. "It makes grown men act like children. Both of you ultimately answer to me, so you both can just hush up right now."

"Come on, that's enough from you too, Angus,"

Rusty protested. "We don't have time to stand and bicker. What's the plan? You saw the moon last night, didn't ya? I hope you have someplace in mind to run for because I don't. What in the world are you doin' out here? Bad weather's comin', and I don't see any cover in sight."

"I was going to ask you the same question." Hachta smiled, patting his blood brother's back.

He and Angus had been friends from the White trapper's first weeks on the mountain, and both had saved each other's lives on more than one occasion. Rusty Steel was the only White man in the Rockies who had an open invite to the Crow stronghold. The chief had often tried to get him to take one of the beautiful widowed women of the tribe, knowing he would make a good husband, but he refused.

Of course, not because they were Indians, but because Rusty had a Flathead wife long ago. But she died like so many others in the past, and he never married again. That didn't mean that he didn't cut up and try to charm every pretty woman he met. Rusty was going on sixty, but in his own mind, he was just a young man of twenty-five.

In the mountains, they had little use for mirrors unless you used them to relay messages at great distances with the sun's reflection. After the arrival of the mirror, each tribe developed a Morris Code type of system. It was easier than building a big fire and laboring over smoke signals. It was a hot and boring job. At times, the reflector device made the same chore easy and got it done in a flash.

There were few mirrors in the compound, at least until Captain Forrester arrived, who liked a clean-shaven face. Then, of course, the arrival of the women changed all that. Once Dahteste got a mirror, Levi could hardly separate her from it. But Steel had little use for such things, especially as they reminded him how old he was. That was something he wasn't pleased with. No matter how hard he tried, he could feel himself gradually slowing down.

All was quiet, and the trees were still until the sun rose a little higher in the sky, but with it came the wind, which hit them like a punch in the face. The pine's tow-whorl swayed, making the stems and even trunks bow. They stretched their necks to gulp down fresh mountain air.

"I've seen people thumped in the head with a hammer with more sense than that fool medicine man," Angus whispered in Rusty's ear.

"He's crazier than a dog humpin' a pig." Rusty laughed.

Angus wrote his name with slow, block cursive like a man who never set foot in a school. "If anybody comes this way, they may see my scratching in the snow if no more powder falls tonight."

"Why in the world would you leave a message, and for who?" Rusty asked.

"Just in case there's somebody else out here stranded like us," Angus replied.

"Well, then we would have company to die with." Rusty chuckled. "Your wisdom never ceases to surprise me."

The Hunt

Levi and Will rode stirrup to stirrup from the closest hunting grounds with sizable game. They trotted their horses across ridges where the snow wasn't deep. This also meant they could be easily spotted, which was unwise in the Rocky Mountains. It was *always* best to travel unperceived. Still, they doubted that many hunters would be out just before a storm was about to hit. Both men had seen the ring around the moon and expected the worst, so they wrapped up their small hunting venture and turned for home.

They had bagged two large elk and hoped to get a third before they made it back to the cabins and safety from the coming blizzard. The light clatter of horses' hooves echoed on the empty stone trail.

"I'm afraid that out here, law and order are little more than precarious ideals," Captain Forrester said.

"Oh, there's law and order, all right," Levi replied. "The Indian Nations have their own laws, and right now, we're probably trespassing. Maybe it's a good thing they're precarious ideas and nothing more."

The hunters knew this part of the mountains like the back of their hands. It was the second season they had provided meat for the crowd back at the compound, and the supplies needed constant resupplying. Levi was the best shot and trapper, with Rusty Steel a begrudging second. And where Johnson went so did the captain. Everyone in the compound had some designated job, and finding meat for the dinner table was Captain Forrester and Will's.

The sky turned orange, leaving the west dotted with rafts of blood-red clouds. Vultures circled high in the sky like fugitives of the fire at the world's end.

"I reckon we best find somewhere to take shelter," Levi said as he looked over his shoulder. "That storm shouldn't hit until tomorrow afternoon, but it's gonna get cold tonight. I expect we'll be home by then, though. But I'd still like to bag that last elk. We have a way before we're out of range of the big game animals. We planned to kill three when we set out, and I don't like to return short."

"Returning short one elk is better than not returning at all." Captain Forrester smiled. "I don't think we want to be out here when the storm hits. Personally, I want to be sitting in front of a big fire, reading a book with a hot cup of coffee warming my hand. Maybe with Betty snuggling up nice and close."

Levi uncinched the saddle and pulled it down, hobbling the horse's rear leg to the foreleg. They camped just over the ridge, protected from the wind but above the snowdrifts. This allowed them good visibility when the moon rose. Even though they were out of the direct wind, it was cold. Frost formed on Levi's beard, mustache, and eyebrows.

They slept in shifts, so someone was always awake to protect the fresh meat from any number of animals. Wild cats, wolves, coyotes, and a dozen more would be waiting in the distance for a moment of lapse. Then they would suddenly strike, stealing the meat the men had labored a week for.

They had packed dung on the mule's back, so they were sure to have combustibles for their campfire because the snow would have covered most of the dry wood. Sun-baked cow manure gave off less smoke and burned hotter anyway, so it was ideal for somebody who wanted to go unperceived. It was even lighter to carry than wood, so it was most mountain men's preference when traveling light.

With gloved hands, they swept the snow off the stone and laid their bedrolls as close to the fire as they dared. Still, the occasional whiff of burning hair drifted through the air.

"So, let's hear it, Will," Levi said. "How's married life goin' for you? It must be easier than for me with a Crow Indian wife."

The captain looked at his best friend with surprised eyes. "I haven't really thought about it too much." He crossed his arms and held his chin in his hand as he considered the question. "I don't really know how to answer since it happened so fast and not long ago. I've hardly had time to get used to the idea. It just kind of crept up on me all by itself. I had no idea I would ever end up married. As far as an opinion on if it's good or bad, ask me in a year." He chuckled and winked.

"That a poor excuse for an answer when your best pard asks ya somethin' so serious," Levi said throatily. He was struggling to talk about it, too, but it was busting out, and he had to vent to somebody. "That's what best friends are for."

"Maybe if you go first, it will get easier." Will smiled, and it reached his eyes. "I don't like talking about something I really don't understand, so I wouldn't know where to start. Plus, you've been married much longer than I have. Why, we just got hitched."

"My biggest problem is with Dahteste. Everything is a competition," Levi griped. "Whether it be shooting, tracking, skinning, or even how to smoke a pipe, she turns everything into a little battle, and we have one every week at least. It wears me out trying to do everything better than her."

Forrester laughed and said, "Heck, even I know how to fix that. Let her win occasionally. I believe you're just as competitive as her. I know you always are with me. What you're tasting right now is a dose of your own medicine." The captain couldn't stifle a loud laugh—it burst out on its own. "That's something that Betty and I haven't suffered, at least not yet. Of course, we've had a squabble or two, but nothing that a few kind words couldn't fix. Of course, I'm married to a White woman from Tennessee, and you're married to a Crow wildcat with War Chief as a title, my friend. What did you expect?"

"Yeah, well, don't get me wrong now," Johnson went on, but slower. "I do love the girl with all my heart—even more than my horse."

"Even more than your horse? Are you sure?" The captain chortled. "You are a strange man, Beaver Johnson."

"Where I come from in Southeastern Indiana on the

Ohio River, anything you love more than your horse is mighty special," Levi explained.

"To me, you sound like you have a dose of Rocky Mountain fever." Will chuckled. "You must have loved your parents more than your horse, too, didn't you?"

"Of course, but that's different," Levi fussed. "That's kin and the same blood."

"I never asked you, but what do they call people from Indiana?" the captain asked.

"Why, Hoosier," Levi replied, puzzled.

"Who's what?" the captain teased.

"No, not who's what," Levi corrected. "Hoosier—it comes from the Indian word for corn, which is *hoosa*." The captain's joke went right over his head. "When Dahteste and I fell for each other, it happened so fast and powerful that it nearly knocked us off our feet. I can still remember how my head spun around and around. My heart nearly busted right out of my chest. That was when we both knew without a word spoken."

"Nothing so serious ever comes so easily to me," Captain Forrester replied. "It was the hardest thing I ever did—facing up to Betty, I mean. Sure, I fancied her, but I just couldn't put the steps together to walk up to her and confront the situation. I could face a dozen Comanche warriors and not run away, but I nearly fled when Betty came after me. I believe if it weren't for her, I'd have gotten stuck between the straw and the hay, and nothing would have come of it. In a year, I will let you know how it worked out or didn't. It's a hard thing to coexist with people, especially if you come from different places. Even Betty and I come from very different backgrounds. You and Dahteste's origins are more similar than ours."

"Who would have ever thought it would all be so complicated," Levi said. "At first, it seemed like a piece of cake. Of course, I'd never lived with a woman or even had a serious girlfriend. In the woods of Indiana, we didn't have any neighbors closer than a week's ride."

"When I went to West Point, all the women wanted to date one of the students," Captain Forrester said. "Maybe even marry, as most future officers were from wealthy families or had high military ties. But I was so focused on my studies and school that I pushed such things aside, believing it would all come with time and in an orderly fashion. Boy-oh-boy, was I wrong."

"All in all, I reckon we did well, all things considered," Levi said. "I ain't exactly the type for a normal woman from back East anyway. I best get used to the competition and get on with things. That's what I'll do. Next time she tries to outrun me, I'll let her win."

"She even tries to beat you at running with those long legs of yours?" Forrester laughed, nearly getting a stitch as tears came to his eyes. "You are a funny man, Mister Johnson. Let me get some shuteye. We've got to get up early and be sharp if we want to beat that storm home. Wake me up when it's my turn to keep watch."

Levi pulled all four pistols and left them close to his hands if he needed them quickly. He cocked two just in case, then pulled his blanket up to his neck and leaned against his saddle. His eyes traced the land before him, lit by a silvery moon.

Chief Hachta

Hours before meeting Rusty and Angus

"I told you it was a mistake to make your pilgrimage this close to bad weather," Chief Hachta chided. "What was I thinking when I let you talk me into going with you? We should have both known better; now, it might cost us our lives. And for what? I don't see any bright lights and flashes from the sky like you told me we'd see, and I haven't seen a miracle either. Promises. Promises are all you ever give me and my people, but we never see anything come of all this, Whisper. You used to be an important shaman and medicine man, but now all you do is send us chasing our tails like camp yard dogs."

"I don't have a choice about what I do," the medicine man replied smugly. "I follow the spirits when they whisper in my ears—I would be a fool not to. That is why the elders gave me my name. Not many men have this gift of visions. I smoked the sacred pipe and traveled to the heavens. That's where I saw the bright lights and flashes in my mind. If you are blind to them, that is your problem. Maybe if you believed more, the spirits would come near, and you could hear them whisper, too. They don't like grumpy old men, though. That is why we're here—to serve the spirits. We are but mortal men, despite you being a chief and me a medicine man. We don't need to understand the why of everything the Indian gods tell us. I am sure they know better than us, so all we must do is follow."

"I don't follow anybody blindly," Hachta retorted. "I'd think you'd know that by now. You tricked me, is what I believe. You didn't want to risk climbing the mountains alone, and you promised me magic so you wouldn't have to go alone. I went against my better judgment. Mother Earth is full of surprises this time of year."

It was true, when the medicine man told Chief Hachta about his visions, he was fascinated with the possibility. Of course, all Crow Indians believed in the spirit world, but few believed in miracles unless they had witnessed one themselves. Of course, it *was* something the chief always longed to see and experience. Still, he was skeptical if such a thing existed. Sometimes, the unexplained was tagged with the name *miracle* because they didn't know what to call it or didn't understand what it was.

The way Whisper described what they would see on their spiritual journey weaved a path around Hachta's curiosity and captured it whole. But even chiefs made mistakes; too many errors in the Rocky Mountains would cost you your life. Of course, the chief and Whisper, the tribe's spiritual guide, were both aging. Perhaps that was what pushed them to strike out like younger men to do the impossible. As time passed, youthful was something that they were less of every day.

The Crow medicine man's face was gaunt and drawn. His black hair was stringy and held in place with a red scarf. His eyes were a faded hazel like a deer's, mistrusting and unusual for an Indian—it had always made him stand out. Of course, Rusty and Angus had heard a lot about the shaman. Still, Whisper generally shied away from or even ignored most White men even when they were in Hachta's camp, and that included men like Rusty Steel, Levi Johnson, and Angus McFarlin, who had all spent time living in Chief Hachta's Crow stronghold.

Of course, the Crow camp was large. In warriors alone, it was a hundred braves strong, and then there were the men behind the fighters who hunted and trapped for the tribe. All the women participated in the daily chores and butchered the meat or cleaned and cured hides. When the hunters brought buffalo skins, the women would make blankets and new teepees and patch up the older, damaged ones. Even the children participated in their common goal, making tools from bones and horns. Nothing went to waste.

The tribe's intention was obvious and straightforward—it was survival. These people who lived in what they called God's country only wanted to live in peace without asking anything from others and happily providing for themselves. Even with the encroachment of men from back East, wild game was still plentiful, and this far north buffalo too—at least for the time being, but that too would change soon.

For Whisper, those who didn't believe in the Indian spirits were simply shadows of visions in a man's mind and nothing more—they didn't really exist. He seemed to live in his world of ghosts and demons more than he did down on Earth with the other mortal human beings and his fellow tribe members. Still, he was revered among his people for his wise actions in the past. Now, his mind seemed to be blinded by his fame, clouding his judgment. The chief even questioned if he really heard voices as he claimed or if he was simply crazy.

"Be careful, and don't think you're too clever." Whisper smiled. "Many chiefs have fallen to the blade, never knowing it was coming. It's dangerous to tempt fate, Hachta."

"Why don't you just shut up," Hachta scolded, fed up. "The day you outsmart me will be the day the moon disappears."

For the briefest of moments, everything froze. They could hear voices in the distance, and although the scent of men was weak, it was still there. Hachta's gaze was like a stone wall reflecting some primal part of his being. The chief glanced at the sun for the time; it said nine o'clock.

Hachta's and Whisper's insides gnashed together as alarm bells rang in their brains. The Indians froze in place as if a syringe full of ice was injected into their veins.

"Blackfeet?" Whisper asked, his voice no louder than a light breeze.

"Maybe," Hachta replied, shrugging.

The fact that they had come close enough to hear them speak before they were aware they were there shook the chief up and threw him off his game. Neither man ever expected to run into anyone in such an isolated stretch of land, especially with the weather that was on its way. But still, he should have smelled them long before or at least felt a gut feeling, but nothing. Then again, they could be expert travelers and stayed downwind and knew how to avoid detection. They obviously hadn't noticed the Crow were there. They could be anybody.

Whisper sniffed, shook his head, and frowned as his eyes widened. Hachta smelled the air, too.

"They smell like White men to me, and not Indians," Chief Hachta muttered.

The shaman's eyes shone with a look of ignorance. To Hachta, it was apparent he wasn't aware of his own lack of intellect. He was blinded by all the fame from the past.

At first, the men they smelled were fuzzy in the distance and were hard to see as the low sun's light reflected off the carpet of sparkling snow, half blinding them. When the Crow chief got a good look and finally saw who it was, his pulse calmed like a receding tide, and his blood warmed. He grunted, curled a sly grin, and motioned to Whisper with his chin. Hachta pressed his lips into a tight smile.

"It's Rusty Steel and Angus McFarlin." The chief grinned. "I thought they might be Blackfeet for a moment. It's much better to run into friends than the enemy."

The chief glanced at the medicine man from the corner of his eye. He knew Whisper didn't like people from back East, whether they were white, black, or brown. For the shaman, this land was reserved for the people of the earth, the red man.

A visit would serve Whisper right, the chief thought. The grin grew so big you could see his molars.

Rusty's dog ran onto the trail, bounding through the snow and barking at the intruders. The big black canine contrasted with the pure white snow. Whisper was taken aback, but Hachta knew Rusty's pet and knew he wouldn't bite them with its master there. Then again it might take a nip at Whisper for being so contrary and ornery. The idea made the chief smile some more.

Rusty Steel looked over, scratching his bushy beard and squinting his wisdom-filled eyes. As soon as he saw Chief Hachta, his strength seemed to rise from somewhere deep inside the aging mountain man, like steam from the earth's core. Suddenly, there was hope. Even though they hadn't yet found shelter from the storm, they had found moral support, and a more knowledgeable man in the wilderness than Hachta didn't exist.

"Sho′ daache Kahee. Becoming old was the dumbest thing I've ever done." Rusty cackled as he walked toward his old friend. "I reckon all four of us are in the same boat, ain't we?"

"Diishootaa," Hachta said, greeting his friends. "I agree; old age is coming at a really bad time. I never imagined it would be nearing so fast."

"Don't tell me you're lost in the middle of nowhere." Rusty smiled.

"Of course, I'm not lost," Hachta grouched. "This is my backyard. My problem is I decided to follow this fool." He made a fist and jerked his thumb toward the medicine man.

Whisper shot the chief a dirty look. He didn't believe it was proper for the tribe leader to speak to the shaman in such a manner before the inferior White men, but the chief just smiled as he wrapped his arms around his old friend, greeting him like a brother.

"Those are some nice beaver pelts you have on those heavy timber sleds." Hachta grinned. "Maybe you could travel faster if you weren't pulling a hundred pounds each."

"What did I tell ya?" Angus grumbled, locking eyes with Rusty. "And you wouldn't listen."

"You too?" Rusty barked. "I'd rather freeze to death than give up such a catch of furs. I ain't seen this quality of pelts for a decade, and I'm not givin' 'em up for nobody. Not for you, not for Angus, and surely not for that turd you call a witch doctor."

"I'm not a witch doctor," Whisper replied testily. "I am a shaman, and one is totally different than the other. A medicine man is for good and wisdom, and witch doctors live in the dark world of the night. One is genuine and the other not."

"I reckon you be the one that's not," Angus retorted. "I've spent entire winters in Hachta's Crow stronghold where you live, and you always turn your nose up at me and spit like just seeing me left a bad taste in your mouth. So, don't expect anything but the same back from me, mister. I don't take kindly to fools and clowns."

"That's enough!" Hachta shouted. "We have more pressing matters on our hands than bickering with stupid people." He glared at Whisper. "Come on, we can walk while we talk and catch up. Let me help you, brother."

Betty Forrester

After the fight, both women retired to separate shelters to lick their wounds and try to clear their heads. Betty was in her and Captain Forrester's room in the last log cabin in the compound. The angry Crow woman had retired to her Indian teepee, which stood in the middle of the large yard. Both opponents were too sick to fight from the massive overdose of liquor. The aftermath and hangover from a bottle of whiskey was something neither had ever experienced. They felt like they were at death's door.

Blacksmith's hammers and anvils pounded behind the women's eyes, and their stomachs were wreaked with dry heaves. Even Dahteste's face was pale, and Betty's was the next step blancher, nearing translucent. The bad breath, dry mouth, and bitter taste were foreign to them, too. Their suffering faces made them look five years older.

When Betty looked in the mirror upon returning to her bedroom, she was shocked at what she saw. It was a bruised and battered woman looking back at her who appeared to be pushing forty. She used two fingers to wiggle a loose tooth, hoping it didn't fall out.

The woman's eyes were crusty, and bloodshot veins traced the whites like roadmaps. Both smelled of whiskey, sweat, and sickness from their grumbling stomachs. Weakness and lethargy overtook their bodies, and their brains went numb. Their hearts were thumping, and their stomachs were doing flip-flops as their minds spun out of control.

Levi and Will had renovated the last cabin in the compound with an additional room. Until the previous day, everything had worked out fine, and the women seemed like they were becoming fast friends. With the deaths of Portland Pete, Syracuse Sam, and Yosemite Bob, the last home was abandoned until the two young couples made some late-season additions to ensure their mutual privacy and moved in.

Of course, there were times in the past when six, seven, or even eight mountain men waited out the freezing winter months confined to one cabin with a single room. Now, they had the space to provide some privacy. The compound and the stables and corral had also grown over the years. The animals were bedded down for the cold days to come with lots of straw and hay.

Betty's blond hair and thin, delicate features with dark shadows below her blue eyes belied her past. Under the beauty and good sense of humor lay a serious woman who loved and lived strongly and simply. She was as uncomplicated and drama-free as a White woman got. Of course, that only went so far. Her father was much like her famous uncle, Davy Crockett. He taught her how to shoot, hunt, and trap as a young girl. Nor was she a little woman by any means. She was tall, fit, and as tough as they come in Tennessee.

Virgil Lovejoy sat on Dennis's porch as he clutched his spyglass. He watched both the last cabin and the teepee for activity. He didn't know what started the ruckus the day before, but it got out of hand fast and nearly became deadly. Dahteste's actions were probably natural when threatened. She was a Crow warrior, but Betty's behavior was totally unexpected. Then again, they hadn't known her long. Of course, Dahteste's life could be followed back to her forefathers in the same tribe among the same people. Her family tree was known to everyone in the stronghold.

The Crockett family was known across the United States, but Davy was one of eight children, and his brother had twelve, of which Betty was one. Who knew whose steps she followed? Until now, she had been a perfect example of an intelligent and educated woman. But unexpectedly, there appeared to be a rivalry between the two, and Lovejoy didn't really know how to proceed. He somehow felt it was his responsibility to steer Betty in the right direction, and Dennis would attempt to do the same with Dahteste, if that were even possible.

They had both asked the women what started the quarrel, but neither one remembered much more than the drag-down punch-up they had had and the destroyed window in the cabin. Joseph was trying to fix up a replacement from the supplies shed, or it would freeze inside that night when the temperatures plummeted.

When Virgil saw both women moving toward Rusty's cabin simultaneously, he jumped up and off the porch, landing at a dead run in the deep snow. With white powder to his knees, he struggled to move forward fast enough to be there before they arrived. His heart started to pound hard between his temples as his eyes narrowed, and he struggled to move more quickly.

Black and ropy locks swung about Dahteste's head as she swiftly headed for Rusty Steel's cabin, her head down and her hands bunched into fists. As soon as Lovejoy got a look at her face, the Indian woman's eyes shone with what looked like innocence, but Virgil instantly knew better. That was just a ruse to cover what was to come. Her white knuckles showed her true fury.

Betty arrived first, curled her fingers into a fist, and lambasted the door a dozen times. Apparently, she thought Dahteste was inside. She didn't see the Crow Indian right behind her.

"Whoa, whoa, now, girls!" Virgil shouted all breathy, waving his hands, trying to get their attention. Dennis and Joseph came running behind him, but they weren't close enough.

Lovejoy saw Dahteste's eyes shift suddenly, and he shouted, "Behind you! Look out!" But it was too late, and Betty didn't even see it coming.

A haymaker hit her on the side of the head and knocked her to the floor. Dahteste smirked and made a funny face as Mrs. Crockett sat on her butt, furious. Her eyes blinked, and she shook her head to clear the fog and ringing in her ears. It pounded distant like an echo chamber. Betty wiggled her jaw and ran her tongue across her teeth to ensure they were all still there. She winced in pain, closing her eyes to keep the tears of frustration from escaping.

"Are you all right?" Virgil asked.

"Uh-huh, maybe," Betty replied and shrugged. The pallor of disappointment crept back onto her face as she pushed herself up and off the floor. The cold air left her cheeks rosy and her nose red.

Dahteste let out a scream as anger filled her eyes. She begged for her hands not to tremble as she bunched them into fists again. Both women seemed to be in a freefall descent into malice and self-destruction, and nobody knew what had set it off. With Levi and Will on a hunting trip, they didn't know what to do, so Walker and Breed tried to go unnoticed for fear the two wildcats would turn on them.

Only Virgil felt obliged to interfere and try to talk some sense into the women before one of them killed the other. He suspected Dahteste would be the victor, but until now, Betty had been holding her ground and inflicting as much damage and pain on the woman war chief as she had on her. Betty felt a power like she had never felt take hold of her, and it seemed to build. She had regained her wits and caught her breath as she swung her head toward Dahteste and glared.

"What in the world has gotten into you two?" Virgil asked. "Who's been pushin' your swings, Betty, Dahteste?"

Lovejoy was the best read of the three men and was more intelligent than Dennis, for sure, and maybe even the marshal. As an enslaved man, he had the luxury of an education provided by his still-hated but reasonable owner, the Englishman Fitzgerald Worstshire III. He was a decent man as far as men who bought and sold human beings could be. Now Virgil had to use his wits to bring the women back to their senses. If Levi and Will returned and found them like this, there would be hell to pay, and Virgil somehow felt responsible for keeping the peace among their little clan.

But before he knew it, the two women circled crabwise, crouched low, ready to strike. It happened so quickly, Lovejoy didn't even see it coming. Suddenly, Dahteste felt fingers clawing through her shirt and clutching at her neck, trying to get a good grasp. Betty had jumped up suddenly and was all over the little Crow warrior.

Suddenly, something hit Betty on the head. The Crow woman stood with a war club in her hand. A drop of blood stretched from the end of the truncheon and into the white powder just off the edge of the porch. Betty's blond hair lay like an abaníco on a field of white.

Virgil Lovejoy held his Bible over his head, screaming, "Stop before you're stricken down! Betty Crockett, you should know better. At least Dahteste is a warrior, and much more can't be expected. Still, you're actin' terribly, and I'm embarrassed for you both. Now stop your strugglin' and tell me what this is all about."

A bucket of water sat on the table in the corner. Dennis had just brought it over, so it wasn't frozen yet. Dahteste grabbed the gourd floating on the surface, and she dipped a drink. Finishing half, she used the rest to wash the blood speckle off her face—Betty Crockett's blood.

"Why are White men always talking about principles and honor and telling the Crow people what to do?" Dahteste asked. "Then they turn around and ignore their own standards. I bet you White *women* are the same. You put on a face like you don't look down at me, Betty, but I know you do. I suggest you remember where you are. I am the wiser woman in these mountains despite you being my elder. For Crow Indians, thirty years old is already an old woman." She spat into the snow to show her anger.

The shadows of a stand of trees edged out to the end of the large compound. Betty and Dahteste both heard voices—the men did, too. The Crow warrior sniffed the air, and she instantly frowned as a biting fear gripped her soul. In a single instant, they all forgot about their personal differences and focused on the noises at the edge of the compound.

"Blackfeet," Dahteste whispered as she wrinkled her nose and crouched with the rest.

Hammers clicked loudly in the frigid air. Their breaths disappeared a few inches from their mouths. Right after they cocked their weapons, the voices stopped. Now, everybody was aware of each other's presence. Did the hostile Indians stumble on their compound? Perhaps they were lost from the snowstorm. All possibilities, but everyone there doubted them. There wasn't an Indian in the Rocky Mountains that didn't know about the large Crow stronghold six hours' ride north. It was risky business for Blackfeet warriors to come so near such large numbers of their sworn enemies, so there must be a good reason.

Everybody held their breath as hearts hammered between their temples and time suddenly stopped. With eyes spread open and mouths a hard line, they waited for what they knew would come. It was only a matter of seconds.

Hunters Return

"I've never seen the likes," Marshal Walker chortled. "I thank my lucky stars I ain't married. Just sittin' here watchin' all this foolishness has proven me right to remain a confirmed bachelor. But it *is* mighty entertaining. I've spent some long, boring winters in mountain cabins in the past, but this ain't gonna be one of 'em." He hooked his thumbs in his belt and belly laughed.

"You and me both," Mountain Dennis snickered. "I reckon I ain't the marryin' type anymore, either. Hell, I'm too old. But I agree they sure are funny to watch when they aren't scaring me to death. I've nearly peed myself twice." He suddenly broke out laughing again and crossed his legs. "I doubt I've ever seen such foolishness. I bet they don't even know what they're angry about. It's like two hens claimin' the same roost. I thought it foolish for that pair to room together from the start. They're as different as night and day. I hope Dahteste don't cut Betty's throat in a fit of anger. She sure has the skills."

"Oh, I figure any niece of the great Davy Crockett will be able to take care of herself," Joseph said. "It must have been a hard life back in the mountain forests of Tennessee. I read her uncle and whole family lived in the woods and hunted and trapped for a livin'. I doubt she be a pushover."

Levi Beaver Johnson and Captain Will Forrester had their heads down and were walking fast toward Mountain Dennis's porch, where the three sat watching, waiting for the next act of the spectacle. They led their horses by the leads, and the dopey mule trailed behind with two elk on her back. Despite the weather, Joseph, Dennis, and Virgil lounged on the adjoining porch and smoked while sipping whiskey-laced coffee and laughing up a storm. Every time one of the two women roared out the front door, sparks would fly, and loud, angry words were exchanged.

"Uh-oh, here comes Levi and Will." Virgil frowned. "They must have just gotten back. Boy-oh-boy, they are in for the surprise of their lives. I'm just glad they returned before one of them girls killed the other. It's been touch and go for a spell now."

They all knew lousy weather would arrive soon, and then total confinement could be necessary. If not, somebody would freeze to death. A cord of wood stood beside the cabin doors. Sure, it would warm up again before the depths of winter arrived, along with survivable temperatures. In the middle of winter, it could be dangerous going to the outhouses, even for short periods of time.

This was an isolated storm and, if they were unlucky, a blizzard and possibly a complete whiteout. Then, they would be confined to the cabins, which were connected with long strings of rope hung on wooded posts a yard off the ground. The network of leads ran between the houses, the stables, and the outhouses. It was imperative when you couldn't see your hand before your face to have something safe to guide you. Icicles hung from the frozen hemp rope as it swung in the breeze in one long, solid piece.

As soon as the two young mountain men stormed onto the porch, Dennis laughed and said, "If ya want a tip for a successful marriage, don't ask your wife when breakfast is ready when she's out milking the cows."

"What?" Levi asked. "Whatcha talkin' about?"

"Where's Betty?" the captain asked. He was dirty, cold, and tired but delighted to be home again and anxious to see his new wife.

"You best sit down, gentlemen," Virgil said. "The horses can wait for a spell. We've got to have a little talk before you see your wives. Pour 'em a stiff drink, Dennis. They're gonna need it."

Levi and Will looked utterly puzzled, but Joseph and Dennis laughed so hard they got a stitch. Virgil didn't even *try* to hide his anger at the two. He chastened them with burning eyes.

The way Dennis saw it, the White and Red women provided quite a circus atmosphere for a change from their usually dull winters, mainly when they were confined inside due to the dangerous weather. Something that hadn't even happened yet. What would come of the two fighting cats, then? Both Breed and Walker were anxiously waiting to see what happened next and how did their husbands plan to settle things down—or would Levi and Will start fighting, too?

"I wish I had some popcorn." Dennis chuckled.

"Ain't ya glad ya stayed now?" He turned to the marshal and snickered. "I bet your man, Rory Breaker, is gonna wish he'd come along. I doubt he made it to Kansas anyway. That's a heck of a ride to just turn around and come back again. Especially as you plan to cross the country a few months from now."

"Nah, he just wanted to get back home for a spell before we took the big wagon train to Oregon City," Joseph said. "I reckon he wanted to say bye to his folks one last time. He told me they were gettin' on in years. Now that we know the trail, I figure we can do it without too many losses. Rory's still young, so I reckon he was just missing his family."

"I'd say it looks like we have a quandary—a conundrum if you may," Virgil said as he eyed the two new arrivals.

Even though Lovejoy had been an enslaved person, he was school taught with a proper education. Not only could he write better than most, but he was also a voracious reader. And that appetite wasn't limited to his tattered Bible either. He read everything he could get his hands on.

"That's called a dilemma, is what that is, no matter how fancy a word you put on it." Joseph huffed.

Levi wearily took a seat, as did the captain. Their questioning eyes locked with Virgil's. Dennis poured each of them a generous glass of whiskey and waited until they drank up.

"Go on, whatcha waitin' on?" Mountain Dennis said. "Trust me, you'll be glad ya did." He coughed into his fist to stifle a snicker.

As soon as Will and Levi turned their glasses bottoms up, angry screams came from Rusty's cabin. A coffee pot crashed through yet another windowpane, as the glass exploded, peppering the porch. Brown java splattered across the white snow. Levi and Will went for their pistols, swinging the barrels toward the commotion.

"Hold your horses, boys!" Virgil yelled as he jumped into the line of fire. "You don't wanna shoot your wives, do ya? Then again, after what you're about to see, maybe ya will." This time, *he* couldn't stifle a chuckle, but the younger men didn't notice.

Dennis's and Walker's eyes danced with mischief and fun, but Virgil was nearing panic. He knew it was none of his business and he should leave it to the husbands, but something told him they would need his wisdom, and things were going to get out of control again. That is, if he could get anybody to listen to him. Dennis and Joseph found it all funny, and Will and Levi hadn't grasped the gravity. They had no idea what was going on.

One moment, all they heard was women shouting, and then suddenly, a bundle of arms and legs came tumbling out the door, across the porch, and into the snow. As they struggled, only the contrast of their skin color gave away who was who. Dahteste and Betty rolled around in the white powder, making a ball as it stuck to their bodies. Little by little, the snow trapped them in a snowball as they struggled. They struggled to the edge of the compound and the open gate and rolled down the path and out of sight.

"That's the steep bit at the top of the trail and the gate!" Levi exclaimed, shocked.

"I bet we're gonna be lookin' at a couple of snow-men!" Joseph laughed loudly and without shame.

"Come on, quick!" Will said. "They must have rolled halfway down the hill by now."

They followed the path of the growing ball of snow. It looked like a steam roller ran through the middle of the yard and out the south gate. Snowflakes as big as silver dollars fell from the sky. In the distance, thunder cracked overhead and rumbled as the Rocky Mountain storm came closer.

When they reached the gate at the edge of the compound and the beginning of the trail south, they couldn't believe their eyes. A big ball of snow, like a snowman, sat stopped in the middle of the trail with arms and legs protruding from all around. Ankles flipped feet as fingers wiggled, but they were obviously stuck. The only thing that wasn't visible was their heads.

"Come on, quick, before they suffocate!" the captain shouted.

Behind the two running husbands were Joseph and Dennis rolling around in the snow by the gate, holding their bellies for fear they would burst from all the laughter.

"I ain't seen anything funnier in my entire life!" Marshal Walker roared. "And I've seen proper circuses back in Kansas. This show is second to none."

Will and Levi pried the two women apart and dug them out of the giant snowball. Luckily, both women were only dazed from rolling down the hill. Neither one could stand without falling again.

"Are you all right, Betty?" the captain asked.

His wife instantly appeared elated to hear the captain's voice as she brushed off the snow. White powder was in every fold of her face and clothing.

"Why is it that you two smell like a couple of polecats?" Levi asked. "You both smell like you slept in a whiskey barrel. What's goin' on, girls?"

Dahteste used her fur cap to dust off the snow. Then she reached up and kissed Levi on the cheek before storming off to their teepee.

"Are you all right, darlin'?" Levi asked the retreating figure.

Dahteste shrugged, looked back, and said, "I'll live." She forced a tight smile as tears rose in her eyes born from anger and confusion.

She made a show of closing and tying the teepee flap. Johnson assumed he was still welcome, though.

"Attaway!" Marshal Walker laughed as he slapped his knee. Angry eyes immediately shot daggers his way, and he zipped his lips as tight as a dung beetle.

"Tell me what's going on here, Betty Crockett," Will demanded. A hint of anger vibrated in his voice. "Are you drunk?"

"Not anymore," Betty said defiantly as she pushed out her chest and jutted her chin.

"And why is it you and Dahteste are beatin' the Dickens out of each other?" Will asked. "When we left, you seemed like there was the makings of a long and lasting friendship."

"That just goes to show ya how little you know about women." Betty huffed. She looked like she got caught in a trap, and she was scrambling for a way out.

"Sometimes women are just jealous of how little men's brains are, so they don't have to suffer fools like women do," Betty spat. The words came out before she could stop them. She unconsciously curled a strand of blond hair with her finger as she bit her lip.

Will drew his eyes wide, questioning why as they

filled with dark clouds, and he became angry. Johnson sniffed and shook his head. He didn't miss that Betty's voice held a tone of desperation. He bunched up his lips and shrugged, shaking his head. Suddenly, the truth settled in, and Forrester's eyes grew sad, and he frowned.

Betty wondered if Will could hear the bass drum hammering in her chest. If her heart rate could be measured, hers would be off the charts.

"As soon as I see you, I get to feelin' girlish again, is all," Betty said as she batted her eyes, hoping the shocked expression on Will's face would go away.

The captain's eyes were icy cold, and he didn't respond to her feminine plea. She paused, not knowing what to do next; pushing hair out of her face, she frowned.

They stood there staring at each other, and nobody said a word. The few agonizing seconds it took seemed to stretch into minutes. Eventually, it seemed like an eternity.

When Captain Forrester turned his back and walked away, Betty's heart sank and filled with dread.

Distant Smoke

"We could heat rocks and bury ourselves in the snow," Hachta said. He blew into his cupped hands, but they didn't feel warmer. "That would keep us from freezing tonight. Tomorrow will be another story."

"Where do you see any dry firewood that ain't ten feet under snow?" Rusty asked. "And we're fresh out of dung. I've done the same thing, but not out here so exposed and not with this wind. If it drifts over us, we'll never dig our way out before we suffocate anyway. Nah, we've gotta keep headin' toward home and hope for the best."

"Hope?" Whisper huffed in disgust. "White men are all alike—as if hope changes anything. Only a fool would believe in something that doesn't exist. But then again, most White men are halfwits."

"All right, then," Hachta said, but now he had a dangerous tone. "Now that you have insulted my blood brother, I expect you to tell us what to do and how to escape the cold. You're such an important shaman, so it should be easy for you. Maybe the spirits will whisper in your ear and tell us what to do. I haven't heard a good idea from you in years, so it's about time. You claim you know everything, so come on, spit it out, and let's hear it. We can't stand here all day. Where's these miracles you talk so much about?"

The chief's anger startled the medicine man, and he took a step backward, but his eyes betrayed the truth. They were filled with hateful envy. It was something that often happened to powerful men. As soon as they got a taste of what great influence was about, they wanted more and more.

Whisper was so angry that before he could stop the words from walking out of his mouth, he blurted, "Maybe we need a new chief! Maybe you're getting too old."

The crack was instant, like a distant thunderclap, and there was no warning. The flat of Hachta's hand left fingerprints on Whisper's red face. It nearly knocked him to the ground as he blinked in shock.

"I'm afraid you have forgotten your place in my tribe!" Hachta thundered. "If you want to challenge me, now is the time and place. I never wait to respond to insults. I deal with them instantly—the moment they occur."

Whisper was so surprised he had said what he was thinking; he was caught entirely off guard, especially after the chief hit him openhanded. Now, the first nail had been driven into the coffin for both men. The shaman just rang a bell that he couldn't un-ring, and they both knew it.

"Now, hold on a dad-gummed minute," Rusty said. "This ain't the time, and it ain't the place, either. What we need is to focus on how we're gonna live through this blizzard. You two can work out your differences if we survive. Now get your lazy butt over here, witch doctor, and help me pull my sled. And I ain't askin', mister—I'm tellin' ya."

Rusty Steel wrapped his fingers around his pistol grip as he glared at Whisper, stopping violence seconds before it happened. Still, he knew the chief would never let such an insult pass. Rusty had always found the medicine man arrogant and asinine. He silently chuckled inside. Maybe he would get what he deserved, after all. He was the most arrogant man in the tribe and, as far as Steel could see, all for squat. All he did was tell fancy stories about things folks can't see. As far as Steel could tell, he wasn't more than a con artist.

Of course, Rusty knew there were honorable medicine men in the Crow Nation and even in Hachta's tribe. Since Whisper was successful with his predictions when he was young, fame followed him through the years. Previously, he went on long journeys alone, searching for meaningful signs of the future, but it had been a long time since he left his cozy tent and wife. It was his lack of confidence in the sudden expedition that provoked him to convince the chief to go with him, even if it was with false promises. But it was true; it was the first time in years the Crow spirits had called out to him and asked him to follow their smoke. He had no choice but to follow.

Rusty exchanged looks with the chief and nodded. Hachta helped Angus grab a strap, pulling the sled together, although Whisper acted like he didn't notice. When Steel growled, the medicine man scurried over, averting his eyes, hoping he didn't say something else he would regret. His sudden outburst had already put him at odds with the chief. That was no small thing and would have to be dealt with if they did live through the coming storm.

Steel would usually refuse help from anyone, anyway. He wasn't the kind of man who sought assistance lightly. But this was different because he had ordered Whisper to do as he was told, which added more insult to injury for the spiritual leader who thought more of himself than his people. Inside, Rusty felt his funny bone tickle, and he nearly smiled.

The fiery sun rose with the color of Steel. After hours of walking where there were no souls save them, a spiral of smoke squirreled obliquely from the mountain peaks. A thunderclap and frigid wind set the trees and bushes, gnashing like desperate beasts. They leaned into the wind. The storm was upon them, and the temperatures plummeted. If they didn't find someplace to shelter, they would succumb to the forces of nature within hours.

"I sure hope that's a manmade fire," Angus said as he squinted his eyes against the field of white. He used the flat of his hand to shade his face. In the distance, a string of black smoke contrasted with the falling snow.

"We better be quick," Rusty said. "We could have a whiteout upon us at any minute, so don't just stand there like one o'clock half-struck. Let's get a move on."

They raced toward the string of smoke, all the while worrying that it would disappear and they wouldn't be able to find its source. The mountain men and Crow Indians struggled up a steep grade covered in ice. It was so slippery that with every three yards they advanced, they slipped back one or two. Finally, they reached the summit, and that was when they saw it.

Angus's eyes stretched wide as he said, "Oh, my God. It's coming from that hole in the side of the cliff. But lookee over there—that's a ladder. It almost looks like it's inviting us in."

"The country is so big here it makes ya feel like an ant." Rusty smiled as he looked around them. "I knew we'd find something out here to protect us from the storm. I had a gut feelin'."

In the distance, a slash was cut into the mountainside. The sun said it was nearly eleven o'clock. Under that was the black hole from which the smoke rose. It lingered in the air until it floated above the canyon walls and disappeared into the wind. Large snowdrifts as high as thirty feet were visible on the valley floor.

Who knew how far down the bottom really was? A man would have to come and visit in the dead of summer to find the snow melted to see the truth. Only then could they discover how much snow lay beneath their feet. They plodded on with their heavy snowshoes.

For the briefest of moments, everything froze like in a picture. Rusty craned his head around in wonder at the power of hope. Right there before them, they had the shelter they needed. Call it what you may, but it was a miracle for three of these four men.

Whisper opened his mouth to brag and claim it was he who brought the smoke. But with one sharp look from Chief Hachta, he snapped his trap shut and bit his tongue. Now, he knew better than to let his true thoughts be known. Like it or not, the chief was the head leader of the tribe and was above even the number one medicine man.

"I reckon that's just what we needed." McFarlin

chuckled. "We're gonna be all right, after all. Things always seem to work themselves out, don't they, Rusty?"

"They sure do, old friend. Now let's go and see who else is in there."

Angus had a calm, resolved look, like a man who had already made his peace with God. He looked at the cave—like he always knew it would be there. As they got closer, the weather began to darken, and they heard thunderclaps somewhere not so far away. Ten steps of a ladder leaned against the cave's floor. A pully stuck out from a large vertical crack in the canyon wall. They assumed it was to pull supplies to the top. As they approached the slash cut into the mountainside, their hopes rose.

"It'll help if the folks inside that cave are friendly," Angus said. "That'll be the icing on the cake."

"It will be their bad luck if they aren't," the medicine man protested, fingering the knife in his belt. "I doubt there are more than one or two men in there. We could kill them easily."

"Maybe we might wanna wait until they prove to be our enemies before we start with the killin'," Rusty scolded and gave the shaman a dirty look. "I find that in dire weather, most folks are accommodating. Maybe it's because they wouldn't want such a thing to happen to them. We're all in danger out here in the wilderness all the time."

The cave looked much closer than it really was. Even though it appeared to be half an hour away, they walked most of the afternoon before standing before the ladder. It was of crude construction. The rope bound two thin trees together with cut branches, making the rungs.

"Is anybody in there?" Rusty called out in English, then repeated the same in Crow. "We come with the best intentions and don't mean nobody no harm. All we want is shelter from the storm."

Eight eyes stared at the dark hole. Most of the cave entrance stood in deep shadows. As they waited, time slowed to a stop, and what had probably been minutes seemed to take an hour. When Angus saw the White man, his stomach fell off a cliff. The stranger's state of mind was evident from the start, even before he opened his mouth.

With one hand, the hermit curled his finger to come; with the other, he wagged no. His frown betrayed his smiling eyes. The travelers instantly recognized a complicated man and knew they had to tread lightly.

"I'm Rusty Steel, and this is my pard, Angus McFarlin. Don't be afraid of the Crow Indians. They're a friend of mine too. This here is my blood brother, Chief Hachta, and his gofer, Mister Whisper." He glanced to see the angry face of the medicine man, which gave Rusty a genuine smile.

The Crow Indians were much more cautious now that they saw the man in the cave was White. On top of that, he appeared to be possessed by spirits. Most Indians were afraid of crazy people and believed dangerous demons possessed them. For this reason, they were cautiously kind when they couldn't steer completely clear.

Both Rusty and Angus took the hermit in stride. He wasn't the first man they had seen who had lost his mind alone in the Rocky Mountains, nor would he be the last.

The Hermit

The albino, Toothpick Vic, was dressed in rags, and his face was wrinkled like an old dog. But his pink eyes were full of life and so piercing it was difficult to hold his gaze. He lived on the side of a mountain well above the valley floor high in the Rockies, where few humans ventured. A forty-foot ladder rose from the bottom to the cavern's entrance.

A pulley system allowed him to raise and lower the stairs, providing a difficult barrier for attack from hostile Indians, outlaw White men, or wild animals. Even bears and mountain lions couldn't reach his refuge. Both had tried and failed, as had red and White men alike.

The old hermit eased down stiffly from the ladder—ten rungs to the snowdrift. The stiff breeze flapped his ragged clothing. The wind moaned like a distant beast.

"I take it y'all be lost," the hermit said. "Come on in, but mind your step. The ladder is a little rickety. Once you're in, pull that door to before we all blow away."

What the hermit called a door was no more than a

mass of mismatched planks on leather hinges. It hung loose and left marks in the dirt where it opened and closed. It was fastened by a leather latch.

The guests sat cross-legged across from the hermit, who didn't seem to remember his given name. Toothpick Vic constantly mumbled like he was speaking to an imaginary friend. The invisible person sat at his side, and he translated everything spoken in a foreign tongue. His pink eyes, lack of eyebrows, and translucent skin made him stand out anywhere but where he lived in isolation.

The hermit sat with a gash for a mouth as he cocked his head and listened to the howling wind outside. Now decrepit from age and stooped over, he survived on the same dead animals the scavengers did on which they fed. His water well was the perpetual snow found at such altitudes. A large clay pot sat in the corner of his cave with a small fire underneath. Shovels of snow filled the vessel as it slowly melted.

In the center of the stone room, a fire burned on a flat gray floor, creating a circle of light in the dome, but the cave continued far deeper into the mountain. Vic knew the only other living things he shared his home with were thousands of bats that were hibernating for the winter. Only the occasional hawk or vulture attempted to breach the entrance, and they did so at their own peril. Some of their bones still lay just outside the cave's mouth as a warning for those that followed.

"If you leave them furs out yonder by the entrance, some critter's bound to drag 'em off to eat," the hermit said. "Anything that ain't in my cave disappears by mornin'. I reckon some of the bigger buzzards could fly off that big old dog in their talons and all. Have y'all all got any bacca?"

Angus pulled out a twist and gave him the whole thing. It was the least he could do for a man who saved his life. He added his coffee and even gave him a corncob pipe he carried as a backup if his ceramic one broke.

The old man was armed with a single Tennessee long rifle. The wood stock was worn from decades of use. Steel traps hung from wooden pegs hammered into cracks in the cavern's walls. The weapon was for defense only. Several knives protruded from his belt and boots. Stones neatly circled the flames and orange cinders. Smoke stained the ceiling black, but some source of air deep in the cavern created a current that swept it out as soon as it appeared.

Thick piles of fur pelts and hides covered the area around the heat source like a plush carpet. Others hung from the walls, stretching on wooden frames, but it was clear the hermit didn't trap to sell his furs. It was his meat source, bone tools, warm clothing, and blankets. A mix of smells filled the room, some pleasant and others not. It created a unique odor, not offensive but still not enticing either.

Of course, Toothpick Vic hadn't always been a raggedy hermit living alone in one of the most isolated places on the planet. Long ago, a time he had now forgotten, he was a soldier and an officer. A deep crease in his forehead and a long scar told the story. He had the Indian wars painted all over his face with powder burns and pockmarks. His raggedy remains of a uniform were blue—he was apparently an officer, but high in the mountains, there were no sides or politics. It was just the albino and Mother Nature.

As he came from a long line of military men, when the war broke out, he immediately joined the army. His superb education made him a captain upon inscription. He was all guts and glory and never considered anything but victory, but that victory he hoped for was lost, as was his memory and part of his mind.

The only blessing was he didn't remember even participating in the bloody Indian wars. For him, it had never even happened. He was spared the memories of all the cruel violence and torture from his soldiers scalped and others, their hearts removed after they were skinned alive. He had peered deep into the eyes of Comanche warriors and lived, which was no small feat. What he had seen was beyond terror. It was impossible to describe.

The thunder moved northbound, and in a half hour, it was booming overhead. The hermit watched his visitors and nodded, but his face was now a mask. Or was it just more madness?

Rusty made a fist with his thumb pointing up and his little finger down and tilted back his head as he tipped a phantom drink down his throat, then looked questioningly at the hermit. His eyes instantly lit up, and he thrust his chin toward the water bucket in the corner and made clucking noises with his tongue.

Angus was already busy making a meal. Bacon sizzled, and the aroma of coffee floated in the air. He stirred beans in a tin pot. Vic sat watching McFarlin carefully as he whispered to his invisible friend.

As they hunkered over their tin pie pans, they wiped

the grease with their fingers and drank from a wooden bucket with a brown gourd. The not-so-distant thunderheads quivered against an electric sky. The hermit sat with his head tilted as he listened and stared at the strangers over the flickering flames. Curiosity filled his eyes, but still, he sat silently. It appeared he had said all he had to say. Yet, he continued to mumble to his spirit friend beside him.

Whisper was getting nervous. He thought maybe the invisible friend of the White man was possibly real. He had heard of such things among shamans but never from White men. Then again, this one had the curse of the pink eye and was clearly mad—even more reason to keep a careful eye on him just in case.

As the thunder moved overhead, everything seemed to vibrate with each boom. They hunkered down in the hovel of a shelter as they spooned more hot beans into their mouths, slurping the grease from their fingers, refreshing themselves with melted ice.

The stiff breeze stirred the ends of Vic's matted, greasy hair. His eyes were set, tunneled deep into caves over a haunted face. He pursed his mouth and shrugged but continued silent as he held his gaze at the visitors.

Sweat beaded on the men's foreheads, but nobody complained. They sat as close to the fire as they dared without being set alight themselves. Inside was darkness, and it smelled of dirt and earth. There was little light save the fire with the rickety door closed against the freezing wind.

Deep in the cave in another dome, overhead was cluttered with a dark-furred mass that shifted, chittered, and breathed. As winter deepened, the bats' metabolism slowed to nearly nothing as they hibernated.

The visitors spread their bedrolls on the frozen stone floor. The entrance to the cave howled as the wind whistled off the stone outside. As the hermit slept, he muttered and struggled like a dreaming dog. In his dreams, he lived his nightmare past. The things he didn't remember when he was awake he lived again every night he went to sleep.

The naked feet of the dead jostled stiffly from side to side in the back of the wagon. Vic pinched himself to see if he was dreaming, but no...it all appeared genuine. He was startled and shocked when he saw his face among the others. Was he dead, too? Toothpick pinched himself again; then he awoke, blinking his eyes, unsure which world was real and which was his imagination. Then, he immediately forgot everything again.

In Dog's sleep, he struggled and muttered in his dreams while kicking his feet as though he were running. Late into the night, Rusty eyed the strange man over the dying flames. The sleeping dog opened one eye, looked at his master, and then fell back asleep. The warm cave made all of them drowsy and calmed their spirits, all but one.

The hermit turned his head, pinched his nose with thumb and finger, and blew twin strings of snot onto the floor. He wiped his hand on his dirty, tattered shirt.

A stickler on manners, Rusty's face clouded, but he held his tongue. It was enough that Vic had saved their lives. A bung-starter hung from one side of his belt and his whip from his hand, and he clearly wasn't afraid to use either one. Thunder quivered, and lightning slashed across the magnetic sky. The streaks of electricity were sucked away and were replaced with blackness.

The wind continued to howl louder and louder until

it sounded like a massive locomotive roaring down steel tracks, hurtling toward them. When they ventured to peek out, the whiteout was so thick they could hardly tell if it was day or night. With the full moon, it all looked the same.

Two days later, when they heard the birds singing outside, they knew the storm had passed. Toothpick was the first to rise, pushing open the door and shoving the snowdrift aside. Everything beyond the mouth of the cave was frozen and windswept. Snowdrifts towered so high they covered lower peaks. The ladder had disappeared in the snow, and not a single rung showed of the forty-foot ladder. Rusty Steel warmed up creakily, as did Angus. The cold made their old bones ache.

Birds awoke Rusty and Angus where they lay in the warm cavern. Vultures' eyes stared from the entrance, inspecting the humans. Hunger gave them the courage to stand fast and not flee and flap away. Victor suddenly lashed out at the vultures with his whip, cracking it against their tails as feathers danced in the air and vanished in the wind. The leather whip lashed out, hitting its target precisely like a well-practiced art.

Yards of wings whooshed as the giant birds took flight and escaped the fall's popper at the end of the braided whip. It cracked again and again right behind them as they fled. Toothpick Vic cackled, and it echoed across the canyon again and again.

Rusty's dog sniffed the air, got up, and walked out the door, lifting his leg and peeing against the rock wall. One by one, the men came out and had a look around. As far as they could see, the land was void of tracks. What looked like Hell a few days before now looked like Heaven.

THE MEDICINE MAN

ONCE THE STORM PASSED, EVERYBODY WAS FULL OF SPUNK and vinegar. They had weathered the blizzard and weren't any worse for wear. As soon as it ended, Toothpick made it clear that the visitors were expected to leave. Vic made shooing motions with the backs of his hands, making his desires clear. He didn't say a word when he pulled the crumbling door closed and disappeared into the dark cave. The visit was obviously over and his guests suddenly unwelcome. At least he had saved them from freezing to death. A stranger man they had never met.

Rusty slapped his hands on his chest and grinned from ear to ear. The clear blue sky was crisp and the air cold, but the danger had passed, and they could all be on their way. Angus rubbed his hands together and pulled his hat over his ears.

"I reckon it's time to head home." Rusty grinned. "How about you and mister witch doctor there? What cha all gonna do? Are ya still gonna chase that miracle or is surviving the blizzard miracle enough for ya, Chief?" Rusty laughed; it too echoed, bouncing off the canyon walls. "We best get those sleds full of furs harnessed and ready to pull. I told ya I wasn't gonna leave my pelts behind. You should thank your lucky stars you've still got yours. If it wasn't for me, you wouldn't."

Whisper frowned and spat into the snow, but the mountain men just smiled some more. They enjoyed aggravating the old fool.

"When we get to the compound and we still have our furs, then you can crow all ya want," Angus replied. "It's still dangerous cold out and we could freeze tonight."

"I have some unfinished business to attend to before I go anywhere," Hachta said in a low growl. "Like I said, I respond immediately when challenged. Prepare yourself, Whisper. Your time has come."

Whisper was so relieved the storm was over and they had survived, he had forgotten he insulted the chief. It suddenly came back to him like the kiss at the end of a hot fist. That, along with Hachta's stare. The chief's eyes bore right through him. Of course, the shaman wasn't a famous warrior like the tribe's leader, but still tribal rules were in play now, and he had bitten off more than he could chew. Now he *really* needed a miracle, or he would probably end up dead.

Hachta pulled his pistols and passed them to Rusty. Angus took both his rifles. Only his knives remained. The medicine man put his pistols on the ground. He didn't trust the White men with his guns. He braced himself and when he looked down, he had knives in his hands. It almost came as a shock. The last thing he ever wanted to happen was materializing before his very eyes. He suddenly understood how big a mouth he had. He must have been crazy to get so sassy with the chief. He knew in seconds he would be dead but at least he would die bravely.

Every nerve in Whisper's body went dead instantly. He suddenly realized the severity of his actions. The medicine man turned long enough to glare at the Rusty, but he continued to smile. Whisper's control of the moment was wrenched from his grasp. That was when blood began to race through his body and his nerves began to fray. He knew he had screwed up but now it appeared too late to take back what he had said. Even he, a famous witch doctor, knew insulting a chief was a serious matter.

"Well, whaddaya say, Chief?" Rusty asked. "Maybe you can hurry it up because I'd kind of like to get on our way." He grinned at the terrified shaman.

Little snowflakes still filled the sky, but the temperature was rising and little by little the flakes became smaller until they eventually disappeared. These were not the flakes the size of silver dollars from the day before. It was just a normal early winter's day.

"It's time to separate the chaff from the wheat," Hachta replied. "If I let this pass, then who am I? I won't have this fool telling lies back at camp. This ends here and now." He turned to the medicine man. "With your life or mine."

The shaman seemed to try to fold into himself and cower before such a dangerous man. *What was I thinking*? Whisper asked himself. He had signed his own death warrant.

"Prepare yourself, Whisper, or I'll kill you where you

stand!" the chief roared. It came so suddenly, the medicine man took two steps backward. He could feel the chief's hot breath in his face.

"Didn't you know, witch doctor?" Rusty asked. "Chief Hachta's enemies have the habit of dying off like deer flies at the end of summer. I've been lookin' forward to this for a long time."

"Me too." Angus grinned. "This'll be a lesson, well overdue."

Hachta surprised everybody when he whipped his bow off his back and around in a large arch and smacked Whisper square in the face. *Thump, thump*—the hardened wood hit Whisper's head and ribs repeatedly as he went down. When the medicine man rolled over on his back, the chief hit him square in the mouth. He coughed and spat up a dozen bloody teeth.

Chief Hachta stood back and examined his work and nodded in approval. A teeth-clenched curse followed.

"That's right," Rusty said. "Be decisive. Right or wrong, make a decision and stick to it. The trail is full of flat squirrels. I reckon you did the right thing by not killin' 'em and all. I really didn't think you would, but there was no sense in tellin' your witch doctor that." He coughed into his fist to stifle a snicker. The moment was too grave for that.

"Hell fire, Chief, you don't need no gun," Angus marveled.

"Get up and wash the blood off your face," Hachta spat. "You're an embarrassment to the Crow Nation. You're lucky I didn't leave you here for the critters to eat with your throat cut. I could have just as easily killed you. This is a lesson and make sure you learn it well. Before you insult someone, especially before dear friends, you might consider if you can kill the man you insulted or not. This time you're lucky because I don't want to have to explain why I killed you to the tribe. There are still a few that look up to you. For the life of me, I don't know why, but they do. I reckon you're a good liar is all."

Rusty sucked on his cud and spat. A half yard of brown juice landed right beside the shaman's head. Brown speckled his cheek and mixed in with the blood.

The chief's bow was composite. It was made of wood, backed by buffalo back, leg tendon with rawhide and gut. The wood was bought from contacts with the Iroquois from far away elm trees near Ontario. It was said to be the best bow wood in the country. As many believed, it didn't have only a single function but served well as a club, too. The hardwood and flex made it hit like a whip. Welts popped up across the medicine man's body and he wasn't acting strappy anymore. The chief was sure he would never tell a soul if he simply thrashed him for poor manners.

Now, with most of his teeth missing, Whisper wouldn't be able to deny the truth. Still, he was a clever liar, and Hachta knew better than to trust him ever again. He had tricked the chief into coming on a pointless journey into the wilderness to find themselves without shelter before a deadly storm. Eventually Whisper had shown his true colors, and his thoughts escaped him. Everything the chief had suspected was true.

Hachta had been the chief of his tribe for a long

time. He knew when and where to act against a member of their stronghold. Some things were acceptable and others grudgingly so, and killing Whisper would have put pressure on his hold as chief. He felt he dosed out the correct amount of punishment to teach Whisper a lesson and any others who got big ideas. Of course, it was routine for the young warriors to challenge the leader, but none of them had the experience the older men did. Being a veteran in battle held much more weight than they believed.

"Get up," Hachta growled. "My friends are waiting to leave. We have kept them waiting long enough or maybe you want some more of my bow?"

Whisper held one hand over his mouth to block the flow of blood from his broken gums. He mumbled something unintelligible as he used his other hand to push him up and out off the ground. Claret spotted the snow red. Wobbly knees threatened to topple Whisper as he struggled to fasten his snowshoes.

"Grab the harness of Rusty Steel's sled," Hachta ordered. "You will pull it alone the rest of the way as punishment. This is how you will beg forgiveness to my friends for embarrassing our tribe and people, the Crow Nation."

Whisper looked over and nearly spoke but when he locked eyes with the chief he thought better and clamped his lips shut to keep words from running out his mouth. He tried to hide the hate in his eyes, too, but it was impossible. It ran too deep and long. Hachta knew he had an enemy for life now. They had always had their differences, but from this day on they were adversaries.

"Don't even think about it," Hachta threatened. "I saw that look in your eyes. Maybe I should kill you just to be on the safe side. Most of the tribe wouldn't mind if I did anyway." He fingered the bone handle of his large knife.

Heading Home

Once they said their goodbyes to the Crow Indians, Rusty and Angus turned for home. It was only a day's walk away now, so they knew they would be sleeping in their own beds by a roaring fire the next day. As simple as their cabin was, it was a luxury compared to the last two days in the hermit's cave. They wondered how Vic survived for what appeared to be years. Still, no one knew much about him since he wasn't much of a talker. He didn't speak a dozen words the entire time, except for his imaginary friend, to whom he mumbled constantly.

Rusty grunted and curled a sly grin as he glanced at the sun again for the time. "I reckon tomorrow we'll be home, sippin' on whiskey-laced coffee before a roaring fire." Dog looked up at his master as he spoke.

"I can almost smell the cabin full of finely cooked food," Angus said. "As soon as we get home, I'm gonna make some elk steaks as thick as a table with lots of potatoes and gravy. There ain't nothin' better than home cookin', and we've got the new storeroom full of wild game meat of every sort and size."

"With the new company to the compound, it won't seem like such a long winter, either." Rusty smiled. "That Betty is quite a talker, ain't she? We could use some new conversation. You've told me every story you know a thousand times."

"Likewise." Angus snickered. "Still, we've got our new adventure to tell everyone about. That will be good for a week at least."

"You best let me tell it first before you begin exaggerating, or soon it won't be recognizable," Rusty said. "It will go from an adventure to a tall tale as soon as it comes out of your mouth. Somebody should hear the actual story before it's passed on and turned into something hardly recognizable to what really happened. You know how the Indian gossip is, old pard."

Steel pulled the cigar from his teeth, turned his head and spat, then stuck it between his lips again. Billows of smoke floated around his head briefly before the breeze swept it away.

"After all this, I see it as clear as a bell," Angus said. "We need to set our feet on the path of righteousness. A man ain't given but one miracle in a lifetime, and I figure we just saw ours."

Their snowshoes and sleds left tracks like two slugs in the otherwise untouched snow—Dog's paw prints circled them. They walked through the towering pines as they swayed in the breeze. Bunches of snow fell from bows, plopping down to the powder-covered ground. Now, they were in familiar territory and felt safer with every mile they neared home. Despite pulling a hundred pounds, they felt light, and a sudden burst of energy overcame them. The journey was almost over, and they had done what they set out to do, despite the hardships. Seeing trees they had lived around for over a decade felt good. They noted the unique scent of home.

Rusty and Angus sat under a pumpkin moon smoking ceramic pipes beside a small fire that night. They had managed to gather the odd bit of firewood as they traveled through the day. At least they would go to bed warm, even if they would awake cold. Buffalo skin blankets covered them as they slept. They were so tired and close enough to home they didn't even take turns keeping guard. Both men sighed a deep breath of relief and drifted off to a peaceful sleep. The canine cuddled up snugly against Rusty, sharing the warmth.

Shortly after the fire flickered out, only the orange coals remained. But as it was small, they soon turned cold, and their surroundings fell into total darkness. Clouds passed between the earth and the moon until it set; then even the silvery glow vanished.

They didn't hear the voices in the night as the Blackfeet Indians passed far too closely for comfort. But without a campfire nor the silhouette of a guard, they were invisible unless the hostile Indians stumbled over their bodies. The mountain men slept quietly undetected, nor did they realize a mortal enemy was nearby.

Rusty's dog opened his eyes and watched, but he sensed not to bark, disclosing their location. Hackles rose on his back as he made a low whisper of a growl. He crouched near his master and prepared to attack if the hostile humans came their way. He knew their scent well and instinctively knew they were enemies.

The following day, Rusty and Angus awoke to finches and hairy woodpeckers hammering on frozen trees. Rusty stretched into a yawn as soon as he popped his head from under his blankets. He slept in a bear skin coat and furry hat. Dog continued to sleep because he hadn't gotten much rest during the night.

"Wake up, Angus," Rusty said. "If we leave right off and don't diddle-daddle around, we'll be home by noon." He poked Angus in the ribs, and the old mountain man grumbled.

"Just another thirty minutes," Angus's sleepy voice came from under hairy blankets. "I need to rest a little more before I start pullin' that dad-gummed sled again. I feel I've been dragging it behind me for a thousand miles."

"All right then," Rusty growled. "I'll see if there's enough dry wood to make a small fire and some coffee while I wait for you to wake up. If you don't linger too long, I'll save ya a cup."

Angus ignored Rusty's impatience. He had lived in the same cabin with him long enough to know his ways. He closed his eyes again, and, in a minute, he was softly snoring. Rusty sat bored, staring into the water pot, trying to make the water boil faster.

They slipped the harnesses over their heads and chests an hour later and began the last short jog home. Not two hundred feet into their last bit of the journey, they saw the footprints in the snow.

Rusty stooped down and inspected the size of the snowshoes, shaking his head. "Them's Indian snowshoes. They're heading in the same direction we are. I wonder who they are? They ain't Crow, and any other tribe around here is unwelcome. Even from here, the big stronghold ain't but a day's walk. Nobody but Blackfeet would be so bold, I reckon."

"Maybe we should abandon the sleds," Angus said worriedly. "Those pelts are gonna cost us our lives."

"Shut up, pull the danged thing, and stop complainin'," Rusty retorted. "We've just gotta pull harder, is all. The folks back at the cabin are well prepared, and they all know how to shoot. I wouldn't worry too much. I figure them walking right by us is another one of those miracles Whisper talks about so much. I don't know how they missed us. Why, Dog didn't even bark." He looked at his canine quizzically and raised his eyebrows.

"I figure he's smart enough to have known not to," Angus replied. "They would have been on us too fast to fight 'em off."

Rusty and Angus put down their heads and nearly ran, or at least went as fast as a man can go with snowshoes dragging two sleds. Still, they were moving faster than the day before by far. Now, they had a real reason to hurry. They knew there was nowhere but the compound in this area to pillage. They assumed the Blackfeet were taking advantage of the coming blizzard to use it as cover in their attack.

As they raced through the forest, Dog ran out front to ensure the coast was clear. They knew the Blackfeet would be nearby if they heard him barking now, but they were ready.

As they followed the hostiles' tracks, they trod lightly as they approached their cabins. They listened, but there wasn't a sound in the crisp morning. That alone was a signal that something was amiss. With five people in the compound, they knew that breakfast brought noises like coughing, banging of pans, and the outhouse door slamming on steel springs.

They could see a single plume of smoke rise into the sky above the pines in the distance when there should be three or more. They listened, and everything continued to be far too quiet.

Rusty whispered, “They’ve all holed up in the main cabin. Otherwise, there should be three strings of smoke from three chimneys. If they’re all together, they know the Blackfeet are out here. But what the Indians don’t know is that we’re behind ’em. Pull your pistols, old pard. If we sandwich ’em in, we should be able to make quick work if Levi and Will hit ’em from the cabin simultaneously.”

“I’m sure as soon as they hear gunfire, they’ll recognize our pistols,” Angus said. “Although a lot of Indians have flintlock rifles these days, pistols aren’t as common. The rifles aren’t our best choice at close range in the forest anyway.”

“We’ve got seven pistols between us and four rifles,” Rusty said. “Maybe we can make ’em think we’re a small army if we walloped ’em and shoot our guns off in quick succession. Even if we don’t hit a target, we might make ’em change their plans. This ain’t gonna be the easy hit and run they expect it to be.”

“They’ll be after the horses first,” Angus said. “They can mix in with our small herd and remain unseen.”

“Hopefully, Levi stored the animals in the stable to keep ’em out of harm’s way when the storm hit,” Rusty said.

“But what if they’ve already let them out since the blizzard passed?” Angus asked.

They moved more carefully as they approached the

last five hundred yards, moving from tree to tree. Rusty and Angus left the sleds to retrieve later and pulled their guns, preparing for what was to come. Now, they crept through the forest with a pistol in each fist and the others ready to draw from their belts. A brace of rifles was strapped across their backs.

When they found the hostile Indians' snowshoes, they knew they were right and were on the trail of men who intended to kill them, if not at least steal their mules, horses, and supplies. What the Indians didn't know was with the mountain men behind them and the fort they planned to attack in front, they were walking right into a hornet's nest.

Rusty stopped and pointed to his nose, and Angus took a whiff. He nodded. For men like these, their sense of smell was almost as important as their keen eyesight.

"Them's Blackfeet all right," Angus whispered into Rusty's ear. "We best crawl the last stretch of land. We can sneak in by the old path we used when we first arrived."

"It'll be too grown over after years of no use," Rusty replied.

"Exactly, but I bet the old trail will still be there if we crawl under the brush. I can follow it blindfolded," Angus whispered. "Nobody's gonna follow us through those briar patches with this snow. Maybe we can make our way to the edge, burrow into the powder the last few yards, and pop up all unexpectedly. The Blackfeet will have their backs to us, so it should be a turkey shoot."

Angus led the way. He and Dennis had made the path years before, but they had traveled it so many times, he remembered every twist and turn. It was true

—it was completely overgrown and covered in snow. Still, the old mountain man did just like he said, and he closed his eyes and moved forward, remembering the trail in his mind's eye as they crawled under briars and bushes. Soon, they were at the edge of the compound. When Rusty crawled up next to Angus, he looked like a snowman. He was hardly recognizable. His blinking eyes were what gave him away.

"Lookee over there," Rusty whispered, pointing. "They're all lined up behind the corral. We were right. They plan to steal the horses and, if possible, flush the boys out and pillage the houses too. But I know Levi better than that. They'll never breach the door or window in our place. It's like a fort. Mind you, they might get into Dennis's and the boys' cabins. I'm sure if they're under threat, they will all be in our place. It's the safest one of the three."

"That's how I built it." Angus smiled. "Easy to get out of and impossible to break in. The only way is to starve 'em out. Maybe that's the hostiles' plans."

"Not with the stock we have in the new storage cellar." Rusty huffed.

The snow drifts against the bushes were four to five feet deep. In seconds, both men disappeared as they burrowed their way in, holding their breaths. They would pop up and start to fire as soon as they were fifteen feet closer. Their pistols were stuck into their belts again, with their coats covering them to keep the powder dry.

When they arrived at the agreed distance, they both popped up and pulled their pistols. A dozen Blackfeet braves' backs stood before them. The Indians were so focused on the horses and the cabin, they didn't check their six and were suddenly in the position for a crossfire. The boys just hoped that Levi, Will, Virgil, and the others were ready and had their ears sharp. With the storm, they probably weren't expecting Rusty and Angus back so soon.

Hostile Indians

Betty screamed when she saw what was unfolding. She clutched an axe handle in two fists and turned toward Dahteste with fire in her eyes. Both her husband and Levi Johnson huddled around the woman Indian war chief. To her, it looked like they were planning against the only White woman in camp. She secretly felt intimidated by the Crow woman, and her natural instinct was to go on the offensive.

Her father had taught her always to be the first to strike, or you stood the chance of losing the fight. Somehow, she saw Dahteste as a hostile. Maybe she wasn't as prepared to live in the wilderness with Indians as she thought she was. A deep fear set into her soul, and she couldn't shake it. It had clouded her senses, and she was acting crazy and wasn't quite sure why.

Of course, they had all heard the stories of captured White women and how they went mad when forced to live with the Indians, even though tribes like the Crow eventually treated them like another one of their people. But Betty had come voluntarily and wasn't captured nor forced to stay with her new husband. Maybe deep down inside, she wanted them to join Marshal Joseph Walker on the planned wagon train, travel to Oregon City, and settle like other normal Easterners.

Then that would mean she didn't know the captain at all. Levi, Rusty, Angus, Dennis, and Virgil had become the only family he had. His folks back home would have disowned him by this time. He doubted he would be prepared to leave his best friend and mentors for a woman he apparently knew little about. In the last few days, she had become an entirely different person, almost unrecognizable from the woman he fell in love with.

Maybe it was the small red woman's Indian ways that put Betty into such a tailspin. Her apparent need to announce her position was much more significant than her common sense. The always sensible woman had turned into someone nobody recognized. It was strange how they had traveled from the South Pass and across what was soon to be known as the Oregon Trail to the Pacific coast and back, and the two women got along fine. It wasn't until they were in Betty's new future home did her instinct of hierarchy came into play.

Perhaps the fame that came behind her famous uncle, Davy Crockett, had blinded her to people she might unconsciously feel inferior to. She appeared to be hellbent on proving herself the superior of the two when everybody else knew she wasn't. This was what shocked and bewildered her new husband so much. He didn't know what to think. Was it going to be a transient situation, or was this the true Betty Crockett—now the newlywed Mrs. Forrester? Had the captain made a terrible mistake, and if so, how was he to resolve it?

As a cavalry captain, he always knew what he had to do. Even though he had lived in devastating situations, losing most of the people on his famed expedition, he never found himself lost for what to do next. Too many men were counting on him for the captain to lose his direction and put their lives at risk. But dealing with a woman, let alone a wife, was another situation, and he had no idea what to do. Of course, he was taught from a young boy to respect women and never strike them, and even though he wanted to do just that to see if he could knock some sense into her, he knew he could never do it. It was against everything he was ever taught. Something that his mentor shared, regardless of the situation.

Unbeknownst to the White woman, Dahteste was a force to be reckoned with. Not only was she a war chief, but she had also earned her title by fighting and killing enemies of the Crow tribe. She was fearless, and despite her small package, she was as mean as a honey badger if provoked. Luckily, so far, she had been either sucker punched or surprised unawares by Betty or had been subdued by Levi and her husband, Will.

"Put that club down right now!" Will shouted. "I said this was over, and I don't like repeating myself."

The captain stood and turned harsh eyes toward his bride. Now, when he looked at her, he saw a different person he didn't quite like. Still, he wondered what set it off. He doubted it was Dahteste's fault, or Betty would already be dead. A White woman, even if she came from Crockett stock, could never hold their own against a veteran fighter like Levi's wife. Then again, Dahteste wasn't about to take guff or aggression from Betty sitting down. Levi had his hands full, keeping her from teaching Betty a lesson she would never forget. Still, he didn't think she would kill her, but she could turn things around so fast the White woman's head would spin.

"Because if she doesn't..." Dahteste shook her head grimly. She didn't need to say more.

Levi wrapped his muscle-bound arm around her tiny shoulders, hoping to keep her close and from not racing off at Betty to tear her apart. Something was pleasing and pure in the way Dahteste looked at Levi. When she blinked, there was certainty in her gaze. She leaned closer and whispered something in his ear. Johnson sternly shook his head and grabbed his wife tighter. The White woman didn't realize how dangerous the Crow Indian was.

"Calm down now, darlin'. This ain't the time or place." Levi arched his brow and asked, "How'd all this get started?" His heart suddenly began to thump in his throat.

The captain sat there staring blankly like he had never seen this woman before. It was like he was looking at a stranger. "Put it down, Betty." But she barely shrugged, evincing a hint of a wicked smile. His wife squeezed her fists, feeling her blood come to a stop in her veins. White knuckles wrapped around the axe handle. Forrester could see her blood speed into overdrive as her eyes seemed to fog over and become crazed. The thought that she had lost her mind drifted through his mind, but he pushed it back into the dark recesses of his memory. That was something that he might not have the strength to face.

As the drama continued, the hostile Blackfeet

Indians crept nearer the cabins, hoping to get close enough to make a surprise attack while the White people were busy arguing between themselves. But little did they know the mountain men had already discovered their presence.

They didn't know a Crow warrior with a nose as good as Rusty's dog was in camp. Soon, there would be a second shock for the Indians of reckless blood. It was sneaking up behind them as they waited to attack. It would all unfold in a matter of seconds.

The five men and two women battened down all the cabins with the heavy timber shutters and closed and locked doors with hefty chains and thick, loud locks. They all gathered in Rusty's cabin. It was the best building prepared against an attack, and the same place they had fought off hostile Indians and White thieves many times before. Gun slats were cut into both the shutters and the door, one high and another low, so there was room for multiple weapons to fire. As the house was dug into the mountain, it was impossible to burn them out or attack from the flanks or rear. The only way to get to the mountain men was a frontal attack.

After Dahteste discovered the presence of the Blackfeet warriors, they had shown themselves several times throughout the day. Usually, it was a single warrior exhibiting how brave he was by running dangerously close to the main cabin. Others were ready to breach the compound and hide behind buildings and porches. Twenty braves closed in on the enemy. They were confident the Crow stronghold would be all locked down for the blizzard, and they had heard the famous Rusty Steel and his partner, Angus, weren't home. Hopefully, they would only find Levi and the captain with Dennis, but they weren't worried about the old man.

"Those must be some brave Blackfeet to come so close to the Crow camp," Dahteste said. "Either that or they're very foolish." She held her rifle with the barrel sticking out the window shutter and the hammer drawn back. She was ready for the attack that she knew would come. They all knew it could happen any second.

A week-old beard stubble darkened the captain's face. It added a few years to his appearance; he already looked older than Levi, yet they were the same age. The problem between their wives was taking its toll on both husbands, not to mention now hostile Indians. The captain had to push their personal issues aside and deal with the life-threatening peril before them, though.

As they waited for the attack, the captain eyed Betty over the brim of his cup. The steam blurred his vision, but it also covered his eyes, so she didn't notice him watching. Her features shined in the firelight and shone warmly, but he maintained his stern face despite his feelings. She had deeply disappointed him, and now he wondered if things would be the same or if would they somehow change. He suddenly seemed to see her in a different light.

Levi could see the corral from the corner of the door's gun slat. Behind that, he saw motions that weren't horses' legs. The clever Blackfeet were using the animals as cover to come closer to the cabins undetected. Of course, they could break the heavy locks with time and rob the other two lodges, not to mention the teepee, although they would find little of value there. Dahteste had already cleared everything out.

The horses were presently in jeopardy as the Blackfeet warriors were preparing to herd them out. Two warriors were working on tearing down the corral fence to lead them out the back and flee. But first, they wanted to see if they couldn't acquire the big prize. Maybe they could even take a few scalps.

First, the hostiles saw the gun barrels sticking out the holes in the window and door. Five rifles pointed at them. Now, they realized they had been foolish to believe these mountain men never sensed their presence. Of course, Rusty Steel and Angus were known for their almost Indian-like skills, and they would have smelled the enemy before they got into striking distance. But they believe the apprentices could not have yet learned enough to be dangerous enemies. They had only been there a year and a half. The leader of the war party suddenly saw they were wrong.

The Blackfoot war chief gave the signal to retreat and decided to settle with the mules and horses. All of them were fine specimens, and they could proudly claim they had stolen them from the famous old mountain men's camp. This would put another feather in the leader's hair.

The clicking of hammers sounded loud behind them. None of the twenty warriors doubted what the metallic noise was. The Blackfeet's eyes grew when they saw the gun barrels pointing at their backs, and they were close enough that they knew their enemies wouldn't miss. Their only escape was to their flanks, and with them caught with their pants down, even that was dodgy. They would have to cross too much ground, leaving them open to the weapons in front of them and the others at their backs. They had unexpectedly walked right into a trap, and still, the war chief couldn't figure out how it had happened.

"Boo!" Rusty shouted, then he shot off both pistols at the Indians' feet. Angus also shot his guns simultaneously, but his were aimed closer and tore at the warriors' clothing. The men in the cabin heard the gunfire and took aim and pulled their triggers, too. Suddenly, pistols and rifles went off like popcorn in a skillet. The Blackfeet Indians turned and ran.

Angus aimed with his other two pistols, trailing the first two to flee. He had two more rifles laying beside him on his blanket in the snow, primed and ready to go.

Rusty suddenly grabbed his friend's arm and said, "There ain't no need to kill nobody today. Had they stolen our horses, it would be another matter, but I can't see killin' men for tearing down our corral fence. If we shot the bunch, the leaders of the Blackfoot tribe would feel obliged to retaliate anyway. So, it's best to let them flee with their honor damaged. They failed miserably, and the war chief knows that gossip always has a way of getting out. One of the warriors, if not more, will be disgruntled by the skills of their leader, and the secret won't be kept for long."

They were promised the spoils and the honor of beating the mountain men in the compound, even if they were the less experienced newcomers. Now, they were going to have to return empty-handed when they had promised the chief and tribe that they would defeat the White men and steal everything they possessed.

Ultimately, they escaped with their lives only because of the benevolent mountain man, Rusty Steel.

Safe & Sound

They could all see the hope and excitement in each other's eyes. Betty curled a grin despite her differences with Levi's Crow wife. For the moment, it seemed like a forgotten subject. Nobody had died from the intended Blackfoot attack, and that was important above all other things. Everybody sighed a breath of relief except for Marshal Walker because he felt cheated out of doing his duty as a lawman.

Attacking White people wasn't something he looked lightly on. Joseph was outraged that they hadn't killed the Blackfeet hostiles to the last man. Dead men didn't talk or gossip. He said they could have buried them in the snow, and nobody would have found them until spring.

As darkness neared, a glowing yellow lantern hung from the side of the entrance of Rusty's cabin. It shined like a beacon in the night. Now, the weather was too cold to sit on the porch. Yellow light spilled out the window onto the wood plank floor. When hazy silhouettes walked out of the dark from the side of the cabin and into the circle of light, rifles were trained their way, and hammers clicked in the dusk.

"Is this any way to greet your blood brother, Rusty Steel?" Chief Hatcha called out as he grinned. "I see you got to the Blackfeet before we arrived. A pity that. I would have taken great joy in capturing them and bringing them back to our camp myself. I already have scouts out searching for them."

When eyebrows raised, the Crow chief added, "I sent up smoke signals with the little wood you two left over in your last camp. I'd have never noticed it if it wasn't for me knowing where to look. We've been following you since we saw the hostile tracks on the land of the Crow Nation. But don't worry, I doubt they will make it back home. I sent thirty of my most veteran warriors. There is no way they'll escape them."

"At least somebody has their head square on their shoulders." Joseph huffed. "I agree with the chief all the way."

Rusty shot Walker a dirty look and said, "I actually didn't think them breaking down the corral fence was enough to deserve killing." The aging mountain man smiled. "Hell, I don't shy away from the occasional fight. It gives us something to talk about in the winter months. What do you say, Chief? Are we gonna let 'em go just this one time?"

"You know I can't do that, my brother," Hachta said. "I can't allow Blackfeet warriors to trespass on Crow land without due punishment. They would do the same were the moccasin on the other foot. If I let this incident go, others will follow, and of that, I have no doubt. If they are killed or, even better yet, captured and brought back to me for torture, it won't happen again—at least for a while. They were thinking they could hide under the shelter of the snowstorm. I am afraid they were dearly mistaken."

"Well, ya can't say that I didn't try," Rusty replied. "We were lucky anyway, Chief. We just happened to survive the blizzard and then had the good fortune to coincide with the timing of the Blackfoot attack. If we hadn't made it back here to the compound when we did, we would have lost our mules and horses for sure, though I doubt the boys would have let them breach the cabin." Steel gave Levi a warm look like he was peering at a son. "Then again, you're the boss, Chief. Hell, we're only here because of your kindness and our friendship. So, you go ahead and do what you have to do. I guess I'll just settle with *us* not doing the killing. Still, it would be nice to live a month in the mountains without seeing somebody die."

"Let me get at my kitchen," Angus said, pushing everybody aside. "I'm gonna make a meal fittin' for Thanksgiving. Who's hungry?"

"With this bunch, it's better to ask who's not hungry." Rusty laughed. "Then you'll never hear a word."

In minutes, Angus did his magic with the cast-iron stove, and soon, the table was covered in food. Steam rose off the hot mashed potatoes, and two-inch steaks were stacked on a large tin platter. No one has yet mentioned the problem between Dahteste and Betty.

Rusty hadn't noticed how they sat on the far sides of the table, as far away from each other as possible, when usually they were like two peas in a pod sitting side by side. Nor did he notice the concerned look on his apprentices' faces. He just figured they were still a bit shaken by all those Blackfeet warriors that were just about to breach their compound.

"How did you know the Blackfeet were headin' our way?" Levi asked. "I agree it was a great bit of luck. I'd hate to lose Trigger." It was his fourteen-hundred-pound Mustang.

"I don't know what I'd do if I lost Midnight, my stallion," the captain said. "Had they stolen our horses, I'd have tracked them down and killed 'em myself."

"They left enough tracks for a blind man to follow." Hachta chuckled. "Then again, it's pretty hard to cover all your tracks after all the snow."

"The same here." Rusty grinned. "When we smelled 'em, we knew they were Blackfeet right off. You just missed 'em by no more than a couple of hours, Chief."

"What in the world happened to you, Mister Whisper?" Levi asked as he eyed the toothless medicine man.

The supposed shaman had welts on his face and neck, and Johnson assumed they didn't stop there. He, too, had lived in the Crow camp for a while with Dahteste and knew the medicine man for his arrogance and dislike for White and Black men from back East. He knew the chief wouldn't appreciate it if he were too nosy, but he could hardly contain his curiosity. He even briefly forgot about the problems with his wife and Will's missus.

"He slipped and fell." Hachta chuckled. "Actually, the man doesn't know when to shut up. He has the impression that he is the spirit's gift to Earth."

Then the chief laughed until tears came to his eyes, much to the displeasure of the shaman, but still Whisper held his tongue. He had learned his lesson fast. He didn't like to smile anymore because he was missing all his front teeth. With his teeth went his arrogance in one swift movement. The chief had given the adequate punishment: no more and no less.

Still, Levi wondered what happened, but he said no more. Hopefully, the chief would spend the night, and the story would come out around the table with some whiskey-laced coffee and tobacco. That always seemed to loosen up Red, White, and Black men's tongues.

A massive fire roared in the fireplace, making the room almost too hot. But they all knew Rusty and Angus felt the cold more as the years passed. They still had to completely thaw out from sleeping in Toothpick Vic's cave. It had been like an ice box, and the chill that set into their aging bones took time to warm up again.

Shadows of flames flickered on their faces and the walls. Just as they were about to dig into the delicious-smelling food, Virgil cleared his throat, opened his tattered Bible, and read a verse from the sacred book.

As soon as he said amen, knives and forks clinked and rattled against tin pie pans. Nobody said a word as they shoveled heaps of food into their mouths. Finally, they cleaned their plates with freshly baked bread, leaving them sparkling. They even sucked on their greasy fingers before Dennis cleared the table and left the dishes to wash after a smoke.

The aroma of coffee floated in the air. Soon, steam rose from nine cups as Angus dosed out just enough liquor to taste but not so much as to make the chief uncomfortable. He was outspoken about the consumption of whiskey by his tribe's members. The chief believed that alcohol had adverse effects on the Crow people, and he always discouraged its consumption.

That was why he forbade his people to attend the Rendezvous. Each time they had, it ended in disaster, so he went himself to trade the furs and ensure there were no mishaps with the Crow. Even then, he did so discreetly, and few people saw him come and go. He didn't like to practice things he condemned. So, if the dose was small, he acted like it wasn't there. Still, it relaxed the warrior after a trying day.

"As soon as spring comes, my right-hand man, Rory, and me will take two hundred wagons across to the Pacific coast," Joseph daydreamed. He meant to impress the chief. "I can see it now. A wagon train that runs as far as the eye can see."

"I figure on this trail to Oregon City you keep talkin' about, the commonness of death will make reference to it almost casual, won't it?" Rusty said. "Funerals will become a monotonous regularity along the way. I reckon the Oregon Trail will be the longest graveyard in America in a few years. One day, I bet the folks will be able to follow the ruts and won't need anybody to guide 'em."

"Why do you have to be so dad-gummed contrary all the time?" Joseph grumbled. "Times are a-changing, old friend. You can't stop the progress machine. It's comin' just like the locomotive is on its way. One day, folks will be able to cross the great United States in less than a week, and my Oregon Trail will be the very start of the entire process. It will mark the way for times to come."

"What I am afraid of is that this change will be the end of my people," Hachta said. "Where is this Oregon Trail you speak of? Is it far away from our Crow stronghold?"

"Yeah, sure, it's a long way away, Chief." Joseph smiled. "You're safe on your mountain, sir."

"From the South Pass to Yellowstone Valley is only seven days walk," Rusty argued. "That means that some of those thousands of folks will make their way up the mountain hunting for wild game or gold. Mark my words, this trail you talk about is no good for us or the Crow Nation."

"Even if I'm not the first one to take a large wagon train across, one will come soon enough anyway," Joseph replied. "I'm just tryin' to be the first of many to come. It's what I do for a living, Chief. Don't take it personally."

Finally, Rusty noticed the silence of the women. Both stared into their swirling drinks, denying eye contact with anyone at the table. He also noticed the occasional scowl from the captain, and he was looking at his wife. Now, he took notice of their every move and their every expression. He noticed Betty had a swollen lip, and Dahteste had a lump on the side of her head as big as a small rock. Once Rusty caught on to what was happening, he wore that reproving-older-brother look when he looked at Levi and Will.

"I certainly hope you two ain't hidin' anything from me," Rusty said. "I've never taken you two for keepin' secrets from your family."

"Tossin' your rope before buildin' the loop don't catch the calf," Kansas Marshal Walker said. "Explain carefully what's going on so maybe we won't have any more violence."

"Violence?" Rusty asked, eyes spread wide in surprise. "Is that why you two have bumps, cuts, and bruises on your arms and faces? I don't like returning to a bunch of secrets, Levi. You best get your tongue a-waggin'."

"It's my place to talk, not Levi's," the captain said. "As far as I can see, Dahteste has only been defending herself. For some reason, Betty has taken to attacking Levi's wife without apparent reason."

"As far as you can see?" Rusty asked.

"I have reason, all right!" Betty said, her voice louder with each word. "Dahteste has turned everybody against me. I'm no coward, either. If someone does me wrong, I don't wait for them to do it twice."

"What in the world is this woman talking about?" Rusty asked. "I didn't quite get your drift, Betty. It's clear that you're mighty upset, though."

The captain suddenly found himself praying to something he couldn't remember believing in. Still, he begged God to give him strength. He didn't know what was happening, but he did know one thing. He wanted his old wife back. The one that stood before him currently, he didn't even know. For the life of him, he couldn't understand what was happening.

"I don't know what's gotten into her, sir," Will nearly whispered. He stared at the smoke squirreling from his pipe.

Everybody began to talk at once, overwhelming both Rusty and Angus. Angus was less vocal but didn't tolerate bad behavior in the compound any more than Rusty did.

"Hush now, all of ya," Rusty said loud and clear. "The only person I wanna hear from right now is Dahteste. Be forewarned, Betty Forrester. You will stay silent until Levi's wife has had her say. Then, I'll give you an equal amount of time to give us your side. In our compound, we have a court, judge, and jury: Angus, Dennis, and me—the original settlers on our mountain. Excuse me, Chief, your mountain."

Hachta nodded and smiled approvingly.

Dahteste shrugged and said, "She came at me first, and I have no idea why. Of course, I defended myself but with a certain restraint. It would have been too easy to kill her, but she is family, so I tolerated her aggressions, returning an equal dose of pain."

Dahteste smiled confidently. She knew she could snatch away the White woman's life so quickly she would be in the spirit world before Betty realized she was dead. It was almost like a game to the Crow woman, although she did hold the sucker punch against Betty. Crow Indians faced their enemies like warriors and sorted out their grievances accordingly. Still, she was also aware that White people were very different than Indians in many ways. She still had trouble adapting to their values, ideas of why they were on their Mother's Earth, and customs. That and the way they smelled different. Everyone but her Levi. He always smelled like mint.

Still, she was as perplexed as anyone why the White woman had turned on her as she had. It was a mystery to everybody but Betty, and so far, she hadn't been able to explain herself. Maybe it was a mystery to her, too.

The Which of Why

Betty stuttered and stammered at first like she was utterly at a loss for words. Everyone present waited patiently on the edge of their seats to hear what she had to say. Until now, she hadn't said much more than jibber-jabber, so none of it made any sense. This was the first time they had tried to talk to her when it wasn't at the end of another lunge at the woman war chief. Betty had sought out every chance she saw open to physically attack Dahteste. She wasn't even sure why, but she felt she was her natural adversary.

Before they arrived at the compound on the journey across the country to the Pacific coast and back, despite their different cultures, they never had a bitter word for each other. Maybe it was because Dahteste was experiencing something as new as Betty. Everything was a surprise and different, and they took it all in with enthusiasm and awe.

But when they arrived at her new home, Betty felt Dahteste rubbed the fact that she was the newcomer in her face, making her feel unwelcome. The Crow woman was pampered and was everybody's favorite. They even put a teepee in the compound's center to make her feel at home. Mrs. Forrester didn't feel they had given her an equal welcome and began to suspect a plot behind it. She felt Dahteste didn't want competition and was prepared to do anything to avoid it.

Dahteste had lived with Levi for some time now and they had had many experiences together. Plus, Levi was almost as much an Indian by nature as Dahteste. Betty was also raised in the wilderness of the Tennessee mountains, but she felt out of place, like she wasn't really part of the family. She thought that the Crow woman did it intentionally, and she resented her so much for it that she was compelled to attack her at every opportunity. She couldn't help herself to resist.

"We're waiting on you, young lady," Rusty said patiently. "Take your time when you talk so we can all understand. Every one of us lives here as a family. Everybody but Joseph, who's a guest—I suppose." He gave the marshal and longtime acquaintance a dirty look. "You can exclude the medicine man, Whisper, but not the chief. Hachta's like our big brother who watches over us so we can all live here on the mountain in peace and harmony."

Betty looked at Rusty longingly, like she wanted to speak but was too afraid to start. Her eyes were big, like a doe's in a hunter's gunsight, just before it bolted for safety or was shot dead.

"Come over here and sit beside me so you don't have to yell, darlin'," Rusty cooed. "I ain't gonna bite."

Betty stood with her eyes looking down. She felt embarrassed for her actions for the first time. Like the others, she naturally looked up to Rusty Steel and felt safer near him. He never made rude remarks nor made her feel uncomfortable. She crossed the room and sat beside her husband's mentor.

"Dahteste..." she said but stopped as she cleared her throat. Betty was clearly shaken up. "I don't know why I feel you are a threat to me. For some reason, ever since we arrived at the compound, I've felt like an outsider, and I believe it was you who turned these good people against me. That's why I'm not part of the family, and my husband is angry with me. I feel I was only protecting myself before you do something worse—maybe get me thrown out of the compound."

Nobody said a word for minutes. They tried to absorb the logic, but there was none, and they didn't get it. If Dahteste had it in for Betty, she would make it known. She might be a lot of things, but she wasn't shy or a liar. Now, it was clear the problem was Mrs. Forrester. Why she thought this way was yet to be determined. Everybody waited for Rusty to speak. He was the official leader of this mismatched family with different bloodlines. He was also considered the wisest, even at times in Chief Hachta's eyes.

Rusty opened his mouth to speak, but no words came out. He harrumphed and crossed his arms and used his hand to rest his chin. He pondered for longer than was expected.

"I'm afraid I find myself in uncharted waters," Rusty said. "I figure the first thing we need to do is make any wrongs right—the which of why that all this happened we'll sort out after. First, we'll get that fire out of you two so you can think straight. From what I gather, Betty had several goes at Dahteste when she wasn't looking, and they were all unprovoked." Betty went to protest, but

Rusty held up his hand, and she bit her tongue. "So, I propose we let 'em fight it out. Maybe a little sweat and blood will sort things out, and Betty can give us a better answer than she just did. It was pretty much more of the same jibber-jabber as before, which ain't cleared up anything at all."

Levi and Will both gasped. This wasn't what they expected Rusty to say. How could he put the women against each other in a fight? Nobody else complained, so they kept their mouths shut. Hachta even nodded his approval as a wise decision. Who were they to judge when they clearly knew much less than their mentor and the Crow chief? They sat by silently but as nervous as a legless dog with ticks.

"This is gonna be interestin'." Marshal Walker chuckled. "It's about time we saw some justice. Even if they are women, they should abide by the same rules as the rest of us. Dahteste sure as hell does, and she's an Injun. Let 'em at it. If she acted like that back in Kansas, I'd have thrown her in jail for sixty days."

"Back in the Crow stronghold, I would have done the same as Rusty Steel," Chief Hachta said firmly. He, too, shot a dirty look at Joseph. He shook his head and thought, *Rusty usually doesn't have such rude friends*. "It is a wise decision, and I see no other option."

"Since they're your wives, Levi, you and Will go get the shovels and clear a place in the yard twenty feet across," Rusty said. "I want a big circle. Then get the sledgehammer and drive a stake into the ground, dead center. It's gonna be frozen like a rock, but you're a big fella, Beaver. I'm sure you can do it. Well, whatcha waiting for? Go on, and when you're done, come and fetch us. There's no sense in all of us getting cold."

When Levi and Will opened the door, the wind blew into the cabin, sending chills up all their backs as it swirled around the room. Even Dog got up and lay down beside the crackling fire. Waves of heat replaced the cold as soon as the door closed. Levi and Will pulled up their collars and leaned into the stiff, cold breeze.

The shovels were in the stables, so they had to walk the compound length with two to three feet of snow. The white powder came up to their knees, making the short walk a struggle. At first, they felt the rush, but as they worked on their task, they went slower and slower. Both men already regretted what was about to come. Since the snow was deep, it took them an hour to make a clearing big enough to do whatever Rusty had planned. Then Will held a two-foot stake, and Levi hammered it into the ground. He went at it like he did chopping wood. At first, it slipped on the icy surface, making the hammer nick the captain's knuckles.

"Be careful, Levi, or you're going to take off my fingers," the captain growled. "What do you think of what Rusty has planned? I know I don't like it much at all. Your wife is as dangerous a woman as I've ever seen, and it appears my wife doesn't see it. I don't want her to get hurt."

The second strike of the hammer drove the spike through the crusty, frozen surface. Chips of ice flew through the air like shrapnel. Three more blows from the massive mountain man's powerful swing did the trick. Pulling out the stake after the duel would be all but impossible. They would have to wait for the first thaw. Even then, they would probably have to use a mule. At the moment, it would stand as a reminder of what happened that day.

"Dahteste ain't gonna hurt Betty," Levi replied. "Had she intended to harm her, she would have done it that first day. She's just trying to teach her a lesson, is all. Myself, I don't see where she gets the patience. Betty has been a handful of late."

Forrester nodded and frowned. "Yeah, you're right there. I don't know what I'm going to do, my friend. What would you do in such a situation?"

"I have about as much an idea as you do," Levi replied. "I figure the best way is to trust Rusty to work it out. We've been in some bad spots, and he always finds a good solution. You know deep down inside he's a peaceful man, but Lord help ya if you get him riled. He's hell on wheels, he is. I've seen him take down five Blackfoot Indians standing as close as you and me and all on his own."

"Let's just hope you're right," the captain said with weary eyes. His wife wore him out more than a Comanche war party. "We better go get the boss. It looks like our job is done, and it's ready to get things started. I wish we could put it off, but we have no choice at this point. Now, it's a compound community matter, and everybody has a say so. I guess the worst that can happen is Betty gets banned from the camp if you're sure your wife won't seriously hurt her. Maybe then, I'd better leave, too."

"Stop already with the negativity," Levi chided. "That's not your way, pard. You watch how Rusty fixes this, and it's all gonna come out fine. I'm gonna need a hot coffee before I come back out here," Levi said. "I'll have to dig out my bearskin coat, too."

Bear claws clicked on Levi's necklace. The captain wore one just like it. They both turned for Rusty's cabin with heavy feet. They tried to put it off for as long as possible, but there would be no getting out of it if Rusty had made his decision. He had the last word in the compound, despite Dennis and Angus being there before him. He was the mountain man's mountain man and was famous across the Rockies and the Yellowstone Valley, not only to the other Easterners but to all the Indians living there.

Some were Rusty Steel's friends who revered him, and others were his enemies who feared him and revered him in a different way. He was indeed more like a half-breed than any White man who had graced these mountains with his presence. He could outfight, outshoot, and outwrestle even the young Crow warrior braves. The Blackfeet avoided him like the plague, but still, when he was away, they tried to embarrass him by raiding his compound, though without success to date. So far, all hostile aggressions had been thwarted. Most of the battles were won by Mister Steel's involvement. Even when he lived with the Flathead Indians after he stopped captaining riverboats, he already had a reputation.

When Rusty met Levi for the first time, back at the Rendezvous, he could see a lot of himself in the young fellow. The old mountain man instinctively knew he had what it took to become a woodsman himself. The captain had lucked out, and Johnson didn't want to split up from his friend, so he, too, was invited. At the end of the day, both men had excelled in becoming mountain men with their mentor's introduction to his way of life.

The Fight

Everybody gathered around the snow-cleared circle. Dog started running about the yard, barking like mad, happy to be out of the cabin. He kicked up snow as he ran around the outer fence, trying to get all humans' attention but failed. They could see the yellow dead grass where the snow was removed. Beside it were two high piles of white powder. A wooden stake was in the middle, and Rusty was tying two ropes to the post, ensuring they wouldn't slip off.

All eyes were on Steel, but he was oblivious to the stares. He was all business. He knew his decisions weighed heavy on those living in their little stretch of paradise. He knew he couldn't make mistakes just like his friend, the chief. Steel's tribe was small, but the rules were the same, despite their numbers. It had always been like that ever since he arrived.

Now more so with not one but two apprentices and their wives. Surprises seemed to be the order of the day ever since they arrived. A fleeting thought passed through his mind. He wondered if their arrival was a good thing or not. Rusty supposed that remained to be proven with time.

Levi and Will had cleared enough ground of snow so the other members of the compound and their guests could stand close by and see the fight without being too near and getting struck themselves. The women had a twelve-foot-wide circle for their combat. Their tethers wouldn't allow them to reach farther and, at the same time, forced them to remain close enough for a strike. The ropes' lengths were only six feet long, less the part wrapped around each leg.

"Levi, grab your wife and tie one ankle to the rope," Rusty instructed them quietly but sternly. "She's right-handed, so tie her left leg. Betty's left-handed, so tie the rope to her right ankle. That makes it fair. We don't want to give anybody an advantage."

The husbands reluctantly led their wives to what they felt was a slaughter. Will nearly balked, but Levi urged him on. Dahteste went willingly on her own, but Forrester had to lead his wife by the arm.

"If you have a better idea, now's the time to speak up," Levi whispered to his best friend. "I'm all ears, but I don't have any other ideas. Heck, who knows; it might just work."

Dahteste put on her warrior mask. She had even painted her face when the others weren't looking. This was something none of them expected, although it was common enough practice for Crow warriors. How could Will's wife see better what the Indian woman was all about?

She looked a little too serious for the husbands, but now it was too late. Betty's eyes spread wide when she saw her opponent. With the scary painted face, this was not what she expected.

"Let me go!" Betty revolted as she kicked her feet. She tried to wrestle her arm away. She even tried to bite her husband, but he squeezed her bicep until she stopped, whining as her husband shook his head and frowned. He hardly recognized his wife. She had somehow transferred into a different person than the one he had married. She seemed more like a stranger than his family at this point.

"Come on now, honey," Will said. "Are you going to give us trouble with this, too? You wanted to fight Dahteste, so a fight is what you're going to get." He sighed in frustration.

It sounded final, and Betty sensed that no matter what she said, this was how it would play out. She began to plan. She knew she was much braver than they gave her credit for. She was born and raised in the Tennessee mountains, which she believed gave her an edge, and she had learned more from her father and her famous uncle than they ever imagined.

When the husbands stood from a crouch, the women were tied. Everybody started to talk at once, making a small roar of excitement. One fighter with a pale complexion stood facing the other with a more terrifying painted face. It was black, white, and red. White incisors were painted on her bottom lips, and red blood dripped from the canines.

Delight flashed in the Crow woman's eyes. She showed no fear at all. This was her bread and butter of every day when she lived in the camp. She had had a dozen warriors under her command.

"There's to be no weapons, but there are no other

rules," Rusty shouted to shut everybody up. "This is the Rocky Mountains, and here we live by Crow rules and laws. Ladies, whenever you're ready, be my guest and make contact." He tried to stay as formal as possible, especially with Hachta in the crowd of spectators. The chief, too, was part of the family. This was something that the newcomers had yet to discover.

Dahteste instantly dropped into a crouch, making her profile all but impossible to strike. Betty stood like a prize fighter, twirling her fists, bringing attention to her upper body. Suddenly, Betty threw a handful of dust into Dahteste's eyes and swiftly kicked her in the crotch. The red woman put her hands between her legs, moaned, and fell over. Nobody had seen Mrs. Forrester grab the dirt, but it immediately gave her an advantage.

Levi went to move, but Angus was behind him and grabbed Levi's shirt with both hands, pulling him back. Angus had expected as much. Johnson shot a hard look behind him, but when his eyes met Angus's compassionate expression, his shoulders relaxed, and he turned back to the fight. He realized he had to control his feelings, despite what happened. It was meant to be.

"Hold steady, boys," Angus growled. "Like Rusty said, there are no rules except no weapons. Dirt ain't a weapon last I checked. It was clever, is what it was."

McFarlin cackled like it was all a big game, but Will and Levi didn't think that way at all. Both men balled their hands into fists as their hearts raced into high gear. Blood pumped through their veins like racing locomotives. They could barely hold themselves back, but the hard stare from Chief Hachta gave them second thoughts. If the chief approved of Rusty's little game, they had better go along. Nobody crossed the Crow leader, not even Rusty Steel. He was the true leader of all humans in this part of the mountains.

The Crow chief was the last man they wanted to offend. He was the one who decided who could live on his mountain and who couldn't. If they did something that offended him or his tribe, they risked being banished from the Rocky Mountains and even the Yellowstone Valley forever or wherever the Crow people lived. If it happened to Levi, it meant he would lose his wife. He didn't see her living among Easterners for the rest of her life. All her family lived in the stronghold, a half-day walk from the compound and higher into the hills.

Betty stood over Dahteste, panting from the adrenaline rush. A wicked smile curled the edges of her lips. She drew back her foot and sent it flying toward the red woman's gut. Levi's wife looked up, surprised. She grabbed her opponent's foot and flipped her on her head. Betty hit the ground hard and saw stars as the sky spun around and around. She shook her head to clear away the cobwebs, surprised that she was staring at clouds.

Betty pushed herself onto her feet and began dancing around the ring, careful not to trip over the rope. She quickly regained her composure. Her fists were twice the size of the small Indian woman's, but there was no fear in her eyes—only anger. She had been tricked, and she wanted revenge.

Dahteste resumed her crouch, and they crab-circled each other. Betty didn't see her opponent's leg as it swept her feet from under her. Suddenly, she found her legs flying into the air as she was toppled on her head again. Like before, she saw stars, and her mind spun out of control.

She blinked back the tears of frustration, jumped to her feet, and lunged for Dahteste. Now, she was as angry as hell and wanted to see blood. Adrenaline pumped through her veins, making her heart roar in her ears.

Betty came from Irish stock and was fighting mad. She screamed as she dove for her opponent's rope. She quickly pulled the small woman off her feet when she jerked it. Her foot was waiting, and again, she gave the final blow. She kicked Dahteste in the temple, and the Indian woman's eyes crawled back into her head. She was out cold.

The spectators' mouths dropped open in surprise. It was an outcome that nobody expected. The White woman with the ruffled hair and dirty face stood over the unconscious Crow woman. Even Betty's face showed her surprise.

"Well, I'll be danged." Angus huffed. "That didn't work out like we planned at all, did it, Rusty?"

"No, it did not," Rusty replied. "I figure we might have just made things worse."

Levi jumped into the ring and grabbed his wife as she came to. She immediately began to struggle to get up and have another go at the White woman, but the fight was officially over. The first one rendered unconscious was the loser, and the one left standing was the victor. That rule was the same everywhere.

"That's enough!" Rusty yelled. "I reckon Betty Forrester is the winner." He looked as puzzled as the rest.

Nobody expected Betty to beat Dahteste in a fair fight. The White woman had proven she did have some of the stuff her Uncle Davy was made of. Maybe everybody had misunderstood her entirely from the beginning. Will had always seen this sweet, gentile lady who would never make a ruckus. Now, he started to believe she was much more like her uncle than any of them had expected.

"What are we gonna do now?" Angus whispered. "I figure we're plumb out of ideas."

"The hell if I know," Rusty replied in his ear. "I thought Dahteste would give her a sound whoopin' and knock some sense into her head, but I was mistaken. Whatcha think, Chief?"

"I think this is the first person I have ever seen beat Dahteste in a fair fight," Hachta replied. "I've never seen her beaten by another brave back in our camp. Maybe this woman from Tennessee is a warrior, too. Perhaps we must look at her in a different light to understand who she is and what she is about. I believe we were all mistaken. She appears to be more like Dahteste than her husband, of that, I am sure.

"There is something in her that is more like a Native American than your typical White woman," the chief continued. "I can't put my finger on it yet, but it will come to me. Maybe I'll spend the night if Rusty doesn't mind and study the situation further. You two obviously are out of ideas. Dahteste is one of my war chiefs, even though she lives here and not with us. You know she will come without question if and when she is needed. Whisper, you can go now. You're no use to me anyway. I've already sent up smoke signals of your disgrace. Go and face more punishment. You embarrassed yourself before me, and now your people will scold you."

The three men huddled together, turning their eyes

to the captain and his woman. Betty's chin was jutted out, and her chest puffed up. She was like a game rooster strutting around the yard.

All the while, Dahteste fumed as her eyes shot daggers at the White woman. Now, she was the one who felt the others were favoring Betty. The table had unexpectedly turned, and Dahteste didn't like it any better than the White woman had. This wouldn't end here if the Crow woman had her way.

Whisper

The day after Whisper's arrival, higher up on the mountain the medicine man quickly snuck out of the Crow camp. All the other members of the tribe were already ignoring him. When he walked around the stronghold, it was like he was suddenly invisible when, only a few weeks before, he was considered a hero. He knew he couldn't get revenge against Crow Chief Hachta, or he would surely die and maybe not pass into the spirit world.

That was something that no man of his stature could ever risk. He had a legacy to leave, even though it was now damaged, perhaps beyond repair. Still, some of his good things would be remembered if he didn't hurt his image even more. Now, he would have to be careful of how he got his revenge.

Some things were unforgivable even for shamans and medicine men. Especially now, whenever he neared the tribal leader's lodge, warriors appeared and blocked his way. He wasn't even allowed to see the chief's home even though he apparently wasn't there. He wondered why he had stayed on to watch two fool women fight. He still didn't think the chief deserved his position anymore, even though he couldn't remember why or when he began to think in such a manner. It was hazardous to make such accusations about the chief in the camp. Maybe the isolation made him too brave for his own good.

Whisper believed that Chief Hachta would need time to think over what he would do about his indiscretion. Now the medicine man was back, and the news was so public, the chief would nearly be obliged to take some formal action against a man who challenged him. The worst thing about it was that Whisper was the tribe's head shaman. This was an embarrassment for everyone in the stronghold. Whisper knew he could never live it down.

The medicine man had only arrived back the day before, but the entire tribe already knew what happened. The Indian gossip was so quick that the news arrived before he could get there. As soon as he stepped foot in the camp, he was ridiculed and called a coward. He held his hand over his lips to hide his missing teeth. White, jagged stubs stood out in a bloody mouth.

The medicine man looked at the ground and rushed for his teepee, followed by a wake of dust. All he wanted was to be alone. But as the anger brewed, so did the ideas in Whisper's head. He began to plot his revenge. He sought restitution, but how?

He was out of the camp and headed for the compound. He had figured out his plan for his last action before he passed on to the Crow spirit world. There was a special place for medicine men, so he knew he was going to a better place. He intended to kill Rusty Steel. This would cause the chief great grief, and he could get even with a White man he despised. Maybe he would get lucky and kill two or three.

But he had only managed to scrounge up another gun beside his old rifle. He knew he wasn't a good enough shot to kill Steel at a long distance. He believed his best bet was to get close and kill him with his pistol. A shot to the face would disfigure him, too, making it more difficult to pass into the spirit world.

Then it dawned on him. Maybe White men didn't have spirit worlds like Indians, or perhaps they didn't believe in an afterlife or anything at all. To be truthful, he had to admit he never really knew a White man and had only seen a few, besides Rusty Steel, whom he had spoken to although reluctantly and was hostile when he could. In the tribe, the mountain man was treated as a Crow. He was even fluent in their language.

Whisper had openly despised White people simply because he was afraid of them and what they represented—the unknown. Deep down inside, there was a bit of a coward inside Whisper, and at times, it surfaced. He hoped his courage didn't fail him now.

He rushed through the forest, sinking deep in the snow despite using the trail all the tribe used. Even though the powder was trampled down, his feet still sank a foot deep, slowing him down; it took him twice the time he had calculated. He suddenly found himself with the day waning and the sun closing in on the snowcapped horizon. He wasn't going to make it before nightfall like he had planned.

A prism of rays of light shot across the sky as, in the east, a carpet of stars rolled out toward the opposite side of the world. Soon, he would be in the dark, and the moon wouldn't rise for hours. Whisper pulled his bearskin coat tight around his body, but still, the first shiver ran up his spine and made his teeth chatter. He put his head down and pressed on.

When it went dark, Whisper found he couldn't see where the trail was. He didn't know the stars well enough to use them to navigate. It was only a five-hour walk, and he had started eight hours earlier. He wasn't making the time it usually took, but then again, typically, he was guided by experts and didn't pay attention to how they did it. He left such things to his subordinates. Now, he wished he had studied navigating the mountains. Everything he had studied and learned by experience didn't prepare him to stalk a man down and kill him.

Of course, he knew he couldn't sneak up on a person like Rusty Steel. Instead, he would walk right into their camp, claiming he came to beg forgiveness of the leader of the Easterners and the renegade warrior woman. Maybe he would get lucky and kill her, too. She ran off to live with the despised White people, and to the shaman, she had become a traitor to her race.

Whisper finally gave up. He felt he was walking in circles. He would try to rest briefly while waiting for the moon to rise. He curled up in a ball inside his warm fur coat and fell asleep as the temperatures plummeted. He didn't notice when his chin whiskers froze, and he slept on. He was so tired from all the nervous tension he slept right through the night, even though he had planned to use the moon to make up for lost time. By morning, his shivering body woke him—that and his chattering teeth.

The medicine man glanced at the sun, and it said nine o'clock. He blinked repeatedly against the bright light, using the flat of his hand to shade his eyes. Vultures made lazy circles overhead. Now that it was daylight again, he got his bearings right and headed out. Hopefully, he wouldn't have any more delays. As the morning passed, the sun bore down, and he began to sweat. The thick bear skin coat was heavy, making him walk slower.

He even considered discarding the coat altogether. He wouldn't need it once he got to Rusty Steel's cabin. After his brief visit, his body of flesh and blood would be dead, and his soul in the spirit world where everything would be better. Curls formed at the edge of his lips as he thought about his life to come.

After some consideration, he realized that he would raise suspicion if he arrived without a coat. He had to be careful to avoid making a single mistake. This was his last chance to get revenge for something he considered unfair. He intended to make at least one wrong right. If he made a foolish move, the mountain man would see or sense it, and once the cat was out of the bag, he would be dead, and Rusty Steel would still be alive, and his death would have meant nothing. It would be yet another defeat to leave as a legacy. This was his last chance to do something right—at least in his deranged mind.

Whisper was surprised when he neared the edge of the compound and smelled Chief Hachta. He would know that scent anywhere. He had been his number one shaman for decades. Now, the chief was who the medicine man most despised. He wondered why he was still there. He frowned on his relationship with the

White men in the compound. If he were chief, he would see them all dead and hanging by their feet to warn any other Easterners what they would get if they stayed or tried to settle on their mountain.

Then, he would burn all the cabins to the ground with the mountain men inside with all their valuables. He would tear down their wretched fence and scatter the stables to the wind. He may even kill their animals out of spite, even though they didn't deserve it. If he were chief, things would be different. Once he was done, there wouldn't even be a memory of their existence. If only Whisper were the tribe's leader and not Hachta.

He followed his nose and soon found himself behind the horses. Much to his alarm, the big black dog was outside and began to bark and growl as soon as he ducked between the fence posts and into the compound. He knew better than to make eye contact with such a wild animal, so he watched him through his peripheral vision and slowly near the cabin one step at a time.

Suddenly, he didn't hear the dog. It had stopped barking and disappeared. Then he heard the growl from behind. The canine had Whisper's coat between the toothy jaws. The dog shook its head hard and threw Whisper to the ground. To his dismay, by then, all the people in Rusty's cabin had poured out and onto the porch. They all roared with laughter. Chief Hachta was standing right beside Rusty Steel. This made the shaman freeze in his tracks as his brain raced for an answer of what to do.

Whisper took a deep breath and decided he had but one thing to do. Carry on with his plan despite his sudden discovery. He had hoped to catch Rusty alone, but even his chief was with him.

"I thought I told you to go home," Chief Hachta growled.

"I did and was ridiculed just like you said," Whisper replied. "Then, after a thoughtful night, I decided I had to return and apologize to these people for my actions. I have now decided that not all White people are bad. Especially your friend, Rusty Steel."

Chief Hachta looked at his medicine man suspiciously. He knew him too well to believe everything he said. But, then again, a good chief always gave a dedicated tribe member another chance if merited. He still had to decide if this apology had merit or not.

"Why, that's mighty big of ya, sparky," Rusty said. "Come on in and have a hot cup of coffee. You must be freezing out there. With all the white powder on your bearskin coat, I'd say you must have slept in the snow."

Everybody seemed to be open to an apology except Marshal Joseph Walker. He didn't believe in all the Indian hocus-pocus anyway. And he sure as Dickens did not believe anything the witch doctor said. He fingered his Colt and wondered what the man was up to. He planned to keep a sharp eye on this one. He knew he was dishonored, and a man with a big ego was capable of doing anything for revenge.

Walker didn't see Whisper as the kind of man to apologize and turn a new leaf. He believed him to be a narcissist void of empathy for his fellow tribe members, not to mention White and Black men. So, with his ego tarnished, he was bound to seek some revenge. It was just a matter of time, but the marshal planned to be ready for it.

Joseph Walker bided his time, but if he saw anything amiss, he planned to put a bullet square between the shaman's eyes. In his opinion, Chief Hachta should have killed him instead of whipping him like a child. Now, he might be dangerous even though nobody feared him. That might be his ace in the hole.

"Tell your witch doctor to come on in and warm up some," Rusty said. "There ain't no sense in all of us sittin' out here freezing to death like Whisper there."

"I'll go and put some more logs on the fire," Angus said, always thinking of others.

McFarlin enjoyed cooking for the bunch and doing what he could to make life more comfortable for everybody. His cabin was always open for all the people in the compound and most of the Crow Indians if they felt so inclined. Angus had spent most winters with his wife, Pine Needle, in her teepee in the stronghold, where it was always warm. He lived like another tribe member, and nobody gave him much notice.

Everybody filed in and sat at the big table right in front of the fire. Then, the chief sat cross-legged on the floor as close to the flames as he dared, and Dog lay beside him. Hachta unconsciously scratched the furry animal's head, making him wag his tail like a broken hinge.

Wrongs Righted

Whisper was the last one to enter the cabin. He eyed the rifles on the wall. He also noted that all the mountain men were still armed, despite being safe inside their cabin. Did they always wear knives and guns everywhere they went? When he was in camp, he only carried a knife for practical purposes.

The chief didn't even carry more than his big Bowie knife when in their stronghold. He bet the Kansas marshal was so paranoid that he slept with his guns in his hands. It's too bad he wouldn't have an extra bullet for him. His arrogance stung the medicine man every time he made a dig at him, but now it was his turn to dose out some punishment. At least he would be able to kill his friend, Steel.

"Hold on, just a minute," Angus said. "I've got a fresh kettle of coffee just about to percolate. Pass me that jug of corn liquor over here, Rusty. We might as well make it interesting." He turned and whispered, "It might settle that medicine man down a bit. Keep your eye on him, partner. His apology didn't sound heartfelt to me."

"I always give a man a second chance." Rusty smiled. "Even if he is a no-count liar and so full of bull, he could fill a wagon."

They both snickered and then they turned back to their unwanted guest. Rusty put on a smile that could fool a Chinaman. Angus grinned so wide you could see down his throat as he rushed around, filling tin coffee cups and giving each a splash of whiskey. When Whisper wasn't looking, he filled his cup half with coffee and the other half with alcohol. He stifled a snicker under his breath.

Whisper hardly drank coffee before then just because the Indians bought it from White men or traded it for tobacco. He knew the smell was odd, but he nearly gagged when he tasted his first sip. It burned all the way down his throat, but he hid his disgust, preparing for his next move. Strangely enough, the way the coffee slid down his throat made him want more despite the taste. It almost instantly made his mind a little warm and fuzzy.

Maybe this White man's coffee isn't so bad after all, Whisper thought.

In minutes, the shaman's cup was empty, and he was wiping his lips with the back of his wrinkled hand. An involuntary smile crept to his lips and stayed, despite his effort to frown. He ground his teeth together, but still, he felt good.

"This coffee makes me want to pee," Whisper said. "I'm afraid I need to step outside a minute."

He got up wobbly and staggered to the door. "I'll

have another cup of that coffee, too, Mister Angus. It was better than I thought."

The medicine man disappeared out the door. Once outside, he rushed to the edge and hurled the yellow poison into the snow. Shaking his head to remove the cobwebs, he pulled his pistol and checked the primer. When he cocked the hammer, the loud click caught him by surprise. At first, he was sure that everybody inside had heard it, and he froze in place. After a full two minutes, he reached deep inside, pulled out all his courage, and stepped toward the door. He flipped the latch with his thumb and pulled it open with his left hand. The pistol was hidden behind the door, in his right hand.

Whisper was so focused on his enemy before him he didn't hear the soft moccasin steps behind him. She hardly weighed fifty pounds. Even though she wasn't a warrior, she was still a Crow Indian and intended to protect her husband.

The medicine man flung open the door with his toe and pointed his pistol right at Rusty Steel's head. The target blinked and frowned down the dark barrel.

"Now it's time for you to die like a dog," Whisper spat.

The chief sitting beside Rusty reached for his knife as Levi and Will doubted what was happening for an instant, which cost them time. Then they, too, went for their guns. The knife in Whisper's back entered seven inches deep at the same time Marshal Walker fired. Brains and the few teeth left splatted across the inside of the door, and the dead body dropped to the floor. The gun fell beside the warm corpse.

"Pine Needle!" cried Angus. "I didn't expect you

home until tomorrow! I sure am happy to see you, darlin'. Have ya come to save our lives?"

She gave her husband a crafty smile as she pulled her bone-handled knife from the medicine man's back. She had to put her foot on his shoulder to get enough leverage to draw it out. Blood pooled on the floor from the pierced heart. She had put everything she had into it and buried it deep.

With the sudden commotion, everybody momentarily forgot about Betty and Dahteste's predicament. A dead body lay by the open door.

"Pull that shut, or all the heat is gonna get out," Marshal Walker said. "Come on, Levi, you and Will drag the body outside. It'll freeze immediately, so we don't have to worry about the stink. We can think about burying him later."

"This man deserves no burial," Chief Hachta said loud and clear. "Put him in the stables for the night. I will tie a rope around his feet in the morning and drag him away from the compound. For men like him, we let the scavengers eat them so they can never enter the spirit world."

"Well, somebody get the mop and bucket," Angus said. "We've gotta get his brains off the door and wall." He walked over to the body, and molar teeth crunched underfoot.

Every man in the room had drawn a pistol, but the marshal had been waiting. He knew what would happen and never trusted anybody, never giving such a man a second chance. He believed they should all learn from the lesson. Sometimes, his friend Rusty Steel was too darn forgiving for his own good.

Levi and Will dragged the nearly headless body

outside as Angus used the mop to scrub the gray matter off the door. They left him in the stables, but he was already getting stiff. The body would be frozen solid in an hour with the low temperatures to come. It was nearing the end of the day.

When Levi pulled open the door to go back inside, arrows singed by his head. They came so close they parted his hair. In a second, six arrowheads buried deep into the timber door. The captain and Johnson pulled it open and dove for cover as Joseph and Virgil returned fire and managed to pull the door to, and Rusty hung the two-by-four in place, locking them in tightly.

Thuds hit the shutters and wooden doors like hailstones. The Blackfeet were throwing everything they had at the cabin, but to no effect. Still, none of them had used a firearm so that the mountain men couldn't aim at the muzzle flashes. The enemy was obviously out there, but they didn't have a target to shoot at yet.

"Let 'em use up their arrows for nothin'." Marshal Walker chuckled. "They must be as dumb as mud."

"I'd say we've soiled their honor, and they're fightin' mad," Levi said. "Now I see how it was a mistake turning the other cheek. They just turned around and tried to bite us."

"I told ya them Blackfeet would be back, Rusty." Joseph grinned. "Your benevolence seems to be backfiring on ya, old pard. You call me hard and all, but you're getting soft in your old age."

"I ain't no older than you are," Rusty spat as he primed five pistols and two rifles. He was as angry as hell and was ready for war with the Blackfeet Indians. He knew they were the same ones they let get away. It was true; sometimes, he was too easygoing when he should have been stricter. It was his own fault, and he knew it.

"Yeah, well, I guess I can't deny it, Joseph," Rusty said. "I should have fought fire with fire. There was a time not too long ago when I would have never even considered letting them warriors off when we had 'em in a crossfire. It was a stupid thing to do. Now, I'm gonna give 'em a dose of lead, and none of 'em are gonna get away."

"To be honest, it rubbed me wrong when you told me you let them slip through your fingers," Chief Hachta said. "I would never let such an enemy escape me if I had them trapped."

"Yeah, but maybe all of 'em ain't enemies," Rusty said. The thudding into the wall continued, but the people inside sat patiently.

"They are to me," Hachta replied. "They have killed members of my family."

"That right there's the problem, Chief," Rusty said. "Just like Whisper figured, all White men are wicked. Some of us are, and some of us ain't. I believe it must be the same for most Indians of all tribes. I know it's like that back East. Lucky for the world, the good people outnumber the bad, so you have to take it all into consideration."

"And how's that workin' out for ya lately?" Marshal Walker cackled. "To me, it looks like your score is nil to nothin'."

Finally, gunshots echoed in the night. Now, the people in the cabin had something to aim at. Betty pushed her way past the men and took a post standing at the left side of the shutter. She had two rifles in his fists and a gash for a mouth. Before anyone could protest, she opened fire.

Dahteste fired the second shot from the other side of the cabin using the door's gun slat. Soon, all four slots were spitting lead. When one person emptied their two weapons, they moved aside and reloaded while somebody took their place and continued to fire. This provided a constant barrage of lead against who knew how many Blackfeet Indians there were, but with all the firepower, they had to be dwindling.

They fired into the darkness for a full ten minutes. Since they were in the cabin, they had nearly an endless supply of black powder and bullets. Soon, the return fire dropped to nothing, and no more arrows slammed into the cabin wall, shutters, or door.

"I wonder what they're up to now," the marshal said.

"I say we sneak out while it's dark and have a look and maybe a go at them while we're out there," the captain said. "I hate sitting in here on my backside doing nothing. Soon, the moon will set, and it will be as dark as the ace of spades. That's when we should make our move and ensure the fools don't vanish into the night. Then we'll be in the same position we were in before, with another enemy on the loose."

"We can't let that happen," Levi said. "I'll go with ya, Will. How about you, Joseph? Are you gonna go, too?"

WHITE WARRIORS

LEVI, WILL, AND JOSEPH CROUCHED BY THE DOOR. RUSTY had the two-by-four in his hands, ready to remove and replace again as soon as the three made their way out. Hearts hammered between their ears as adrenaline boosts shot through their bodies. Everybody was on edge.

"Ya ready, boys?" Rusty asked with raised eyebrows.

"I reckon I'm as ready as I'm ever gonna be," Walker replied.

They drew back their hammers with a click and closed their eyes to adjust them to the darkness before bolting into the night cover.

The marshal gritted his teeth and tensed his muscles, ready to burst into a run. They were headed for Dennis's cabin. They could hide under the porch if they could make it there unseen. Then, they could evaluate the situation. If not, they would have to fight from where they stood. It was dark, though, so they would make difficult moving targets. They knew their surroundings like the backs of their hands while the Blackfeet were on unknown territory.

Rusty suddenly opened the door just wide enough for Levi's massive shoulders to pass through. One, two, three men ran by, and just as Angus was about to pull it shut, another one ran out and into the dark.

"Who the hell was that?" Angus asked wide-eyed. He looked around the room to see who was missing.

Rusty blinked, shook his head, and replied, "It was Betty Forrester. The captain's wife." The mountain man was clearly puzzled and nearly lost for words. "What in the world is she doin' out there with Blackfeet Indians attacking? I've never seen nothin' like it. She's either brave as hell or as dumb as a turnip."

"She wants to show us she is a warrior, too," Dahteste said, surprising everybody. "Now I understand. She is much more like me than we ever thought. She is proving she, too, is a warrior, even if she is White. Maybe this famous uncle has more to do with the way of this woman than we thought. Maybe she was already a warrior in a past life. She may have been raised much like me if she grew up in the Tennessee wilderness with mountains."

Chief Hachta nodded at the revelation. "She is right, you know. It all makes sense now. What she did was natural for a warrior man or woman. We ignored her value, and she felt she must prove herself. And that she has. Now, I only hope she survives the night so we can welcome her to the family like the brave woman she is. I am the first to admit I was wrong. I thought she was crazy."

"Well, I'll be," Rusty said. "You're as right as rain,

Chief. Who would have ever thought? Keep a sharp eye out there now. We don't want to shoot one of our own."

As soon as Levi raced into the night, he heard Will and Joseph right behind. Then he heard someone else's pattering feet behind that.

"Be careful, boys; somebody else has come with us," Levi whispered.

"And who's that?" Will asked.

"Your guess is as good as mine, but make sure you know who it is you shoot," Levi replied.

"It must be Virgil," the captain said. "He's like that. At least they'll never see him in the dark."

When Betty decided to run for the door just before Rusty shut it tight, she was torn between going or not. Finally, her sixth sense told her to go for it, despite the apparent danger. But she wasn't afraid. Hostile Indians had attacked her before when the Squirrel wagon train was nearly wiped out. Suddenly, she found herself outside in the cold and the dark. She could hardly see her hand before the face.

Still, she was as firm as a rock. She prayed to her uncle, may he rest in peace. She asked him to give her the strength to save the day and show them she was as valuable as most, if not all. Betty wasn't just another pretty white face with blond hair and blue eyes. She hated it when men took her for what she looked like rather than for what she really was.

Tonight, she intended to prove to them all that she was a mountain woman as much as they were mountain men. That, plus she was as much a warrior as Dahteste. That was what she most desired. Respect from the only woman who felt like a friend for a long time. Sometimes, women and even men had to fight or even become enemies before they could become fast friends. It was a test of wills.

The men ran out the door and turned right for Dennis's cabin. They could hear the Blackfeet rustling in the bushes at the edge of the compound. The snow was up to the second rung of the fence so that they could get that far unseen. But white powder didn't stop bullets. The mountain men only had to figure out where they would hide as if *they* were attacking the cabin. Then, they would direct their fire there.

When Betty squeezed between the closing door and the jamb, she bolted left and found herself at the edge of the compound on the south side nearest the enemy. This was just what she planned. To strike first before anybody knew they were there. She had three pistols in her belt and a scattergun in her fist. The White woman ducked as she raced for outside the confines of the fence. She dove into the first snow drift she saw then she listened carefully for signs of where the enemy was.

She immediately heard them moving at the edge of the fence just a few yards away. Despite the darkness, when the Indians stood to duck through the fence to make their attack, she saw their silhouettes. Betty swung her shotgun toward the enemy and fired both barrels. Lead pellets sprayed five Indians as they fell to the snow, dead or wounded. She dropped her rifle and pulled out her pistols. She didn't hesitate and put two rounds into the heads of two painted braves. Their eyes spread wide in shock as they fell and vanished under the snow.

Now, she was down to her last bullet. A winged warrior rushed her, but she pulled the trigger, and blood poured from a hole in his chest. Her heart sank when she realized she was out of ammunition and had no time to reload. There were still a half dozen Blackfeet too close for comfort. She pulled her knife, waiting for their attack. Even if she perished, she had proven herself. Maybe she could take one last warrior with her to the grave.

When bullets began to thud into everything around her, Betty dove face down in the snow, burrowing as deep as she could. The three mountain men rushed the fence in a hail of bullets. She heard them zing overhead and slam into the enemy. The Blackfeet returned fire, but the White men were already on top of them. Knives flashed in the starlight as rifle butts slammed into skulls. Moans and death songs filled the air as the men fought hand-to-hand.

The last three hostile Indians tried to run for safety as the mountain men reloaded, but there wasn't enough time. Joseph spat and swore; he didn't want one of the enemies to escape.

"Get your knives, boys!" Marshal Walker shouted.

Three chunks of steel closed the distance, tumbling through the air as three blades pierced the fleeing hostile's backs. They fell face down like they were hit in the head with shovels. Claret turned the white snow dark as warm blood pooled beneath the dead.

When Betty heard men talking in English, she pulled her face out of the snow. Standing above her, looking down, she saw the only man she wanted. Captain Forrester peered down at his wife, smiling from ear to ear.

"You saved the day, darlin'," Will said, shaking his head in wonder.

"What in the world got into to ya, girl?" Levi asked.

"You made a difficult task easy. You killed half the hostiles before we even got started."

"I'd say she's a feisty one, your wife, Levi." Marshal Walker laughed as he nudged a dead Indian with the toe of his boot. "These hostiles got so many holes in 'em they look like pincushions."

Betty tried to hide her shaking hands, but Will offered his to help her up. She emerged from the snow and wrapped her arms around him, fighting back the tears. These weren't tears of frustration like before but tears of joy. Her heart was bursting with happiness.

"Maybe now you'll understand who I really am, honey," Betty whispered. She laid her head on the captain's shoulder and sighed. Finally, she felt like she had shown them all her true identity, even to her loving husband.

Despite her bravado, she felt safe in her husband's arms. Now, she had proven herself, and the struggle was over. The anger she had for Dahteste suddenly fell away and vanished altogether. Now *she* knew who she was, too. It was about time Betty really knew herself. Now, the confusion and the anger disappeared. All her frustrations ended with the clash between her and the Blackfeet warriors. It was true; she had won the day.

Fast Friends

Dahteste Johnson and Betty Forrester sat beside each other on an enormous bearskin rug before the roaring fire. They stared into the flames; their reflection danced in their eyes. The waves of heat made Dahteste sleepy, and she lay her head in Betty's lap and, in minutes, was snoring gently. Shadows flickered on the cabin walls as the men played poker at the dinner table. The dandelion wine had fermented, and a jug sat in the middle, while full glasses sat before each player.

"It came out a tad sour this year," Rusty said after gulping down the glass and then puckering his lips. "Did you put the right amount of sugar in the wine barrel, Angus? You're always stingy with the brown sugar, ain't ya? And why is that?"

"Because you and everyone else in this room has a sweet tooth, and you're always stealin' my stock," Angus replied. "Your coffee is never sweet enough, is it? Do you see a sugarcane plantation near abouts? We've gotta ration it like everything else we store from year to year.

If it don't grow on trees, we have to buy it at the Rendezvous or go all the way to the Boise trading post."

"I don't know about you, but my coffee of a morning is sacred," Dennis said. "I could never get my eyes wide open without it."

Betty curled up beside the Crow woman, and she, too, fell asleep on the soft fur. Her Irish white skin contrasted with Dahteste's dark-red face. Blond and black hair mixed as they slept.

"Those two sure are somethin'." Levi smiled. "I thought they were gonna kill each other for a spell."

"I never imagined Betty had all that penned up inside her busting to get out," the captain said. "And here we thought she was something she wasn't. Just because she came from back East doesn't mean that there aren't wildernesses there, too. I just never put the two together. She was one of us all along, and we treated her special for being different. The last thing Betty wanted was to be treated as an extraordinary beauty when all she sought was to be seen as an equal. Not just a White woman men like to look at. One day, she told me she wished she was born ugly."

"Nah, you're joshing, right?" Marshal Walker asked. "I'm ugly, and when I was young, all I wanted to be was good-lookin'." He laughed at his humor.

"No, sir, I'm not," the captain replied. "It shocked me too when she said it, but now, I understand. I believe all of us men are guilty of gawking at pretty women at some time or other. Then, all we see is the outside; we never give the real person the time of day. I've seen Rusty guilty enough times of the same crime." They all laughed, but Rusty blushed as red as a cranberry.

Pine Needle and Angus sat on a bunk in the corner.

They hadn't seen each other for weeks. She showed him the new beads she had made for him. It made her White husband grin like a possum.

"So how many rigs did you say you were gonna wagon master across the entire United States?" Rusty asked. Mischief danced in his eyes. "I can't remember right. Was that five hundred, or was it a thousand?"

"Did the marshal say a thousand?" Levi asked, surprised. "I thought it was a few hundred at most."

The mountain man cackled momentarily, waking the sleeping girls, but they were again snoring softly in minutes. It had been a long night and day before that. Only the men kept awake with whiskey-spiked java and tobacco. Virgil sat at the table because he liked watching the game but didn't believe in gambling. Joseph didn't believe in *not* gambling when playing poker. If not, he didn't see the point of the game.

"I raise ya a dollar." Rusty smiled.

"A dollar?" Levi retorted. "I thought the maximum bid was two bits. That's too rich for my blood. I'm out." He tossed his cards on the table. Two deuces lay face up.

"Dagnabit, you would have to drop out when I've got a hand good enough to win somethin'," Rusty grumbled.

"You must be the worst poker player in the world, Rusty." Joseph laughed. "You smiled like a chimpanzee as soon as you saw your hand. You might be the best mountain man in the Rockies, but you're the worst card player west of Missouri."

"Well, ya can't be good at everything." Rusty chuckled. "I never said I was perfect. I only said I was pert near."

"That's exactly how exaggerations happen. People start to stretch the truth, and we ain't even left yet. It was two hundred wagons and not a thousand," the marshal said. "That's the biggest wagon train ever crossed this here United States, clear to the Pacific Ocean. Rory is supposed to be waitin' for me in Independence, Missouri. We were gonna start farther down the trail, but I figured if we're gonna do it, we might as well go the whole way. If not, somebody else will claim the record, and what we did won't count for squat."

"So, what are you takin' on such an arduous expedition for, Joseph?" Rusty asked. "Ain't you gettin' old for young men's foolishness?"

"That's what keeps me alive and kickin'," the marshal replied, smiling. "And why did you and Angus put yourselves in harm's way fetching them beaver from so high in the mountains? It nearly cost ya both your lives. At your age, you are returning to where you trapped critters some fifteen years ago? And this time of year? It was to prove you're still willing and able, just like me. We were born for this stuff, boys. There's no sense in denying it. I reckon we won't change until the day we die."

"He's right, you know," Virgil said as he puffed on his corncob pipe. "I believe if a man is able and willing, he can live his last day just like his first. It's just a matter of mental attitude. If you think negatively, nothing will come of your plans and dreams. Positive thinking will keep you on an even keel, though. I might look like I'm aging outside, but from inside, I'm still just a lad. It's all about how you feel and how you look at life. Don't expect nothin', and you'll never be disappointed."

Depths of Winter

From outside the three cabins the only sign of life was yellow flickering lights in the windows. Nobody stayed in the teepee when it was so cold. You couldn't beat a stone fireplace to keep warm. It was early in the morning and the only people awake were Rusty and Angus. They were cleaning beaver pelts to sell in the summer when Rendezvous time came around. The extreme cold-water furs were of the best quality and would bring top dollar at market. It had been risky business, but the trip had been worth it in the end.

The skins had been salted and hung up and allowed to dry in the cool air of the storage cellar. They thawed them out to be fleshed and dried again. The skins were folded over, fur to fur for storage. Now it was time to soften them. Rusty and Angus carefully scraped the hides with knives and rolled them over the edge of the dinner table then massaged them with their hands. Rusty and Angus even tugged them back and forth between them, pulling and twisting until they were soft and pliable.

Only Dennis was allowed to assist in curing the valuable beaver pelts. Experience made all the difference in the final product. But recently the aging mountain man got up later every day and he was the first to go to bed. Old age was setting in on at least one of the original inhabitants of the compound. It was something they knew would catch them all one day.

Snow covered the cabin's roofs and stables. The horses huddled together to keep warm. Their breaths showed in the frigid morning. Straw was piled high around their shelter. Coyotes howled in the distance welcoming a new day. Rusty looked out the window, but the only tracks were to the outhouses and back. The ropes between dwellings were frozen stiff.

The day after the Blackfeet attacked the mountain men, they left their bodies lay where they fell. With the freezing temperatures, they wouldn't smell even if they were left there a couple of days. Members of their tribe came to collect the dead under cover of darkness so they could give them proper Blackfeet burials. This would allow them to be sent off to their spirit worlds, something important in all the Indian Nations.

During the collection to bury their deceased, the people living in the compound didn't leave the safety of their home. They all waited in Rusty's cabin, as it was the best place for defense. They believed they would come peacefully, though. Rusty's dog let them know when they weren't too far away, giving them time to lock down just in case it was a trap. At this point they believed anything goes. In the Rocky Mountains it was always that way.

Among the Indian men were women, too. Many were the widows of fallen braves. Even though the

Indians had tried to kill them, Rusty and Angus demanded their customs be respected, something that rubbed Marshal Joseph Walker wrong, and he let them know about it. He believed Rusty was getting softer every day.

Levi and Will had dodged a couple of bullets when Dahteste and Betty made peace. In the end it was all a big misunderstanding. Luckily nobody got seriously hurt along the way. Now they had become so close they were more like sisters than just friends. Just like their husbands, Johnson and Forrester.

As the sun began to rise in the sky and the temperatures became softer, the people living in the compound made their way to Rusty's cabin for breakfast like they did every day. Angus had complained at first. There were too many mouths to feed when he was used to cooking for only him and Rusty. But they all liked his skills as chef so much he now delighted in the task. Especially when he was bathed in compliments every morning. What better way to start a day? He made the best White man's grub in all the Rocky Mountains—at least according to the cook McFarlin.

Mountain Dennis, Virgil, and the marshal were the first to arrive. This too was normal for this winter. The couples took longer to leave their warm nests then the single men. They stomped snow from their shoes at the door and took a seat in their usual places.

"Mornin', gentlemen," Joseph said, "and you too, Rusty."

The marshal laughed.

"No more than you step through the door and you're hackin' on me again." Rusty huffed. "Stop with your sass or you'll do without breakfast. You'll have to cook for yourself and I've et your cookin' and it ain't a pretty thing to see."

Angus and the others all laughed. It was the same every morning since the marshal came back with Levi and Will and Will's new bride, Betty. Joseph was a contrary person but with time he grew on them just like he had on Rusty years before when they first met. Then again soft lawmen didn't live very long in Kansas. They had to be as tough as nails. It was difficult for Walker to soften his ways, but little by little he was becoming easier to live with.

"Mind your manners now, or it'll be a cold winter sleepin' with the horses in the stables where you belong." Rusty chuckled. Eventually even Walker found it funny.

The smell of hot biscuits filled the air. A jug of maple molasses sat on the table to appease everybody's sweet tooth. Outside, the sun said it was nearly nine o'clock before Betty, Will, Dahteste, and Levi joined the table. By then the biscuits were cold but the couples seemed not to notice.

Everybody there was one big happy family even though none of them were really related. It just goes to show that you don't have to have the same blood running through your veins to be family. It's all in the heart anyway.

Rocky Mountain Fever

Levi Johnson Mountain
Man Scout 16

This book is dedicated to my daughter Kimmy. Many of my fondest memories in life were all the moments we shared.

Love you, Dad.

Gold Fever

Finally, the heavy snow stopped, and the temperatures began slowly rising. The mountain men and wives in the compound even started taking lunch on the porch, if the skies were clear and the sun was bright. Being stuffed in the cabins for the whole winter made them edgy, and they felt the need to visit Mother Nature surrounding them. Tempers were short, and everybody needed fresh air.

The out-of-doors was what they wanted after weeks of isolation and cold. Their only visits outside had been to tend to the horses, bring in wood, or visit the outhouses. To break the boredom, they tended to the stables and animals, and each owner would visit their horses or mules every day.

Rusty's dog was the most in need of his freedom. The first day they spent time on the porch, he ran off, and they didn't see him for hours. His owner wondered if something happened to him, but he returned as always. They had been together since the day Rusty and Dog found each other. He barked, ran, jumped, and played in the snow. His coal-black coat of fur stood out boldly in the white powder.

That day, Levi and Rusty were the first to step outside and take a seat at the porch table. Johnson instantly smelled something as he sniffed the air. Despite the rising sun, the cold made their noses red and runny. They pulled their coats tight and settled in.

"Is that burning wood?" Levi asked, sniffing. He turned his eyes to his mentor. "Do you smell it, or is it my imagination?"

"No, sir, you smell it all right," Rusty replied. "It smacked me in the face as soon as we set foot on the plank floor—that and the cold. I reckon we've got unwanted visitors. It's just what we need after all that mess with the Blackfeet Indians. The wilderness don't seem to give a man a break."

"How do you already know they're unwanted, Rusty?" Levi asked. "They could be somebody lost and need direction. Not everybody has ill intentions, boss."

"I know they're unwanted because I don't tolerate STUPID!" Rusty spat. "Any man who makes a fire around here in the daytime and they don't have permission to be on the mountain are either stupid or lookin' to get scalped. Have a peek above those trees. See that trail of smoke in the sky? Do you really think we're the only ones that's gonna see it? I figure they're lookin' to get shot, and I might just be the one shootin'."

"You reckon, boss?" Levi asked. "I thought you were goin' softer on folks instead of being so contrary like before." Levi coughed into his fist to stifle a snicker.

"I figure some of that hackin' Joseph does on me about gettin' soft is probably right. A man seems to get more tolerant as he ages, but it's a good way to get yourself kilt in the wilderness. Get the guns, and let's go see who it is and exactly what they're up to," Rusty said. "From the looks of the smoke, they're on the other side of *our* mountain. I take about as kindly to trespassers as Chief Hachta does. If he finds these folks before we do, they'll be done for. He gets all riled up when more White men show up and decide to settle. We better be good Samaritans and send whoever is on their way before there's trouble. I reckon how I treat 'em will all depend on how they act and who they really are. I may be a tad on the hard side, but you know I don't shoot women."

Levi laid his hands flat on the table and pushed himself from his chair to have a better look. Black soot and vapor rose like a thick string into the clear blue sky. There wasn't a breath of air, and it seemed to vanish in a raft of cirrostratus high above with the circling vultures. Johnson spun on his heels, and boot heels hammered the floor. He pulled the door open, rushed for the fireplace, grabbed Rusty's and Angus's rifles, and turned to head out again.

"Where are you runnin' off to all of a sudden?" Angus asked. "What's the big rush?"

"Trespassers is all." Levi smiled. "Rusty gets all riled up if somebody makes camp on the mountain. But he's right; it's better we run 'em off before a Crow war party catches 'em. They're burning wet wood, and it's smoking something awful. I doubt it'll take long for a Crow hunter or scout to see—maybe one of them Blackfeet if they survived and are still around. If we can smell it, they probably can, too. Rusty says they must be stupid."

"Well, for once, he's right." Angus chuckled. "Any

White men who would make a fire during the day on Crow Chief Hachta's territory ain't only stupid, but they're crazy, too."

Out the door and to the gate, then the mentor and his apprentice headed west to see what they could find. The smoke continued to swirl into the clear blue sky. It was seen for miles.

Angus shook his head, talking to himself. "I don't know why they go lookin' for trouble. I figure enough finds us all on its own."

After racing through the woods for an hour on trails only they knew, the mountain men climbed the last ridge before looking down to the other side and into the next valley. As they reached the summit, something tore at Levi's grizzly bear coat. He looked down and saw the ripped sleeve. The second bullet nicked his ear, and blood trickled down his neck as he slapped it like a pesky fly.

That was when they heard the first gunshot report. The second came shortly after. The mountain men dove for cover and rolled back down the hill behind them. When they scrambled to the top again, this time, they did so with caution. Their reckless actions had bitten them quickly, and they weren't about to give the shooter a second chance. Whoever these trespassers were, their intentions were as clear as water. They were out to kill both Rusty and Levi—maybe anybody who tried to run them off. What was still unknown was who and why.

"I'd venture to say that these fellas are unfriendly," Rusty said snappishly and winked. "It's a good thing they ain't sharpshooters like us. Otherwise, we'd both be dead and not sixty minutes from home."

"Whatcha mean? That fool nearly shot my earlobe

off," Levi growled. He pulled off a long bandana and wrapped it around his head to stop the bleeding. "They're good enough shots to wing me."

"Why, that's no more than a scratch," Rusty tittered. "Now, let's focus on what we're doing and see what's goin' on down there."

Rusty put his rifle to his shoulder and looked for something to take a bead on as Levi pulled out his spyglass. He traced it across the landscape below. Johnson stopped when he saw something moving behind a tree. In the distance behind that was the string of smoke.

"There he is," Levi whispered. "Just follow the trail of smoke down, and you'll see a tree about another hundred yards this way. That's what they're hidin' behind. You keep an eye on these rascals, and I'll see if I can flank 'em. Maybe we can shoot 'em in the legs and put 'em out of commission."

"Why don't you shoot him in the chest or head?" Rusty growled. "That's what he intended to do to you, son. There ain't nobody out there but ne'er-do-wells. If we don't take this seriously, we might be the ones to die today."

"Let me make sure these shooters are alone," Levi said. "I doubt a couple of fellas would come out here on their own, but ya just never know. I know I wouldn't when I first got up here in the Rockies. It's too dangerous when you don't know the land."

Levi had another careful look with his spyglass, behind the men with rifles and toward their camp. "They've got two horses and four mules, so they're plannin' on packin' somethin'. I'd say they ain't just passin' through but are here to visit for a spell. There're sacks of supplies around the campfire. I see picks and shovels, too—that and gear for pannin' gold. Everything I see says they're prospectors, and ornery ones at that. We know they've got good guns and know how to shoot."

"This bunch is too stupid to know how dangerous it is, but they're just about to find out," Rusty panted. "If they're after gold, they won't be alone. The fever does strange things to people. It makes men go to places they would never risk normally and turns them into something they weren't."

The frontiersmen watched for another ten minutes to ensure the trespassers didn't turn and run, but they stayed right where they were, like they weren't planning on going anywhere. They were obviously looking for gold.

"That's what greed does, Beaver," Rusty whispered. "It turns normal men stupid. But I've never heard of any gold around here, nor has anybody else. At least not till now."

Levi slid back down the hill and ran for the shooters' right flank. Both trespassers were right-handed, taking cover from behind the tree, so if they wanted to shoot from cover, they had to shoot from the same side. Johnson would come up on their left, behind a rock. They would have to wheel their barrels around their backs to take aim. Hopefully, Levi could kill them in time before they took a bead. If everything worked out as planned, Rusty's shot should follow right after Johnson's. There was no room for mistakes this time.

In the year or so since Levi lived in the compound and with the Crow Indians, he had learned not only to hunt wild game but also to hunt men. This he did with the same deliberate calm and concentration as his mentor, who was one of the best. He also knew that one wrong move or a bad calculation could cost him his life.

Johnson crawled down a shallow gully, heading for the closest spot to the shooters as he could get. This was land he knew, like only Angus and Rusty. He knew where every rock and blade of grass was, even under the snow. Levi poked his head over a rock. It gave him a small amount of cover so he could have a peek and still be safe.

That was when he saw there were three shooters and not only the pair. This was his second mistake. Two prospectors had long rifles held to their shoulders. The other had a brace of pistols in his fists, and they looked like they were getting ready to rush Rusty Steel, his mentor.

Levi took a bead and pulled the trigger. Rusty's shot immediately followed suit. Both chunks of lead hit their marks. Two of the trespassers fell over dead from carefully placed headshots. They never even knew they got hit. Then Levi screamed and ran for the last man standing with a pistol in each fist. His arms pumped like steam engine pistons, and his stomach jumped to his throat as his face glistened with sweat despite the cold.

That was when the last shooter standing saw the large mountain man barreling toward him. It was clear he meant to take his life. The trespasser's eyes spread as his dead companions lay at his feet.

His pistols were short enough that he could easily swing them left and into the mountain man's path—Levi's third mistake. Johnson suddenly found himself staring down two barrels. He already sensed he had made too many serious miscalculations. Maybe there are errors he could never take back.

Levi wasn't quite close enough for a sure pistol shot, but he knew he would get fired on if he didn't fire soon. He pulled both triggers, and the pistols recoiled in his fists. The man standing in front of him fired simultaneously. They were both thinking the same thing.

Flame and smoke followed the bullets out of the barrels as they raced for their targets, crossing each other's paths. Time stopped as both men gritted their teeth and waited for the expected impact.

The third aggressive prospector dropped to his knees and toppled over. Levi grunted, doubling over before he passed out.

Longshots

Four mountain men sat outdoors on the porch, waiting for Angus. Their breaths disappeared a few inches from their mouths. They finished breakfast as they eyed the smoke in the distance. They heard two faraway cracking sounds. The marshal cocked his head and focused as he closed his eyes. Angus was filling tin cups with java. Bubbles popped from the spout of a percolating kettle as steam arose from five untouched coffees. The rich aroma filled the air.

"Maybe they're just scarin' off the trespassers," Marshal Joseph Walker said. "I doubt a few lost hunters will pose much problem for the likes of Rusty Steel, especially with Levi at his side. I kinda feel sorry for the trespassers already. We know they ain't Indians because there ain't none of them born that stupid."

"You just never know who you'll run into in the wilderness," Dennis said. "It's usually the last people you'd expect."

"I've never seen anybody even near beat Rusty in a scrap," Angus bragged. "I've seen him take on a war party alone when he was young. Once he was declared king of this part of the mountain, the hostile Indians usually steered clear. Then he made peace with the Crow, and now they protect us as well. We live in peace now, but you know how those Blackfeet are. They just won't give up. Maybe it's just out of spite because the Crow and us get along. They sure are a cantankerous bunch."

"It'll be spring soon," Virgil said, "and time to head down the mountain to the Rendezvous. I have a list of needed items as long as my arm." He scratched his face with a brown hand and grinned a full mouth of straight, bright teeth.

"I almost regret the trip down to that circus," Dennis said. "Last year, it worked out so badly with the Squirrel family and all, maybe I'll sit it out this season. I've been to fourteen so far and figure it might be time I let it be. We spend most of the time drunk, anyway, so what's the point? I can get just as drunk here and won't have to deal with all the chaos the trappers meet brings. You know that most of them who belong to trapper brigades are outlaws running away from back East. Mostly murderers and thieves, they are. Somebody can bring back my list of needs. You'll take care of that for me, won't cha, Virgil?"

"It's a long time between now and then, so you might change your mind." Virgil smiled. "Nothin' is written in stone, my good friend. You just wait until warm weather comes back around. I always feel friskier in the spring and summer months." He laughed, and it echoed in the crisp air.

"You're just gettin' old, is all, Dennis." Joseph chuckled. "I reckon I'll be the same in twenty years."

"In twenty years?" Dennis bellyached. "You ain't that much younger than me. You're just so full of yourself, you think you're still a youngin. Let's see how old you feel after you've taken those two hundred wagons on what you call the Oregon Trail. Why, it doesn't even exist yet, and I ain't so sure it ever will, and here you've already named it. It's all in your mind, Marshal. If ya ask me, it must be the most asinine thing a friend of mine has ever thought about doin'."

"And since when are we friends?" Joseph retorted. For him, what he called the Oregon Trail was a touchy subject. It was a passion that had turned into an obsession.

"If we ain't friends, then whatcha doin' stayin' in my house?" Dennis snorted. "I don't break bread with anybody but friends and the needy."

"I reckon I'm needy, then, ain't I, pard?" The marshal chortled.

It was only a three-week trip from the compound to the South Pass. That was where the marshal crossed the Rocky Mountains with the missionaries. He had hired Will, Levi, and Dahteste to help. The pay was so good they couldn't pass. They had made it there and back and had proven it was possible. Now, the marshal wanted to do the same but in large numbers—two hundred wagons with as many as a thousand people, if not more. Then there were the horses, mules, cattle, and goats, not to mention the chickens. It would be like a small town walking across the country beside wagons.

"I know for a fact Chief Hachta is dead against what you're plannin' to do," Angus said, eyeing the marshal under hooded eyes. "I agree with Rusty. It's gonna bring lots of noisy people to Yellowstone Valley, and then they'll be far too close to us here in the compound. Some of 'em are bound to stray and end up here where we live. You just watch and see."

"I reckon the Blackfeet won't take kindly to them trespassing in the valley either," Dennis fussed. "They're gonna stir 'em up somethin' fierce, and any White men around will pay."

"Black folks, too," Virgil said. He occasionally pointed out his race, but usually, it fell on deaf ears. He was one of them, so they didn't see him differently, just like Dahteste. "I reckon everybody's gonna get angry, but not at first. It'll take time to come to a boil."

"That's right, Virgil," Joseph said. "It'll take years for the trail to get up to speed and become a well-traveled road. We'll be long dead and gone before that happens. Hell, maybe my trip will be another disaster, and nobody'll follow us. It won't be my first failure, and I doubt it'll be my last, either."

"Yeah, like mine, back when I was in the US Cavalry," Captain Forrester said. He had been silent for the last hour as he focused on any sounds in the distance. Levi Johnson was his best friend. "In the end, hardly a man survived. That's why I came west with Levi. When we met, he was scouting for the army and was attached to my patrol. After the Comanche nearly wiped us out, I latched on to him for lack of anywhere else to go. Lucky for us, Rusty Steel liked Levi from the moment they met. I doubt he'd have taken me on my own. I was just another soldier to them back then. It really wasn't that long ago. I wonder how he and Rusty are doing right now."

"Easterners are what the local Indians hate," Angus said. "They know we live like they do and don't intend to build a trading post or town. That's the last thing I'd want. As long as they need us to barter for steel tools and coffee with the occasional rifle, we're more valuable than we are a problem. Just as long as we behave ourselves."

"I'm surprised the chief didn't mention Betty when Will brought her back and she moved in. At least Hachta knows the marshal will be leaving as soon as the weather breaks," Dennis said. "Lucky for them, Pete, Sam, and Bob passed. If not, I doubt he'd have taken it so well. I figure he has a number in his head and won't tolerate any more trappers settling in. We must have a full quota by now."

"No matter how much you keep hackin' on me, I'm still gonna do it," the marshal said. "If anybody is prepared, I reckon it's me. I've lived just like you boys, trappin' for a living, and spent more time than y'all combined searching for new passages west. Like I said before, if I don't do it, somebody else will because everybody will know it can be done. I reckon I like trailblazing, is all. It has a nice ring to it: The Oregon Trail."

"What you want is to have somethin' else to brag about." Angus guffawed. "As it is, you spend most of every day talkin' about yourself."

"You're just jealous, is all," Joseph said.

"I wouldn't trade places with you for nothin' in the world." Angus smiled, wrinkling his face like an old dog. "Why would a man in his right mind trade this paradise for a dusty trail, desert, and hardships? What do they have in Oregon that I want and don't have here?"

"How about the Pacific Ocean? Hell, I guess I'm fiddle-footed, is all," Joseph admitted. "I've been that way all my life. Whenever I decide I've found the perfect place to live, somebody tells me about somewhere else, and off I go again. If the truth be known, the grass ain't hardly ever greener on the other side of the fence. Then again, if I don't go and see for myself, I'll never know. Maybe I'm just too curious for my own good."

Twenty minutes later, when more shots echoed through the towering pines, the mountain men exchanged glances. No words were needed—the gunfire brought frowns. They hurried to the door for their weapons. In seconds, they turned for the porch again, but they were armed to the teeth this time.

A cold breeze rushed through the room when the timber door opened. Rusty's dog slipped past the men, racing across the porch toward the buck-and-rail fence with his nose to the ground. He howled as he broke into a run, scenting the path of his master. The others legged it behind the black furry canine. Only Mountain Dennis knew the old path. In the distant past, they had used it to sneak out of the cabin. Then they could flank their enemy, unseen.

As they ran, Virgil shouted to Betty and Dahteste, who were stepping out of their cabin, "Stay here and keep an eye on things. Get your guns ready, just in case. We'll be right back."

When the original trappers occupied the mountain, they were at odds with all the local Indians. In the beginning, when Mountain Dennis, Yosemite Bob, Syracuse Sam, and Portland Pete lived there, it was a running battle from one short peace treaty to another. It wasn't until Steel arrived from the Flatfoot tribe did they gain the respect of the local Crow Indians. Back then, it was the first time Rusty saved Chief Hachta's life.

They had done the same for each other on more than one occasion in the following years, making them fast friends and eventually blood brothers. That made it possible for everybody to benefit from this peaceful agreement with a handful of mountain men. But it wasn't meant for anyone else. Trespassers without permission were dealt with harshly to discourage others who might decide to follow in their footsteps.

Sloshy, dirty snow covered the trail. They could see the old path as they headed for the other side of the hill. The second round of gunfire gave them a boost of adrenaline, and they raced up to the summit like their pants were on fire. The fact that they might be too late crossed all their minds. Lungs heaved as moccasin-covered feet hammered the trail, splashing melting snow as they roared onward.

When they reached the hilltop, Virgil pulled out an old, cracked spyglass. He saw the three trespassers right away. They lay in pools of their own blood. Rusty Steel kneeled over the motionless body of Levi Johnson.

"Lord, have mercy on his soul," Virgil said as the blood drained from his face. "We've gotta hurry down there. It looks like Levi's gotten shot."

"Shot? Levi?" Will stammered, blinking. "Give me that spyglass, Virgil."

Captain Forrester's face turned as pale as a ghost when he saw his best friend lying still on the ground. It looked like Rusty was working on him or something, so there was a chance he was still alive. He could see a dark stain under Levi's body with the small telescope. He instantly realized it was a pool of blood.

"Come on, maybe we can help," the captain said throatily as he blinked back tears.

Rusty was so frantically busy that he didn't even hear the other mountain men nearby.

"Come on, let me give ya a hand," Marshal Walker said. "I've done this before. Let's drag 'em out of that blood first. We've got to clean things up here and quickly. Come and help me, Virgil. Between us, we can help best. Rusty, take a break, old pard. We ain't gonna let 'em die." Joseph stubbornly shook his head.

Will gasped when he saw the gunshot wound. Levi got hit on the right side of his chest. The bullet punctured his lung. Bloody bubbles popped from his mouth and the wound.

"Come on," Joseph said. "We've gotta roll 'em over."

Rusty refused to leave Levi's side, so the three carefully turned the body face down. Johnson moaned, more unconscious than not.

"Thank God for that," Virgil said. "It's a through-and-through. It must have been a fifty-caliber round. At least we won't have to dig the bullet out."

"Yeah, but we've gotta keep his lung from fillin' up with blood," the marshal said. "It's a good thing he's young, big, and strong, or he'd be dead already. A round from such a bullet would kill most people from the shock."

When Rusty realized the severity of the situation, he breathed out a long breath of air. He felt dizzy and had to steady himself against a tree. He said all breathy, "Don't let 'em die on me Joseph, Virgil. I've got the feelin' he was tryin' to save me from gettin' killed. These three dead men were gettin' ready to rush me. Hell, had

I known he would get shot, I'd have stood up and let 'em shoot me. I'm nearly an old man, and he's just beginnin' his life." He shook his head, and his face turned red when he had to wipe a tear away with the back of his wrinkled hand.

"Now that we know there's no lead in his body, we better get 'em back to the cabin where we can dig deeper and see what we can do," the marshal said.

The marshal nodded, and Virgil said, "If the hole is big enough, I could sew up the lung front and back. I've got proper catgut back in Dennis's cabin. I hope to have a needle small enough. With my reading glasses, I might be able to do it. It could be his only chance. If not, he'll drown in his blood."

The gasp was unanimous. Levi had always seemed indestructible, but now he was lying there, knocking on death's door. Virgil's lips muttered as he read passages from his worn Bible. His finger traced under the words, then he closed his eyes and said a desperate prayer. There wasn't a man there who didn't make a plea to God in their minds. They were family, after all.

Rusty pulled out his massive Bowie knife and chopped down two young pines. They used their fur coats to make a stretcher. Will, Rusty, Virgil, and Joseph each grabbed a handle as Virgil dabbed at the blood. The mountain men moved as quickly and carefully as they could, racing against time, trying not to move the body too much. With each movement, Levi seemed to pump more blood.

Luckily, they were close to home, but now minutes, maybe even seconds, counted. Nobody knew for sure, but it was as bad as any of them had ever been shot—

even Will, who had lost his arm in battle. His empty sleeve flapped in a breeze that suddenly arose. Levi was out cold, and now he didn't even moan.

Fort Boise

"Read all about it!" the boy yelled as he waved a newspaper in his hand. Bundles wrapped in string lay beside his feet. "Read all about it. Gold strike in Yellowstone Valley and the Rockies! Read all about it!"

The journalist listened from his office window. He cracked it open to let in the cool air. It was already warming up, and Perry Weston hated warm springs and summers. He preferred even terribly cold winters over July and August. The newspaper owner had big plans for his recently struggling rag. One day, he would call it *The World*, and the entire Western United States would read it. He was waiting for the day the Idaho Territories were free from the treaty with Great Britain and it could become an official territory. Maybe then even a state.

From the time in 1818, when French trappers arrived in the lush green valley and the winding Payette River lined by cottonwoods, to then, the town had grown. That was why Weston currently named his periodical *Les Boise*, like the French originally called the fort. The current day name of Fort Boise was christened in 1834.

The Hudson Bay Trading Post in the southwestern part of the territory on the Snake River was at the center of growth as Idaho was included in the British fur company's Columbia District.

The sizable fort was surrounded by a stockade of poles fifteen feet high and covered in sun-dried adobe bricks. He knew that one day in the future, it would be a bustling city, and he planned to control the news and, with that, the politics. Now was the time to plant the seeds and draw more people to the settlement. With the population would come the need for officials, and his influential tabloid would vote them in. He could see it all unfold in his mind's eye.

That was why the journalist invented the news of the gold strike in the Yellowstone Valley and mountains above. In three days, he sold more newspapers than he had in the previous month, and the sales were still spiking upward in a vertical line. He smiled as he heard the hawker sell his wares. *Hear all about it*, he thought. *GOLD*. A smile curled on the edges of his lips.

Soon, travelers would invade the town, and many would either stay in Fort Boise and go no farther or continue to the mountains and find nothing, only to return and abandon their plans, leaving them in town just the same. It was a long way back to anything that resembled civilization, and many would become trapped. He had no consideration for the adverse effects it might provoke. All that mattered to him was his audience. It wasn't even about the money. It was all about power.

Perry wanted a dramatic increase in the Fort Boise population and was willing to trade anything for success. The publisher was surprised at how well his little lie had worked. Maybe he would add a few juicy details for the following week's edition. He could hardly wait to see how well his plan continued to generate more sales and widen his reader base. It was breaking all expectations.

Wagons rumbled down the street, churning up brown sludge. Men walked with their boots covered in mud, well past their ankles. Mules and miners assaulted the trading post as a line of grizzly-looking men grew outside. The saloons were full and overflowing onto the porches despite the cold weather. It was already getting warm for the people who had passed the winter in town.

Mister Weston grabbed the gold chain of an expensive English pocket watch, pulled it out, snapped the lid open, and checked the time. It was nearly noon; time to eat. The journalist always dined at the busiest restaurant in town, even though it was far from the best. As a matter of fact, it was the cheapest and brought all sorts of humanity. Of course, they all had a story to tell or to be overheard, and Perry was forever hungry for news.

Where better could you hear men's dark secrets than where they mingled in one place of all races, ages, and walks of life? The common denominator was money. Everybody was poor or a trapper or tracker of some sort. Some were even Indian fighters. Most men had five cents for a meal a day, though. It kept many people alive with just enough nourishment to survive.

The only rich man sitting in the restaurant was alone at the corner table. He was so frequent that after time, nobody seemed to notice him anymore as he strained his ears to eavesdrop. He had also become a proficient lip reader if they were Americans. The same skill was less than reliable when reading the lips of Scots, Brits, Swedes, or the French. Sometimes, a patron would talk to the bartender, and he would point out the journalist. Many men wanted to spread their fame, so they gave Perry stories or bits of news willingly. Some hoped even to become famous.

Often, he printed the events precisely. This far west, it was often unnecessary to lie because something interesting was always happening. But there had been no earth-shattering headlines until the gold strike revelation. Of course, the column mentioned undisclosed sources, hinting they came from Washington without being specific. Perry had mastered his trade and knew how to spin a yarn that was not only believable but impossible to prove untrue.

Only Perry knew it was a lie, but then again, who could deny it wasn't true if they hadn't gone there and tried to find gold themselves? It was impossible to accuse the newspaper of right or wrong or hold them responsible. Long ago, he had learned to write articles that sounded like something other than what they were, playing with people's subconscious as he wove his magical words. He always made sure none of his falsehoods could come back to bite him.

Of course, people believe what they wanted to believe. Striking gold was in the back of many adventurers' minds, and the news of a strike so close would make many men crazy and greedy beyond control, causing them to lose all their willpower. They had already begun to count money that they would never find. It was all a fantasy, yet real in their minds. Such men were impossible to stop once the fever hit them.

What Perry had put into motion was unstoppable

now, not that he would have it any other way. Within days of the release of the first publication, thousands of fortune seekers headed for Yellowstone Valley. Most of them hadn't given things like hostile Indians or landowners a second thought. Others knew there would be dangers but were prepared to kill for a place to stake a claim. Gold made men do things they never thought they were capable of doing. It seemed to change every man it touched.

Among these were also men of reckless blood—men who had already committed crimes against the laws of humanity *and* the Almighty. They, too, were always interested in easy money. Many didn't consider the hardships the miners suffered. Most thought they would arrive and find nuggets as big as silver dollars laying on the ground, waiting to be picked up. Many were that naïve. Especially the way Perry worded his headlines. He made it all sound so easy and with apparently nothing in the way to stop them from all getting rich.

From his article, they derived that the supply of the precious yellow mineral was as endless as the Rocky Mountains.

The Wives

Dahteste and Betty sat at the dinner table, frowning. They felt abandoned not only by their husbands but by the other mountain men as well. The Crow woman suspected Levi and Rusty had snuck off early to have a spell on their own. The women would never admit it, but they were jealous of their husbands' time with their friends. Then again, it was only natural that they wanted them all for themselves. Day-to-day life in the Rockies was so unpredictable that nerves ate at their stomachs every time their husbands rode off without them. Even Dahteste, although she would never admit it nor show it in any way,

"Where do you think they went with Virgil yelling up a storm?" Betty asked. "The others didn't even look back. Did he really say we should get our guns? I wonder what's wrong now. We seem to run from one problem to another."

"We have our pistols and rifles, so don't worry," Dahteste said as she fingered her guns on the table. "Life in these mountains is always uncertain. It would help if you tried to learn to exist with it and flow with every day like the current in a stream. Don't fight it, but ebb with it like a tide. Things will work out. They always do."

The women's long rifles leaned against the wall; the Crow woman had her bow hung on the chair-back, and a quiver of arrows strapped over her shoulders. They stared out the window at the end of the buck-and-rail fence where the men had disappeared an hour earlier. Curiosity filled their eyes, but there was fear behind that, too. The thought that their husbands wouldn't return always lingered in the back of their minds.

"I didn't see Levi or Rusty with the others," Dahteste said. "I wonder where they went. I guess the others are following them. I feel like going with them, too. I'm not the kind of person to sit back and let others deal with problems. I can take care of myself."

"Right now, we're in charge of guarding the cabins and all the horses and mules. I won't risk that on my own, so you must stay with me, my friend. Sometimes, we have to listen to others. That doesn't mean they're trying to boss us around. I guess it's really a sort of compliment. That means a lot if they trust us with the cabins and their cherished horses. Of course, our husbands love us more than their horses, but they care for them like family, too."

"I wouldn't be so sure of that," Dahteste replied, dead serious, never taking her eyes from the fence. "In my tribe most warriors spend more time with their horses than their wives."

The Crow war chief continued to thumb her pistol's hammer in anticipation. It was almost like she wanted the challenge. Betty clearly wasn't afraid, but she was still exhausted from the fight with the Blackfeet and, before that, her best friend. Till that day, she didn't know where her courage to make a solitary rear attack on the Blackfeet had come from. She was much stronger than she had ever imagined and believed she had her Uncle Davy to thank for that. Good blood ran through the Crocketts' veins. Then again, she *was* from Tennessee.

Flames caressed logs like long fingers in the fireplace, sending waves of heat crackling across the cabin and shadows dancing on the walls. More warmth radiated from the cookstove in the back. Sun spilled into the window and cast light on the floor. The women waited in their buckskins. Bear fur coats hung from wooden hooks on the wall. An empty gun rack stood over the chimney.

Steam rose from cups, carrying the aroma of coffee through the air. Betty drummed her fingers on the wooden table impatiently. For once in their lives, the women didn't seem to have anything to say. Now that they had indeed become friends and no longer wanted to kill each other, they had talked themselves out and unveiled all their past and darkest secrets. Now, they waited in silence for whatever was next to come. In the Rocky Mountains, surprises were usually nasty and, at times, even deadly.

The first thing Dahteste saw was Rusty, Will, Virgil, and Joseph carrying what looked like a stretcher. The blood drained from her face. When they reached the cabin, they saw Dahteste looking out the window. Her eyes spread as she rushed to the door. By the time they hit the porch, it was open, and Betty was standing beside Levi's wife with pistols in their hands. Suddenly, the Crow woman's face turned into a mask. She showed no emotion and refused to display even a hint of fear. She puffed out her chest—her mouth a hard line.

She was a war chief and had seen injuries like this, and she knew what she was looking at. There were no mysteries here. Still, she put on her bravest face and held back all the emotion building up and bursting to explode from inside. Dahteste refused to shame herself and have an outburst, which would help nothing at all. Virgil's skills were the only thing that would save her husband. He had sewn up many wounds but never tried to do anything as complicated as this.

Betty wrapped her arm around Dahteste's shoulder. Dennis used his arm to clear the table in one quick sweep. Cups, a jug, and nicknacks hit the floor in a clatter. Broken ceramic scattered across the wood planks. There was no time to linger or explain what had happened. Now, they all focused on saving Levi's life.

"The problem are his ribs," Virgil panted. "They're already busted, but we'll have to pry 'em apart wide enough to sew up the punctured lung. Will, you and Rusty grab a couple of pliers. You'll both have to pull 'em apart while I try to sew the holes up. I'll get the catgut. Levi's still gonna bleed some, but his lungs won't fill with blood. At least then he'll have a fightin' chance to survive."

"Who shot my husband?'" Dahteste croaked. Only her voice gave away her true feelings.

The room went silent as blood pooled on the dinner table under Johnson's shot-up body. Lucky for him, he was out cold. What was to come would be impossible to do if he were conscious. Virgil was good at sewing up the usual cuts and gashes a man gets while working with steel traps and cold hands in freezing water. This was much more delicate, though. He had to make sure that he repaired the lung and didn't damage it more, or Levi would undoubtedly die.

Virgil rummaged in his medical kit and said, "Dahteste, here, grab this hammer. If your husband begins to come around, you're gonna have to give him a whack on the noggin. If he moves while I'm patchin' 'em up, it'll make a difficult job impossible. I know it sounds harsh, but the option ain't really an option at all, so bite your tongue and do as you're told, and we might be able to save your husband's life. At the moment, it's as touch and go as it gets."

Lovejoy had already found a hooked needle and had threaded it to make the stitches. Luckily, the exit wound was large and relatively easy to get to his lung, so they started with the gunshot hole in his back. Rusty and Will moved in to grab half a rib each in the teeth of steel pliers. They cringed as Levi's ribcage cracked and popped. But Virgil ignored it and got to work.

Angus was already busy by the piping hot cook stove boiling large metal pots of water. Steam rose, blurring his face. He was as shocked as Betty and was having a hard time keeping a brave face. McFarlin busied himself in the shadows of the corner of the back of the cabin, trying not to look at Levi as they operated on him. The aging mountain man was stunned into silence.

"Light a lantern, Betty, and hold it out so I can see what I'm doin'," Virgil said as he fussed with the wound. His face glistened with sweat. "Grab another one and hold it up on the other side, Dennis. I need all the light I can get, especially when we get to his chest. That's gonna be the stickler. This one's almost done."

"Who shot my husband?" Dahteste asked again. She locked eyes with Dennis this time, as he was the only one not busy, but he couldn't hold her stare. The other men held onto Levi's body in case he came around, and they had to try to restrain him.

"I didn't see what happened, darlin'," Mountain Dennis sniveled. A tear ran down his cheek, and he quickly wiped it away with the cuff of his shirt. "Rusty and Levi were the only ones there. I did see three dead miners, though, so I reckon they already killed the men who did this. What miners were doin' up here in the mountains, I can't say, but they were obviously up to no good. Otherwise, why the violence?"

Dahteste Johnson sat silently, but it was apparent she didn't accept what Dennis said. She was furious and wanted to know the facts, and then, if revenge were possible, she would seek it herself, regardless of the outcome. Nobody was going to trespass on Crow land and shoot her husband, no matter who they were. Then and there, she swore to herself she would find out everything about what happened, or die doing so and wreak the wrath on all those responsible.

Betty Forrester was shocked, to say the least. She had always seen Levi so big and strong and capable, it was hard to believe somebody shot him and he was lying on death's door. She cried openly, although she didn't sob or make a scene. Tears silently rolled down her face in abundance, splashing on the floor—a tiny pool of salty water forming at her feet.

When Lovejoy finished sewing the lung, he used thicker catgut to draw the broken skin together, pulling each stitch tight before tying it off and going to the next. When he was done, they carefully rolled Levi over on his back.

When he gasped, their stomachs jumped to their mouths, and hearts hammered between their ears. Dahteste didn't hesitate and thumped him on the head with the hammer, and out he went again. He hadn't even managed to open his eyes.

"I don't think you had to hit him so hard, do you?" Will winged. "You might kill him with that big old hammer."

"Let her be. She did right," Virgil scolded. "Pull steady now, boys, on my call. Three-two-one!"

The rib on his front was nearly twice as thick as the one on his back. Both men struggled to pull the separated bone apart and not tremble, causing Virgil to make a mistake. They also had to keep in mind they couldn't crack or chip the break any more than it was, or it would be impossible to set. That is if Levi made it through the next bit of the crude operation.

"More hot water, Angus!" Virgil shouted nervously, giving McFarlin a jarring look. "And take these over to boil so they sterilize. If the wound gets infected, it will all have been for nothin'." He handed him the bloody surgical instruments. Lovejoy's hands were red up to his forearms.

Circles of lamplight mixed with sunlight coming in the single window in the front of the cabin. Virgil squinted through old wire-rimmed glasses, his eyes six inches from the needle and Levi's lung. One lens was cracked, and a string held on a stem. They were so magnified, his pupils looked like giant black disks. He constantly mumbled the Lord's Prayer repeatedly while hyper-focusing on the task at hand. He had never had to patch somebody up with such an injury, and he felt the responsibility heavy on his shoulders.

Time seemed to slow to a stop, especially for Dahteste and Will, Levi's best friend. The one-armed captain looked at his pocket watch every two or three minutes. His nerves were jagged as he gritted his teeth. While he watched, he seemed to forget to breathe. When he suddenly got dizzy, he came around and filled his lungs, like a gasp in reverse. Even Angus at the back of the cabin heard the sound. The anxiety levels soured to the clouds.

"Quick, Betty," Virgil huffed, "wipe the sweat off my face. It's runnin' into my eyes."

Betty grabbed a clean rag and dabbed Lovejoy's forehead and cheeks with one hand as she held the kerosene lamp in the other. The frontiersman doctor continued to work. He blinked the salty sweat from his eyes and continued to mumble his passage from the Bible. Levi still breathed shallowly and laboriously.

"Give me a bit of that cane stock in the back," Virgil said. "Find a thin, hollow one so I can use it as a straw. Cut off about eighteen inches for me."

Angus rushed to the corner and rummaged in what was thirty bits of wood and cane. When he found a good piece, he pulled his knife and sliced off a piece about the length of his hand and forearm.

"Will this do?" Angus asked as he passed the short straw to Virgil.

Lovejoy nodded before sewing the last bit of lung and skin. After dipping the cane in hot water with a pair of forceps, he carefully poked it through the bullet hole. Virgil wrapped his lips around the straw and drew, sucking in his cheeks. He turned his head, spat out a mouthful of blood, and retched. Dark red claret splattered into a metal pot. The next time, he only drew half a mouthful. He emptied the lung as well as he could and wiped his mouth with the back of his hand. The strain now showed in his eyes.

"Come on, Virgil," Rusty said. "We're almost there."

Lovejoy took a deep breath and began to sew the last few stitches of Levi's right lung. When he was done, he helped guide Will and Rusty to set the rib bone back into place. Then he sewed the entry wound up tight. As it was smaller, the job looked neater, but still, Virgil worried. He wasn't trained to do such a complicated task with only country skills. He was concerned he had somehow made a mistake. When he was done, with the help of Dennis, Rusty, and Betty, they wrapped his chest in bandages. There wasn't much more they could do for now.

Finally, their black friend sat back in the nearest chair and exhaled, exhausted. Virgil dropped the hooked needle on the table. Finally, his hands began to tremble. Rusty and Will looked at the pliers in their bloody hands. They dropped them on the table like they were poison. It was one of the hardest things they had ever done, and they all knew it was far from over.

"Now y'all can get him off the table and cleaned up," Virgil said. He had bags under his eyes. "Drag one of the bunks over here by the fire and pile on buffalo skin blankets top and bottom. The last thing he needs now is to get a chill. We'll have to watch him closely for the next few days and wait to see if he comes around. All we can do now is pray. If you haven't talked to the big man upstairs for a while, I'd say now is a good time, boys. I have an extra Good Book if ya need one."

Miners or Thieves?

So many people managed to acquire a copy of the *Les Boise* newspaper, headlining the gold strike, that it caused thousands of men to be suddenly bitten by the fever. Those affected by the article dropped what they were doing and headed for Yellowstone Valley. As Perry predicted, many traveled via Fort Boise. That included individuals from all walks of life. Even a few women were on their own, as well as the wives of professional gold miners.

Greenhorn beginners made up a large portion of the wave of wannabe prospectors, people who had only read about and dreamed of being a miner and striking it rich. Now, they saw the opportunity to do just that. They could see gold dust and nuggets in their mind's eyes. Their heads were full of images that clouded all reason and somehow made them feel like they were special enough to strike it rich like others they had read about in dime novels.

It was a land grab for the best-looking spot to start to prospect. The first men there would win the prize of the best locations. Those after would take what was left, and the stragglers got the dregs where it was almost impossible to work. With every gold strike, it was the same. Everybody on their way imagined driving stakes into the ground and making their claim. All that on property they somehow believed, as Americans, they had a right to own. For some reason, ownership by others had never crossed their minds since it was in the wilderness. From what they heard, any land they could hold belonged to them.

Of course, there was no documentation or claims offices. A man who wanted to make a stake had to resist, and his firearms would be what enforced his declarations of ownership. All understood that much. They were also aware of what the dime novels called claim jumpers, who would be heading for the gold fields to fleece those who found the precious mineral. Many would disappear, and others would take over an already working find.

A campfire burned, reflecting in four men's eyes. An A-frame tent stood with the flaps open to the crackling flames. Smoke squirreled toward the sky, disappearing into the night. Coyotes howled at the moon in the distance. A silvery glow covered the land, casting long, hazy shadows. The smell of coffee barely covered the odor of sweat as it danced on puffs of air. A breeze whistled through the pine trees, making them sway at the top. Millions of tiny lights dotted the sky lightyears away, pulsating like living things.

"How far do you think we have until we arrive at Yellowstone Valley?" Enoch "Irish" Mills asked. "This has been a longer trip than I expected. Of course, I have long ago become accustomed to spending days in a saddle. Mine was specially made for me and how I mount my horse, so I'll suffer less than average. A good horse, saddle, and tack is the secret. That and a sharp set of spurs if trouble shows."

Enoch's grin stretched from ear to ear at the mere thought of some more action. He loved his role as an outlaw. Enoch couldn't think of anything he enjoyed more, at least for then. He knew he would soon tire and search for something more interesting. He could only survive for so long with people of little wit and intellect. He hated conversing with stupid people. When possible, he shot them as soon as they became boring. Then, it was worth his time because they provided him with entertainment.

He looked at the sun to check the time. "Two days more, I reckon," Garret Cage replied. "With the weather warming up, I don't see it taking more. But I'd bet my money on the mountains above the valley for the best place to start. Most of the rock formations we're lookin' for I'll find up there somewhere. I'm not very good at searching for good spots on flat land. It looks like we're the first ones here, though. The worst of winter's past, the roads are just travelable, and I don't see any tracks. That or anybody travelin' is off this main stretch. I'd rather take the risk out here in the open, making good time. I doubt many highwaymen would take the chance with four of us."

"As far as I'm concerned, let 'em come on ahead," Mike Melons said, his fat jowls sagging. "I wouldn't mind somethin' to break the boredom. It seems like we're never gonna get to the gold fields."

"If it were easy, everybody and their mother would be on their way right now," West chuckled. "You're lucky we ain't walkin' like some fools behind us." Of the four, Tanner looked more like a cattle hand than an outlaw. Then again, that was the point—not to appear to be what they were.

"They'll be riding their mules, stupid," Enoch said. "Anybody that's going to walk will never get to the gold strike in time to find a good claim. Any fool knows that."

"Remember who you're talkin' to the next time you call me stupid and fool," West Tanner snarled as he slipped his hand into his coat. His eyes narrowed as he wrapped his fingers around his gun's grip.

"Knock it off," Garret growled. "Sometimes y'all act like children. We aren't here to argue or to play around. This is serious business. You might not think so, but somebody believes they own all this land. The idea is to keep our eyes on the target, grab the gold, and get the hell out of there. Remember, this is all about quick and easy money, but be forewarned, if you stray, we'll end up with squat. We ain't rustling horses this time, boys. You're gonna have to get your hands dirty for a change, but you shouldn't have to worry about getting shot."

"I don't see anybody around here to shoot us or anybody else," Melons said. "Who's gonna want to own this land anyway? It's too far away from everything. There ain't a building one within a hundred miles."

"That doesn't mean it hasn't an owner," Enoch said, looking around. He suddenly felt as though somebody was watching them. "I've read that various Indian tribes claim ownership of all this land and protect it as their own. I've forgotten the names of the tribes, but there was more than one, two, or even three."

"How many Indians do you reckon are livin' in the valley and mountains above?" Tanner asked. "I can't see there being very many since we haven't seen a soul for a week. People leave tracks and signs of habitation. I ain't even seen any kilt and skinned animals."

"I doubt anybody really knows how many Indians inhabit this part of the West," Enoch pondered. "How could they know when only a handful of people have ever been recorded traveling here? I fancy the idea of us being the first White men to set foot on some piece of land. There have been White men here before us, but not many, so there must still be some undiscovered areas. Exploring a new valley or passage is one of my dreams."

"I beg to differ as far as inhabitants," Garret said. "I read that every summer they have a trappers meet somewhere close around here where lots of wild frontiersmen come and trade with the big fur companies and Indians. The article said they come in the hundreds. Maybe most of the White folks around attend the meet, but I bet that's only a small portion of the Indian population who show their faces. Most tribes don't kin to Easterners. When you get a bunch of White men together this far west, somebody is bound to take a shot at what they might believe to be a hostile. All this might not be as uncivilized as you think. I believe they called the trappers meet the Rendezvous."

"Hopefully, we will all be rich by then, or it could become a problem," Enoch said. "With that rag of a tabloid, everyone within five hundred miles will get wind of the gold strike shortly. I wonder who reported it. There must be a few miners up here already. Maybe we could jump their claim. That would be the easy way to go about it. We could steal what they have, dig some more gold, and be gone before most miners arrive. By summer, this place will be teeming with characters of questionable nature—such events as this Rendezvous breed pickpockets and thieves. If they hear there's gold near, they'll turn their attention to the miners and forget the trappers. Mark my words."

"I'll say it again, let 'em come," Mike growled. "I ain't shot anybody for six months or so. I'm gettin' itchy for some action, but there ain't anybody around here to even rob."

"Like I said, focus, men," Garret said louder. "We came here to get rich on gold and not fight and kill everybody behind us. If we can come and go unperceived, all the better. Sometimes, it's better to make as little noise as possible. Especially if you don't know the enemy's strength."

Enoch had only arrived in America a decade before but had taken to the West like bees to honey. It fascinated him to live the things he had only read of until he traveled west of the Missouri River. Of this group of reckless men, he was by far the smartest, most educated, and perhaps the evilest, as well. He came from an excellent Irish family. The well-to-do Dubliner couldn't remember ever wanting for anything, and Mills' desire to seek adventure had little to do with money. He was after excitement, and the more he got, the more extreme he needed. For him, it was almost like a drug.

Enoch loved living the life of an outlaw. It sounded much more romantic than being a lawman or local politician—all things he first considered. Still, he recognized he didn't have Garret's instincts or skills. That was what made him so dangerous. He could almost feel what would happen before there was even the slightest hint for the others, Mills included.

Enoch was an educated man and believed in a matter of months, if not weeks, he could learn all his fellow travelers had to teach him. Cage wasn't a genius by any means, so Mills believed it was only a matter of learning. It never crossed his mind that developing some of the skills involved took years. It wasn't all about brains.

These men were only there because they believed it was a way they could get easy money, just like when they stole or rustled but in vast quantities. They didn't see significant profits from stealing horses or robbing travelers, which was dangerous business. Too many outlaws were doing the same back in Kansas, so the competition meant lower prices, resulting in small profits. Everyone but Mills struggled for money from time to time.

Occasionally, Enoch would circle around and check to ensure no Indians or other miners were following them close by. He lazily wheeled his horse off the trail and rode back two miles, flanking the road behind the gang members. When he was close, he pulled his horse to a stop, closed his eyes, and listened. A curl appeared on the corners of his lips—he heard voices in the distance.

Enoch kicked his leg over the horn and slid out of the saddle. Sludge splattered his boots when he landed. After tying his horse to the nearest tree, he advanced toward the voices. Two feeble travelers led aging mules. The equipment on the mules' backs said they were serious miners. Mills finally was close enough that he could hear what they were saying.

"I can almost smell the gold nuggets," the short, fat

miner said, then spat a brown stream of juice into the dirty snow.

"I don't smell nothin' but pines and mud," the tall, skinny prospector said. He sniffed again and asked, "Is that perfume? I'm sure there ain't no whores out here."

Enoch casually stepped onto the trail behind them. He held a brace of fine English pistols in his fists. Neither man had heard the click of the hammers. They were completely unaware of the outlaw's presence.

"Ta-ta said the wee leprechaun." Enoch chuckled and then shot them both in the back before they could turn their heads.

The aging prospectors fell over, burying their faces in the mud. Their mules bolted with the sudden cracks of gunfire. Hammering hooves disappeared into the distance.

Smoke streamed from the barrels, and the smell of cordite filled the air. The ginger-haired outlaw calmly returned to his horse, shoving hot pistols into his belt. Climbing astride the American Paint, he returned to the trail his partners were riding. As he galloped along, he whistled the Irish tune, "The Jolly Ploughman." He had heard it was number one back home in Dublin. You would never think he had just murdered two men, let alone shot them in the backs. The curl on his lips turned into a smile, and finally, he began to laugh. He sounded a little like a madman. The look in his eyes momentarily changed.

Enoch rode up behind his associates in crime, bumping his horse down from a trot to a walk. He tried to hide his grin but failed. He felt alive and was biting at the bit for some more fun.

"What were those gunshots I heard?" Garret asked.

"You do know you just gave away our location. What were you shooting at, anyway?"

"I scared off a couple of prospectors that were dogging our trail. They looked like they intended to overtake us. Of course, we can't have that, can we?" Enoch smiled as wickedness flickered in his eyes. "If there are Indians in the vicinity, I am sure they must already know we're here at any rate. I doubt we're as clever as we think." The European smiled.

Garret Cage eyed the Irishman suspiciously. He held his tongue, though. What he did out of sight mattered little to the most experienced man of the group, but it did indicate further Enoch's character. They hadn't known him for long, and at first, he seemed like an excellent addition to the gang. They had heard he wasn't afraid of anything. Time would tell if that was true or not. He sure was a strange man, and the other two gang members felt the same. Maybe Enoch would grow on them. Then again, he could get killed along the way.

Enoch Mills was the kind of man you would never expect to be a killer. His four-day ginger stubble, curly red hair, and fair skin disguised the devil in him. He wore expensive clothing, including a white shirt when he could. He also rode a fancy saddle. His pistols were English and of the highest quality, with detailed engravings and shiny chrome plating. His rifle he bought in Missouri. They had all seen him use his guns, and they knew he was a dead shot with both pistols and long rifles.

Once you saw him shoot, it instantly changed your opinion of this meek-mannered look. Yet, not even the other outlaw gang members imagined the killer that hid inside the innocent-looking façade. They all imagined him as an evil man, at least as bad as them. If only they knew the depths of his cruelty. He was a lovely looking man with a heart of cold stone, void of feeling, sympathy, or pity for his fellow man.

They traveled all day but finally entered Yellowstone Valley at the end of a long ride. More snow had melted there, and the sun shone brightly as it neared the world's edge. The slightest hint of spring was in the air. As they looked up, they saw more mountains towering over them. Some stretched into cotton-like clouds.

"That's where we need to go," Garret said. "I have to admit, I agree with Enoch. If we can find the prospectors who found the original strike, we might be able to take over what they think is theirs. Unless they have an army up here, I doubt there'll be a challenge. So, you boys look for signs of gold diggers, and I'll keep an eye out for the right rock formations in case the fellas who struck it rich have already retired. Maybe there's a strike up there waitin' for us all on its lonesome."

Trespassers

The alarm was called as soon as the small hunting party raced into the Crow stronghold. A trumpet-like sound from a hollowed gourd resonated between the mountains, echoing off sharp cliffs and steep stone walls. You could hear it for miles. The tribe members poured out of their teepees and headed for the chief's lodge at the center of the camp. Every member knew it would be of the utmost importance.

It had been years since they called the central alarm. It indicated the warriors were to come armed and prepare their ponies for war. The hunters and elders would help protect the inside of the camp against attack. Even the women would stand and fight.

Nobody knew what it was, but it was apparently serious, and everybody knew time was of the essence. Mothers carried papooses on their backs, and others had a child hanging from their breast as they scurried for the main lodge. Such an alarm would affect them one and all, making them scramble as quickly as they could.

Chief Hachta stood at the edge of the stronghold with a long lance in his right hand and a pistol in his left. His expression was chiseled in stone, his mouth a hard gash. A red face surrounded fiery eyes as his anger boiled, soaring higher with every breath. Eagle feathers hung from his long black hair. Scalps were sewn into the sleeves of his buckskins. He waited patiently for his people to amass.

Once his tribe was assembled, he said, "There is a caravan of Easterners on the trail to Yellowstone Valley. They come from Fort Boise. Some early White scouts have already climbed our mountain. Tatanka and his hunting party saw them, and they had mules loaded down with tools. He believes they came here to stay. The Blackfeet in the valley have already sent up smoke signals. We must do the same and tell all our people to return to camp. There will be danger everywhere."

"How many White men are coming?" War Chief Wanata asked, blinking his eyes in disbelief.

What they had heard in the rumors of the Indian gossip for the last decade was happening before their very eyes. Still, it took some of the tribe's members time for it to sink in. It was hard to believe it was genuinely happening when, deep down inside, most of them disbelieved such stories. Now, they had been proven wrong, and they would probably have to defend their homes.

"I translated the Blackfoot smoke signals, and it said hundreds of men with mules and tools were coming, and they are traveling fast," Hachta replied. "Some more unreliable sources said maybe even a thousand. A few are alone, and others in groups of two, three, maybe even five or six. I don't have the full details yet. So far, they have not joined together to become one army. Time will tell if that happens or not. Then it will be a bigger challenge."

"What should we do now, Chief Hachta?" Wanata asked. Everybody held their breath as they waited for the answer.

"If I am not mistaken, the Blackfeet will let the first few trespassers slip through and make us, the Crow, test their strength," the chief replied. "Maybe even more than a few. They are clever and use any tool they can find to attack us, even while they are under attack. Then, they will strike them from behind. The gossip said the army of Easterners are all armed, so they do not come in peace."

"My men are ready, Chief," Wanata said with a dry mouth. "We have three war parties out scouting for our enemies. Smoke signals will bring them back. I don't want my braves in the forest unaware of what is happening."

"Make a ring of warriors to surround our camp. Station them far enough away to be able to surprise anyone who approaches but close enough to reach home if you encounter too great of numbers. I want to make sure no Easterners enter or even get near our homes. Anyone that nears is to be taken captive; then we can make them talk and find out exactly what is going on. We must get out in front of this, or we might get overrun. I am taking serious steps because we don't know what is coming. It is better to be safe and prepared than dead and sorry."

A flurry of activity consumed the inhabitants of the large Crow stronghold. Never before had the camp been threatened in such a way. Of course, their Blackfoot enemies had attacked them over the years, and the Crow, the Blackfeet, in retaliation. But now they had a mutual enemy, so everybody focused on the threat of trespassers on Indian land.

They would have to sort out their Blackfoot enemies later because an armed force of a thousand Easterners was too great a threat to their very existence. They couldn't spare a brave on their lifelong enemies. Hachta believed the chiefs in the valley would feel the same. They would pinpoint the bigger threat and focus their attention there.

Smoke signals filled the sky as mounted ponies charged out of camp—smoke squirreled from several campfires. The Crow women were busy making many meals for the men. If the braves had to leave camp on an arduous journey, they needed full stomachs and extra food ready to go. Hemp sacks were filled with dry tack and goat skins with fresh water.

Warriors cleaned their rifles, checking their powder and lead balls. Also, they checked the few pistols in the camp and others made extra arrows in case of war. Even the children helped set the feathers. Braves made up clay bowls of paint and covered their faces in green, white, and red, and the Indians, with scalps in their belts, made yellow handprints on their ponies. They all prepared through the day as the warriors scouted their perimeters.

Later that day, hammering hooves were heard in the distance racing toward the camp. Wanata entered the camp at a gallop, bringing his pony to a sliding stop before jumping in the air and off his mount. He gobbled air, red-faced, struggling to talk. The horses' lungs sounded like rusty saws. His sweat made his war paint run, making him look even more fierce. The war party's ponies shifted their feet as they nickered, neighed, and snorted nervously.

"We saw White men's footprints," Wanata said. "Five sets of boots in one and four in the other, but I am sure there are more. All the horses wore iron shoes. I heard gunshots in the distance, too. There were several shots, and they sounded like they came from Rusty Steel's part of the mountain. I didn't dare go to see what it was with only a few men. I think you are right, Chief. Hundreds of trespassers are coming to the valley, and the scouts have come first. We must prepare because the people following them won't take long to arrive. Then, we will have too many enemies at once on our hands. We must figure out how to stop them."

"Rusty can normally take care of himself, plus he's White," Hachta said. "I have no idea how the trespassers will behave if they find the mountain men up here living on Crow land. Maybe they will get the wrong impression and think they, too, can settle here and stay. They may plan to treat Rusty and his people like they have treated us in the past. What I do know is that we must kill all the trespassers. There are too many coming to scare away. Prepare for war, people. Wanata, send two braves on fast horses to get Dahteste. She has an obligation to the tribe and her warriors. This is no time for personal matters. Our people's vitality is at stake, and her loyalty always comes first, even if she is married to Levi Johnson. These are dangerous times."

That night, drums echoed through the evening as the coyotes howled at the moon. Painted men hammered their feet on the ground as they danced around flickering flames. Large fires burned across the camp as everybody continued to prepare. Dozens of streams of smoke vanished into the night. So many teepees stood in the stronghold they seemed endless. Two hundred ponies raced around the corral at the back of the canyon. A serious movement was just about to begin.

Hachta tilted back his head, closing his eyes, letting his face bathe in the moonlight. When he opened them, he stared at the heavens for a sign. He saw thirteen falling stars, each vaporizing as they hit the earth's atmosphere. Then and there, the chief knew something big was about to happen. That was the sign he was dreading. He knew it would be bad but didn't know how bad. He felt significant change was about to overcome them, and they wouldn't be able to resist.

Knock, Knock, Knockin'

Sweat ran off Virgil's brow, down his face, and dripped off his chin like a leaky faucet. His shirt was drenched with dark stains. Still, his hands trembled an hour after the operation was completed. An empty glass sat before him, and a jug of sour mash beside that. His breath smelled of liquor, and his body smelled of sweat. Everybody was gulping down spirits to settle their nerves. They were all run ragged with tension and lack of food and sleep.

Only Dahteste and Betty refrained. Levi's wife because her chief frowned on drinking spirits, and although she lived in the compound with the mountain men, she was always a Crow Indian warrior first. Like her chief, she ignored a small dash in her coffee but never had enough to affect her mind—except that first and last time when she and Betty drank a whole bottle.

That was when they started to fight. Neither could recollect why it started, but in the following days, they remembered as clearly as if it were yesterday, and both regretted what had happened—especially the horrendous hangover. They wanted nothing more to do with spirits. Still, in the end, they believed they had become even closer friends for it. Every cloud seemed to have a silver lining if you waited patiently and looked hard enough.

Dahteste believed it was a perfect example of how bad liquor was for her people. A brain dulled by alcohol was dangerous if a problem suddenly emerged, and sometimes, like in Betty's case, it made people change, and she created the issues. The substance blurred her mind and left everything foggy, not to mention the sickness that followed. It obviously made Will's wife aggressive beyond belief, so she swore off anything more than a dash in her coffee like her friend. They had both learned their lesson the hard way.

Levi lay on the cot, but he didn't stir. His face glistened, and his body was soaked and feverish. The young mountain man's breathing was harsh, and he struggled to draw air into his damaged lung, but he was alive. Most men would have already succumbed to such a gunshot wound. Then again, Beaver Johnson wasn't your garden-variety mountain man. He was more like Rusty Steel every day. Being born and raised in the Indiana forests gave him an edge when he arrived in the Rockies, and with his mentor's guidance, he became the second most famous White frontiersman in the mountains.

Dahteste sat cross-legged on the floor beside her unconscious husband. She chanted a Crow tribal song to call the Indian gods to heal his spirit. Her people believed only then could his body heal. But a dark cloud seemed to hang over Levi. He continued to linger between death and life. He was unconscious for two days, and his breathing shallower every hour. His wife kept him hydrated with a small cloth dripping water onto his chapped and cracked lips. She patiently cared for him twenty-four-seven. Only her tired eyes gave away how she really felt. Her face continued to be a mask, and her mouth a hard line.

Virgil said, "Sixty-six percent of a human's body is water. Twenty-two percent of bone is too, along with seventy-six percent of muscle, eighty-three percent of blood, and ninety-five percent of the brain is made up of water. With the lack of food, Levi's body will use his muscle mass to feed on, but without water, in his condition, he would die in three days, tops."

"Why, you sound more like a real doctor every day. I reckon it's from all those books you brought from the Rendezvous last year." Rusty smiled. "What would we do without cha? Levi wouldn't still be here, that's for dang sure."

Virgil blushed, rubbing his toe on the floor, making a clean spot in the accumulating dirt and dust. With them all spending all day in the main cabin, they endlessly tracked mud inside, much to Angus's dismay. McFarlin chased the compound dwellers around the room with a broom as he grumbled, but it was inevitable. At least it helped keep him busy when he wasn't cooking.

Strangely enough, McFarlin was the most visibly affected by Levi's devastating injury. He moved around like a zombie, bumping into walls and family. He was uncomfortable with the cabin being so full. Nine bodies made him edgy, but it was what it was. For now, all eyes were on Levi Johnson as his chest erratically rose and fell.

Virgil pulled his eyes from the floor and said, "A person can live three minutes without air, three days without water, and three weeks without food. I call it the rule of the big threes. If you keep that in mind when you travel, you'll know if you're walking into a situation suffering from one. Your focus diminishes by dehydration, too. It makes your brain cells shrink, resulting in short-term memory loss, making it difficult to count or focus on one thing. Water increases focus and reduces mental fatigue. That's why I told Dahteste to drip water on his lips all day long. It ain't much, but hopefully, it will be enough for him to survive. If he don't come around in the next day or two, we can do the same with chicken broth."

"Them's egg-laying chickens," Angus huffed. His hens were like his pets, and they even had names. He would be hard-pressed to pick one for the slaughter.

"If it means we can save Levi, I'll kill the whole bunch," Rusty growled as biting fear gripped the aging mountain man's soul, but it quickly turned into anger.

"I say we go back and check out the site of the gunfight," Marshal Walker said. "We should have already done it. We might find a clue. We can't all sit here and watch Levi all day. I know y'all are upset and don't wanna leave his side, but it ain't gonna do him no good, and it won't help keep the trespassers off y'all's mountain either. That's somethin' we're gonna have to do on our own."

"I agree." Rusty blew out. "Let's get back out there before somebody else shows up and messes up the tracks. You're right; we've waited far too long. I guess my mind was on the living and not the soon-to-be dead."

The lowering sun sprayed orange rays of light,

which spilled through the glass and into the main cabin. The windowpanes outlined bright rectangles on the wooden planks. The breeze blew steadily, but the gusts bent the trees at their waists.

Rusty sat with a gash for a mouth as he cocked his head and listened to the wind. He closed his eyes and dreamed of better times. About the day when Levi and Will came with them to the mountains and eventually their compound. Beaver learned about the ways of the wilderness with amazing speed. He was like a dry sponge, absorbing every morsel of information.

Johnson's breath was trapped somewhere in his body, and he couldn't breathe right from the damage. He was drenched with sweat, and his hair was matted to his head. His skin was pale, bordering on translucent. They watched as his pulse throbbed at his temple from an erratically beating heart.

Rusty began to get his weapons together to clean them and check his lead and powder. He was ready to go right then. The others looked at the marshal with raised eyebrows.

Captain Will Forrester pinned up his sleeve and then scratched his three-day growth. He stared at the marshal, waiting for him to finish.

"It's gonna be dark in a couple of hours," Walker said. "We don't wanna fly off the handle 'cause we know there's more of the same out there. You've gotta control your temper, friend."

Rusty's eyes grew wild and angry. "I don't need to control my temper. I need people to quit pissing me off," he growled.

"We can set out an hour before first light since we know the area. That way, by the time the sun rises, we'll be at the ridge where we can peek to ensure nobody else has shown up. I hope the Crow warriors don't take us for trespassers."

"You'll be ridin' with me so the Crow won't give ya no trouble," Rusty said. "Since I'm blood brothers with Chief Hachta, they wouldn't dare shoot one of us. Then again, if we run into one of the other tribes, it'll be a different situation. The smoke signals have called all the five tribes to join as one against the common enemy. That may make things more complicated since others have permission to trespass. Outside the compound fence, we might find just about anything or anybody."

Late into the night, Rusty eyed Levi over the dying flames. Every few minutes, he squinted to see if he was still breathing, finding himself holding his breath in anticipation. When he saw Levi was still alive, he sighed and fell back to sleep for another twenty minutes before he was startled from a nightmare and stirred again. The damper on the bottom of the chimney flue howled as the wind whistled off the stone chimney outside. Dog slept beside Levi like he was standing guard. In his dreams, he kicked his feet as though he was running. Maybe he was having a nightmare, too.

The following day, Rusty, Angus, and Dennis warmed up creakily, as their aging bones were stiff the first thing in the morning. All three men rubbed their hands together as close as they dared to the flames in the fireplace. Heat radiated across the single-room cabin. Steam fogged the windows, making mysterious objects seem to waver outside.

"I wonder if we're gonna find somebody else out there where Levi got shot," the marshal said. "If there were friends among the party, the bodies should be buried if they're Christians."

"You can pert near count on it, Marshal," Dennis said. "Where there's three cockroaches, there's bound to be more."

"We can't all go, now can we?" Walker said. "Some of us are gonna have to guard the cabins. I wouldn't put it past part of these men headin' our way thinkin' we've got something of value. As I said, a good number of the folks that run for the gold fields are thieves who plan to steal what some hardworking miner just dug up. The problem here is there ain't no gold, and when they don't get what they came all the way here to get, they're gonna start lookin' for something else to make the trip worthwhile. That could mean our belongings."

As Rusty's anger increased, his strength seemed to rise from somewhere deep inside, like steam from the earth's core. "Everybody has to pay like those in the past paid before us," Steel whispered. "Nobody shoots my friend and lives to tell the tale."

When Levi came out West, he was alive with possibilities. It was evident from the start that he was built to be a mountain man. He was already a first-class trapper and dead shot before he left his home back East. In a short time, he was already recognized as the second-best marksman in the Rockies, if not number one. It was pretty much a toss-up between the young mountain man and his mentor. He had learned so much, so fast, he was now surpassing his teacher in frontiersmen's knowledge.

They assembled on the porch as they prepared to leave. Orange light cast circles on the floor as they checked their guns and prepared for whatever was to come. Will and Joseph walked toward the cabin with the horses' reins in their fists. The animals groaned and snorted at the early hour.

Mountain Dennis, Angus, Virgil, and Betty had to stay behind. If they were attacked, four rifle positions and the protection of the main cabin would suffice unless it was an army.

"Don't worry, family," Angus said. "There ain't nobody gonna get into my cabin. It's been tried over and over across the last fifteen years. I doubt a bunch of green Easterners will do what the Blackfeet and other outlaws couldn't."

Rusty shrugged, looked back, and said, "Everybody connected to this deserves to die. Just 'cause they weren't there when Levi was shot don't mean they don't share the responsibility." He locked eyes with Angus as his friend nodded. Steel knew what he was thinking, and it only fueled his resolve.

Dahteste jumped onto her pony's back as it shifted its hooyes in anticipation. He was ready and raring to go along with his rider. She carried every weapon she owned and had painted her face fot war, like when she fought Betty Forrester.

"Are you sure you don't wanna stay here with your husband?" Marshal Walker asked. "We can take care of this for ya, young lady."

"I'm not a lady," Dahteste spat. "I am a Crow war chief, and if you don't want me to go with you, I will go alone. To me, it is the same. Your choice, Marshal."

"You don't mince around with words, do ya," the marshal replied. "To be honest, I reckon it would be best if we went with a member of the Crow tribe. Maybe Rusty ain't as famous as he thinks."

"There you go again, hackin' on me like always," Rusty said, giving the marshal a jarring look.

Those remaining stood on the porch as they watched the others ride to the end of the compound and out the gate, only to vanish into the dense trees. They all wondered if they would see them again. Somehow, the delicate balance of nature and the residents seemed upset. The string that tied them together appeared to have frayed and was about to break.

Snow sloshed underfoot. It was all they heard as they silently walked through the dark of night. The moon had set long ago, and the only light remaining was from the twinkling stars. Rusty knew this part of the mountain like the back of his hand, though, so they all followed in his footsteps so they wouldn't make a sound. Captain Forrester was two steps behind his mentor.

Will, too, had learned to become a mountain man from Rusty Steel, but unlike Levi, it was an arduous task, and he was still behind his best friend in many of his functions. He knew he could never trap as well as Johnson because Levi seemed to be able to think like a beaver, always knowing where they would surface at the edges of the water. Where he lacked in knowledge, he made up for in courage, though. He carried a pistol in his white-knuckled fist as his thumb caressed the hammer.

Enoch Mills

Ten years earlier

On the ship over to the land of riches beyond most men's dreams sat Enoch in a luxury suite. Of course, he already had the money most people aboard the vessel sought, but he was after something else. It was a much more elusive item than mere wealth. Mills was after extreme adventures. He had become bored with everyday life and decided to go out and find the action because it obviously wasn't coming to him. The last thing he desired was to live the life his father did.

When he was still at home and studying at a private elementary school, his father told him he had two choices to make. One was for Enoch to be accepted to study at Trinity College, founded in 1592. To be admitted as a student, he had to come with a recommendation from a lord, earl, or duchess, if not a princess or even a king. Yet his father couldn't work out the issue with the royalty and thought he should consider his second suggestion, too. He believed Enoch could also make a good philanthropist like himself.

Both were noble trajectories for an affluent young man to take. His father had done both. After graduating from Trinity College, he retired as a British Army colonel, only to become a philanthropist, mostly because he could afford not to work and spend his riches on admirable issues across Ireland. He said a man had to leave a legacy—at least a Mills did. There was much to do, and he welcomed his son on board his journey.

The problem was Enoch Mills was itching to go west and see what few men had. He had read all about the pioneers forging new trails toward the Pacific coast, and he desired to join the ranks of the men searching for better ways to cross America. He longed to go to the rugged towns and forts on the Indian frontier. Life in Dublin wasn't in his dreams, so he gave Lord Ellsworth Mills the bad news.

He wasn't meant to follow in his family's footsteps as his father had. He was destined to explore the world for new discoveries. He wanted to be free and mingle with the population, from which, to date, he had been sheltered. He had no idea of how everyday men and women lived. He knew he was from an entitled family and was very different from the vast majority of the population. Now, he desired to mingle with all colors and races—even the dangerous American Indians. Nowhere else in the world offered such journeys through the unknown wildernesses.

Enoch was on an ocean liner with another two thousand people in a matter of days. His room was on the upper deck. The one below was for the second-class passengers, and in the lower bowels of the beast traveled the third-class untouchables with the cattle, mules, and horses. Many were thin and apparently near starvation. Somehow, they had managed to acquire the money for the passage and blindly took a chance, hoping for a better place. Life for the lower classes in Ireland was challenging, to say the least.

These people were escaping the beginning of the potato famine. Many were from Connaught and Munster, where the situation was more pronounced. But they all knew the worst was to come and fled Ireland by any means possible. Some sold everything they had, and others even sold their bodies. Some stole to acquire their passage, and a few were even murdered to get away from what they already felt was a prison. They took a chance attempting to escape the famine or, if they failed, heading off to prison in Dublin's Kilmainham Gaol.

An escaped chicken flapped its way across the deck, squawking as its owner chased behind it, grabbing for its wings. People slept on piles of straw on every surface. A choir of snores created a din. There was a pungent stench coming from the poorly ventilated area. Vapor trailed from the massive smokestacks on the upper deck of the vessel. The lines of steam intertwined as they followed the white ship, quickly disappearing in the sky.

In Ireland, everybody looked the same, and Enoch came from a sheltered background. He had little contact with immigrants other than a few Englishmen or Scots. Even the latter was considered undesirable to some of the wealthier Irish. There had always been a rivalry between Ireland and Scotland. Now, all that didn't matter to the young man because he was about to be swallowed up by the vastness of a new frontier and a new land. He believed it to be the perfect choice as it was a distant, foreign place, but they also spoke English —or at least a facsimile of Enoch's native language.

He had considered Australia or even India, but too many White men had already conquered these frontiers, so they weren't new and alluring. Mills desired the virgin and unknown land America offered. He planned to travel the country extensively, crossing from the Atlantic Ocean to the Pacific Ocean and everywhere in between.

The first thing he planned to do was outfit himself properly. He had read book after book on the best firearms and all the kit he would need for his journey west. He even planned the horse he wished to buy. If nothing else, Enoch was thorough. He didn't miss the smallest detail, from a compass to saddle and bridle. He brought two of his guns with him. He had a brace of the best English pistols on the market and planned to purchase a Hawken rifle with a thirty-four-inch octagon barrel bored to 50 caliber. It was made in St. Louis, Missouri, right there in the United States. Mills had it all planned out.

He imagined it all as the ship yawed in the North Atlantic Ocean with the usual rough weather. But his cabin was heated directly from the massive steam engines somewhere deep inside the ship's guts, under the many decks. He stared out the porthole at the freezing North Atlantic's huge swells. Sea salt accumulated on the outside of the glass. Incredibly, seagulls flew just over the surface, snatching pieces of fish as tuna ravaged a school indifferent to the weather.

It seemed like a dream as Enoch soon found himself on a westbound train. His horse was in the cattle car, and his saddle lay in the rack over his head. The country outside gradually changed from a lush green to more arid land as it flashed by the window of his private compartment. But his environment was just about to change completely. He was nearing his objective. He took a moment to wonder how this new influence would change him or if he would remain the same. He couldn't imagine everything that was about to happen as he traveled farther west.

When the locomotive's brakes began to screech, sparks flew from the steel tracks as the train jerked and jolted and slowly came to a halting stop. Gathering his things, Enoch walked to the steps and dropped onto the wooden landing before a small shack. The train's shadow stood long, leaving him in the shade, but the temperatures still seemed unbearable. Over an open window, the sign said: Railroad Station Tickets Sold Here. Inside, a white-haired man sat with bottle-bottom spectacles perched on the end of his vein-covered nose.

Enoch stood before the counter, staring at the man, but he didn't look up. The Irishman hammered the bell, sitting on the tabletop with his open palm. Clearing his throat, he asked, "Is anybody here?" He stared directly at the railroad man, but he still took his time to look up. Finally, the clerk locked eyes openly, showing his boredom.

"Can I help ya, mister?" the ticket man asked with a Western twang. "You must have just arrived. Am I right or not?"

"Why, yes, I have just arrived," Enoch replied. "And what does that matter to you?"

"Oh, it don't matter to me a'tall," the railroad man replied, grinning. The lack of teeth made his lips hang loose and flap when he talked. "You seem to be the one in a hurry to get nowhere. Things don't move so fast this far west, fella. The sooner you get used to that, the sooner you'll stop bein' disappointed."

"Disappointed?" Enoch asked. "Why would I be disappointed?"

"Because I just closed." The man pulled down a shade and walked out the back door, leaving Mills standing with a puzzled look.

The Irishman quickly learned that most people west of the Missouri River didn't care for Easterners and their ostentatious ways. Now, no one looked like him, and although it was what he wanted, it made him feel uncomfortable. He thought he stood out like a baby duck in a flock of vultures.

Over the years, Enoch changed in many ways, but unfortunately, none for the better. The first day he was forced to kill a man or be killed, he discovered something deep and dark—he liked taking lives. Or maybe it wasn't exactly that he liked it, but it was more like he didn't mind. He felt no remorse at all.

Of course, like all his family, he was a trained marksman with both rifle and pistol and a champion fencer. This had proved to be imperative during his first months in the West. When he hit Kansas, he rented a hotel room for a month while he decided what he was to do next.

Years later, Mills somehow became involved with a small-time Kansas outlaw gang without an apparent leader. They found themselves hanging out in the same saloon. He jumped at the chance, hoping he would be the one to take charge. He hadn't been so bold as to dream that he would have his own outlaw gang one day. Now, he was with the experienced robbers and rustlers —West Tanner, Mike Melons, and Garret Cage.

At first, Mills mostly rode along on cattle raids over the border or highway holdups. They had him watch their rear and hold their horses when it was a robbery. During rounds of rustling, he was just another man with a gun who didn't hesitate to fire and hit what he aimed at—an essential asset for an outlaw. Despite the gang inviting him to join, he didn't feel they liked him.

He believed they needed another gun to warn off contenders, sheriffs, and marshals. He was also amazed at how little law there was in Kansas. A handful of United States Marshals were supposed to control the entire population and were failing miserably. Back in Ireland, a petty thief could expect to be locked in a pillory at the least or even tarred and feathered, during which many died. This punishment was even extended to the silk scarf thieves because all the wealthy carried them, and they were often expensive.

Enoch was the only literate member of the gang, so of course, when he read about the gold strike in the Rocky Mountains, at first, he debated telling his partners or not. Still, he couldn't see himself setting out on his own yet. He still felt he had a lot to learn to survive solo. He kicked it around for a day before he realized while they were in Fort Boise, the other gang members were bound to hear the rumors and decided he had to tell them then and there.

The outlaw gang sat at a saloon table. Enoch cleared

his throat and read, "Listen to these headlines, gentlemen: Gold Strike in Yellowstone Valley. Here, it says you can pick up gold nuggets right off the ground. How far away is that from here?"

"Gold?" Mike asked with greedy eyes. The effect was instant. "Are you sayin' there's gold somewhere around here close by?"

"It's four hundred miles or so, I reckon," Garret replied. "We've been travelin' three or four days for every hundred miles, so it'd be a couple of weeks. Then again, it would depend on the terrain, but more or less, that's what it would take."

"If it's in the newspaper, there'll already be miners there holdin' gold," West said. "It's easier to steal what's already mined than dig it up. It saves us the work."

"My paw taught me all about rock formations, especially around areas with gold," Garret said. "If there's one there, I betcha I can find a vein. If we can pick gold nuggets up off the ground, we don't have to kill anybody to get rich."

"I don't care how we get the gold as long as we get lots." Mike grinned. "I never imagined we'd find anything in this God-forsaken land. Maybe it's a good thing the law ran us out of Kansas."

"And all over a few scruffy horses," West Tanner griped. "I can't believe they put a bounty on us for a few nags."

"Ten dollars each isn't much of a bounty, now is it?" Enoch chuckled. "Any respectable outlaw would have a hundred dollars on his head if not five hundred or even a thousand. I don't think we have to worry about bounty hunters or a posse. We aren't worth enough money to get off a bar room stool."

Two days later, they were heading for Yellowstone Valley and then up to the mountains above to search for signs of geological formations that indicated a vein of gold was nearby.

As soon as they crossed a portion of Yellowstone Valley, they saw Indians. They rode fast ponies and brazenly defied them by standing on nearby hillsides, apparently void of fear. The travelers didn't know they were looking at Blackfeet Indians. When they saw them, they all four thought they would be dead in minutes. The stories Enoch had read to the other men from dime novels left them with an inherent fear of red men.

"Come on, we can make it to the top of the next mountain if we keep up our pace," Garret heaved.

They stopped and gobbled much-needed air. The altitude made it hard for the unaccustomed men to climb, and they fatigued quickly and were out of breath. All four got stitches in their sides.

West Tanner kept looking behind them, wondering if the Indians from the valley floor were following them. He fingered one of the pistols in his belt.

"I believe it'll be better if we rob somebody that's already struck it rich," Tanner said as his eyes darted around. "I doubt we survive if we stay around here too long. Somethin' tells me there's a lot more Indians around than we thought."

"I believe being first was the best thing to do," Mike said. "Now, I'm not so sure we shouldn't have come with a larger group, though. I figure out here in the wilderness, the only safe way to travel is in numbers."

"We've always been fine with just the four of us," Garret said. "Soon you'll be scratchin' at the dirt, peckin' at worms like a hen. I thought you were outlaws, not a bunch of grandmas."

"Let's stop for a spell, make a fire, and put on the kettle," Mike winged. "I doubt I can stay awake for the rest of the day without a rest."

Half an hour later, coffee floated in the air. The fire crackled and puffed steam from the green wood as black smoke snaked skyward. All four men were oblivious that they were giving away their location to every hostile in the area.

"That coffee went through me like poop through a goose," Enoch said. "I'm going over to those bushes. I don't see any Indians anymore. I don't think they left the valley. They only wanted to scare us off their land."

"Be careful," Garret said as his eyes shifted around. "Shake a bush until you're done, so I know you're all right."

If Enoch was concerned, he hid it better than anybody they had ever seen. He strolled fifty paces to the edge of dense vegetation, pushed some bushes aside, and disappeared.

"Dag-nabbit," Garret grumbled under his breath. "That fool's gonna get kilt."

Despite Cage's concerns, the bush continued to rustle as he kept a sharp eye out for anything that moved. Enoch seemed to take forever. Garret blinked, and when he looked up, he realized what they had done. A dark trail of smoke rose into the sky, lazily drifting with the breeze and into a raft of low-hanging clouds.

"Put that fire out right now," Cage spat, but it was too late.

Garret heard them before he saw them. It was only

the crack of a single stick, but still, he was so concerned about the Indians he suspected they were trailing them right then. He jumped straight into action.

"Quick, get behind that thick tree. Somebody's followin' us," Garret whispered. "I've seen 'em twice, but only in a flash of buckskin. I still don't know for sure if they're Indians or not, but they ain't dressed like us."

"Get your rifles ready, gentlemen," Melons said as curls crept onto his lips and delight danced in his eyes. His rifle's hammer clicked.

"White men," Tanner whispered as the mountain men came into view. "Maybe that's the miners the newspaper was talking about. Let's kill 'em and steal their gold. Maybe we can head right back down the mountain without gettin' scalped."

The bang rang out nearly in Garret's ear. Melons stood with his rifle to his shoulder as smoke wafted from the heavy barrel.

"You fool," Garret said, wiggling his finger in his ear. Tanner's shot followed, and they saw the big mountain man slap his head. "Nearly but not close enough."

Enoch heard the first two shots when he pulled up his britches and fastened the buttons. They came from the outlaw camp, so it was outgoing fire. He wondered what was up. Then, there was a long silence. He sighed out a breath of relief. They were probably shooting at some wild game.

Then, more shots came, accompanied by a scream as hackles rose on his neck, but contrary of what one would expect, a smile curled on the edges of his lips, and a fire began to glow in his eyes. Enoch's adrenaline began to boost, and his palms began to sweat. It was almost sexual how it felt. But he knew he had to sneak off, or he could walk into a trap. He didn't know what or who he was up against, so he slowly pushed himself deeper into the bushes as he watched one mountain man kneel before the other.

Mills smiled. It was a good shot. He wondered if they were the miners from the *Les Boise* newspaper.

The Caravan

Initially, the caravan of miners stretched out for dozens of miles. Many of them had run into each other while purchasing stock in the trading post at Fort Boise. Others camped outside the fort. There were too many to pitch all their tents inside. Still, some snuck off into the night, and others in apparently different directions, one and all intending to trick the people behind them. Miners hated to be followed and were all of a suspicious nature. Anyone who had mined or panned for gold already knew how crazy things could and probably would get.

Nobody could see the single travelers or small groups before or behind them, but they still knew they were there. As they moved forward over the four hundred miles to West Yellowstone Valley, they inadvertently bumped into each other along the way. Every time someone was delayed or had an emergency stop, they found men like them on the same path. Eventually, they began joining each other's groups as they felt more vulnerable in unknown territory and small numbers.

Since all the prospectors and tag-a-longs were unknowledgeable of the land they crossed, they naturally found comfort in continuing with companions. The caravan of people quickly began to grow. During the nearly two weeks it took to travel from Fort Boise, they all gathered into four groups. When they started to near Yellowstone Valley, some thought about sneaking off to run ahead of the others. The first man to make a claim in the right spot would become rich beyond their wildest dreams.

They knew blood would flow for the rights to the best land claim if they all arrived simultaneously. Still, they were torn between other evils and were hesitant despite the apparent dangers. Everybody had heard the stories about Indians and what they did to White men and women when captured.

The hostile Indians' ways of torture were countless, from dipping naked bodies into freezing rivers time and again to skinning them one thin strip at a time. They had read and heard rumors that women were made slaves and forced to submit to the warriors who captured them. Many believed in such a case, death was always preferable over a life with the heathens. The hostiles were famous for their skills at keeping their victims alive for extended periods of time, making the captives suffer unimaginable pain to the very last second of their lives.

They had also heard that it was best to shoot oneself before allowing capture. The countless ways the Indians found to take a man's life left them in awe, and every variation seemed more horrendous than the other. Of course, whites were also guilty of torturous crimes.

When they tarred and feathered an outcast or thief, the subject often died from the experience. The bubbling tar burned off their skin. With such burns, many never recovered. If a hangman did a messy job, the victim also suffered as they dangled at the end of a rope until they strangled.

Strangely enough, these same men didn't recognize that such treatment was barbaric. For them, stringing men up and covering them in feathers seemed normal and was never called torture. It was almost a carnival-type event in both cases, and this deliberately inflicted pain came in more forms as well.

Surprisingly, Enoch found the American Indians' imagination incredibly interesting and mentally noted every variation. The Irishman went as far as admiring them for their dedication to such an unusual task. He even fancied taking a crack at it himself were the opportunity to arise. It seemed that the longer he lived in the lawless West, the broader the path his evil streak became.

Many of the gold seekers wondered if it was true that they could pick up gold nuggets directly off the ground. Most of them doubted if it would be free of hard labor, but a gold strike would make them rich beyond their wildest dreams just the same. A few of them were desperate, and this was their last shot before they gave up on life. All of them had nuggets dancing in their minds and suffered from a different kind of Rocky Mountain Fever—gold fever.

There had been no violence between the prospectors for now, but they all expected the worst as they came nearer the supposed strike. The men were visibly becoming increasingly edgy with each mile they left behind. Soon, tempers would rise, and the first signs of violence would spark a chain reaction. It was something they all knew was inevitable, and now that they were arriving, nothing could stop it.

A thunderclap and a frigid wind set the trees and bushes gnashing like forlorn beasts. The prospectors leaned into the cold wind as they trudged forward. The old miner leading the first group turned his head, pinched his nose with thumb and finger, and blew twin strings of snot, wiping his mustache on his flannel sleeve. Cloud cover stretched from horizon to horizon. Thunder moved quickly overhead, booming, making them hunker down. It made the ground quiver as lightning slashed across an electric sky. They could feel the static electricity in the air surrounding them.

"This country is so big it makes me feel like an insect," the second miner said. "I ain't used to seein' so many miles. It almost makes me uncomfortable."

Rain began to fall, slanting through the trees, denting hats, and sagging brims. Puddles quickly formed, reflecting the black cumulonimbus on the surfaces. Water poured off the crowns like tiny waterfalls. The snow suddenly turned brown and began to melt. The horses' hooves sunk into the mud-filled trail. They finally had to stop because the visibility was so poor; they worried they would stumble into the Indians they had all seen recently. The hostiles had been taunting them for two days, but they made no aggressive actions so far.

Finally, the rain stopped, and they pulled out dry buffalo chips to make fires. The dark cloud cover quickly disappeared on the western horizon, bringing stormy weather to other parts of the Rockies. Rays of the sun fell through the leaves like the recent rain. Having as many as three seasons on a single day was typical. Heavy wool coats were removed and hung to dry on low-hanging broken limbs. In minutes, the nearly smokeless campfire came to life, and the aroma of coffee mixed with that of the pines.

The first group of prospectors to arrive in Yellowstone Valley were left speechless at the breathtaking beauty. They immediately began to eye the best spots visible. But before they could even consider making camp, the Blackfoot Indians showed themselves again; this time, they weren't shy about it. Powder flashes appeared in the distance as bullets plowed into the dirt before them. Fragments of stones created shrapnel-like barrages against their legs.

Before they knew it, they had Blackfeet Indians on their front and both flanks. They had nowhere to run but up and into the unknown mountains above. It appeared as though the warriors approaching them intended to push them out of the valley and up toward the snowcapped peaks. Of course, the miners complied. They had never imagined so many Indians living there in the wilderness. Over fifty braves nearly circled them, and they all wore fierce masks of war paint. The prospectors had never seen such frightening men in their lives.

"Come on, boys," the self-appointed leader, Snaggletooth Wilson, said. "The hostiles look like they mean business."

The trespassers didn't need to be told twice. Some

had already bolted up the first trail they saw that climbed upward. They didn't give it a second thought but instead ran for their lives, hoping the forest would provide them with cover and they could hopefully escape with their lives. They had been caught so off guard they didn't return even a single shot. Then again, if they killed one of fifty, they could guarantee their demise then and there.

Seventy percent of the group of gold seekers were totally green, and this was the first time they had ever left their counties, and they were all east of Kansas. Suddenly, they found themselves on the frontier of the Indian wars and had no idea how to proceed. Strangely, as soon as the danger passed, their minds turned once again to the gold, as though they didn't want to think about the threat but focused on the yellow mineral and the reward they somehow felt they were due.

As soon as they began to climb, Snaggle whispered to his best friend, "Maybe we ought to cut these greenhorns loose and let them fend for themselves. All they're gonna do is slow us down."

"Let's wait for a spell more to make sure those Injuns ain't gonna follow us up the mountains," Boone Cannon said. "I doubt these fools can hit a buffalo if it's ten feet away, but the numbers seem to make the Injuns back off."

"Those soulless heathens didn't back off," Snaggle retorted. "They could have killed us all in minutes in a crossfire. I believe that, for some reason, they wanted us to climb the mountain and not only because we were on their land."

"Then, what other motive could they have?" Boone asked.

"That's what we're about to find out here in the next few days," Snaggle replied.

For the first hour, the men nearly ran up the mountain despite the steepness in various stretches of trail. Snaggle and company finally stopped them for a moment to catch their breaths.

"We can have a ten-minute break," Snaggletooth huffed as he tried to gobble more air.

The two experienced miners' dirty buckskins contrasted with the brand-new clothing the greenhorns wore. Their coats were cotton and wool, while the true prospectors wore fur coats and slept beneath buffalo hide blankets.

"Whew," one of the greenhorns said. "I reckon those Indians feared us more than we feared them. I figure that they see us as dangerous fellas with modern weapons." He laughed nervously. "Get ready for the progress machine, heathens. It's gonna roll right over 'em just like a steam roller. They'll be as flat as a tortilla when civilization is done with 'em."

"Lay off your pontificatin'," Boone spat. "You have no idea what you're talkin' about, fool."

"I ain't seen anybody try to get away and run so fast since somebody shoved a banana in my pants and let a monkey loose." Snaggle chuckled.

"That's about as sincere as a two-dollar funeral," Boone added, then spat a stream of brown juice into the muddy snow.

The fiery disk was the color of steel as it hung in the sky. When Snaggle looked, it said two o'clock.

"Let's stop for somethin' to eat," another greenhorn whined. "I don't have the strength to take another step. I feel faint and all."

"Today, there'll be no stopping until the sun sets," Boone said. "We need to put as much distance between us and the hostile Indians as we can today, so we won't stop until it's too dark to see. But be forewarned—anybody that don't keep up gets left behind."

Defending Their Homes

"Pull that door to before we all blow away and Levi gets a chill," Virgil growled. "All I wanted to do was change the air some, not turn the place into an icebox."

The wind moaned like an unseen beast. Despite the cold, it was getting slightly warmer, and they tried to remove the stuffy smell. Lovejoy claimed the dropping temperatures would help remove bacteria from the cabin, further reducing the threat to Levi's life.

Betty pushed a wisp of hair out of her eyes as she faced Pine Needle, Angus's wife. She forced her lips into a tight smile. Now, they sat side-by-side, waiting. They waited for Levi to come around and recover from a bad gunshot wound and the others to return from a dangerous task. The smell of death lingered in the air. Most of the men stood a chance of losing their lives. The women tried to hide their deepest fears. Betty's husband could be anywhere out there in the forest. She silently prayed for his safe return.

Suddenly, everybody in the compound heard hammering hooves in the distance. They were instantly on their feet and rushing to the gun racks. Hammers clicked like clucking hens. The intruders were upwind, and the smell of sweat and fear filled the air.

When Angus and Dennis rode in holus-bolus, everybody ran for the porch to see what was up, and they were all brandishing firearms. Pistols filled the men's hands as the women peered down rifle barrels pointed at the end of the yard.

McFarlin waved a rifle over his head as he screamed, gigging his horse on, "We've got outlaws on our tails!" His eyes locked with Pine Needle's. She saw the seriousness in his face. She put the rifle's butt to her shoulder and squinted down the gunsight. Despite the cool air, her face suddenly glistened as she blinked sweat from her eyes.

Dennis squeezed his hand around the grip of his pistol as his heart rate flew off the charts. At first, they didn't hear the assailants as they took cover and aimed for the buck-and-rail fence. Angus and Dennis continued to race across the yard and headed for the back of the main building, where they could take cover and tie the horses out of harm's way.

Sliding to a stop, they quickly secured their mounts, removing their rifles as they swung down. Just as their boots hammered on the porch, a dozen men jumped the fence on horseback. Ten animals made it over; two stumbled, tumbling, and the riders got thrown to the ground with a thud. One was unconscious, and the other was dazed and confused as he sat blinking on the ground. He looked around like he couldn't remember where he was.

The dozen men attacking the camp were disorganized, and once inside the compound, they didn't seem to know what to do. Puzzlement showed on their faces as they began to fire at anything that moved. They wheeled their horses in circles, trying not to expose their backs when they weren't sure exactly where their targets were.

"Get down, quick!" Angus yelled, and they all dove for cover.

Chunks of lead slammed into the front of the cabin and the porch roof posts. A gallon jug of moonshine exploded on the large table, sending ceramic shards through the air like tiny bullets. Neat holes peppered the glass panes as they cracked like spider webs. Blue gun smoke made their figures hazy. It was even more challenging to locate the mountain men as they hid patiently on stand-by until they were signaled.

"Wait for it!" Angus yelled over the din of bullets. "Any second now. Hold your fire and keep your heads down until I say, then give 'em all ya got."

The gunfire suddenly dwindled and then abruptly stopped. The two thrown riders continued to sit in the slush as their heads spun. They couldn't seem to get onto their feet. Their horses were spooked; they ran off quickly, jumping the fence again without a rider. One of the thrown aggressors had a broken arm and was trying to make a sling with a long bandana. Still, he seemed dazed and muttered to himself.

The rest of the men found themselves with empty guns, all at the same time. Nor had they killed anybody. The thieves came for gold, which one of the other prospectors claimed was there. It was said the witness was a ginger Irishman.

"NOW!" Angus yelled, popping to his feet, and carefully taking a bead.

McFarlin had planned it perfectly. He instantly recognized the amateurs and greenhorns. There wasn't a single veteran frontiersman in the lot. He knew just by their clothing and the way they recklessly spent their bullets. Now, they were rushing like mad to reload their pistols and rifles.

Like fools, they had emptied their weapons, and now there was no one to give *them* cover. Unlike their attackers, the mountain men and women selected each target, firing well-placed bullets. They took the intruders down like ball-toss dolls at the county fair.

The sudden silence seemed almost deafening. The contrast was overwhelming. Angus looked around, ensuring everybody was uninjured as he clucked like an old hen.

"Cover us while we make sure none of these rascals are playin' possum," Angus said as he jutted his chin at Dennis.

They quickly crept the long way around the buildings down the edge of the fence, coming to the downed enemy from the other side. They maintained an angle, so they didn't cross their friends' fields of fire, putting each trespasser down for good with carefully placed shots. If they weren't headshots, then they were shot through the heart. These men wouldn't be joining any more gold raids on innocent people.

"Virgil, you and Dennis help me while the ladies keep us covered with their pistols," Angus said. "You can both sit and watch from Betty's house. If you see anything move, shoot it."

"What if it's Will and Rusty?" Betty asked, worried.

"They'll know better than to walk into camp without making it known who they are," Angus said, narrowing his eyes. "Rusty's a professional, ma'am. Crow Indians won't be comin' around these days either, because they'll all be busy scalpin' trespassers."

"Dennis, you, Virgil, and me can dig these dirty dogs a shallow grave just outside camp," Angus said. "With the warm temperatures, we wanna get 'em underground before they start to stink. Then the scavengers can dig 'em up a little at a time for all I care. In two days or three days, I doubt there be much left. It's too dangerous to go out into the forest without a twenty-man escort, so we'll have to make do with what we can."

"Let's get this done before somebody else shows up," Dennis said. He cocked his head to listen carefully. Sunlight reflected off his gold tooth.

All three men had a shovel in hand as they scraped aside the melting snow. Then, they used picks to break the surface. Once they were eighteen inches down, the ground was frozen solid. The picks bounced off the hard surface like it was made of steel.

"I reckon we're gonna have to bury 'em shallower than I thought," Angus said. "It'll just make it easier for the critters to drag 'em away. A pack of coyotes should make short work of this bunch. At least the bodies will be out of sight."

They used mules to drag the dead outlaws to the carved-out indentation and then covered them with dirt and brown slush. They rode their horses over the freshly dug graves to cover the scent and pack down the earth, making it more challenging for the scavengers. Yet, they knew in the end, they would dig them up unless the dead men got buried six feet under. Even then, they usually piled rocks on top to discourage wild animals further.

Virgil was torn between the right thing to do and what he knew he had to do. Unfortunately, they weren't the same. Sure, these men had attacked them with every intention of killing them, so they had to take their lives to save their own. Still, Lovejoy usually felt it was his obligation to bury the men he killed regardless of their status with God. It had always been the right thing to do, and he followed that rule through his adult, free life. Even though he knew it was their only choice, he still suffered indignation for the dead.

"Do you think that's the last of 'em?" Virgil asked. His voice held a tone of desperation.

"I hope so," Angus replied, shrugging, "but I doubt it."

McFarlin noticed the pallor on Pine Needle's face as he squeezed his fists, feeling his blood come to a stop in his veins. Right then, his stomach fell off a cliff.

More pounding hooves thundered up the same trail as the last. Clouds of horsehair rose in the sky, along with tiny dust particles.

Betty's blood rose with a jolt of panic as soon as she saw the look on Angus's face. It was rare that he showed his fear.

Mrs. Forrester's eyes stretched wide as Angus said, "Oh, my God."

"Quick, inside the cabin, everybody!" Virgil yelled. He ushered the women in first, and then the other men followed.

The compound dwellers all rushed inside before the enemy came into sight. The timber door slammed, as did the heavy shutters, gun slats, and all. The banging door sounded foreboding, like a tomb. For the second time on the same day, they were about to be assaulted.

Five rifle barrels protruded from the front of the cabin. The people inside peered out the gun slats, wondering when they would strike. Then, suddenly, a string of riders came trotting into sight one by one.

"One, two, three, four, five," they each called out, identifying their targets before firing. The new arrivals opened the front gate and rode right in, and they were all brandishing weapons. This was not going to be a friendly visit.

Every bullet needed to count, so they guaranteed two people didn't fire on the same target. Extra loaded rifles stood beside them, and pistols covered the table. Gunshots rang out simultaneously, echoing across the valley, making it sound like a hundred guns. Five men dropped from their saddles, splashing into the mushy snow.

They got blown off their saddles and onto their backs. They sightlessly stared at the heavens as white clouds reflected in their dead eyes. The marksmen turned, dropping empty rifles and grabbing loaded guns. Five more shots immediately followed, and more men tumbled from their saddles.

With ten men down in seconds, the rest of the riders began to falter, and some of the horses started to squeal and groan as they side-stepped and bucked at the smell of fresh blood. Confusion washed over the intruders as five more gunshots rang out and more bodies splashed in the now-red mud. Blood splatter covered the ground.

Men wheeled their horses, looking for a way out as confusion fogged their minds. They couldn't see the gate and their escape from the death trap. Every time the people in the cabin fired, five more outlaws died. They were scattered across the yard like seashells on a deserted beach. Everything was stained red and gray. Before they managed to get their horses turned around in the right direction and relocate the exit, twenty men died as bullets fell on them like hailstones.

Now, the gold thieves saw this wasn't an easy target like the Irishman had told them. More than half their party lay dead in the bloody snow. The survivors wondered what happened to the first party sent against the supposed aging miners with few weapons. They had picked the wrong spot to try to steal some easy money.

It had been a turkey shoot when Enoch Mills had told them it would be a piece of cake.

The rest of them bolted for the valley, hoping to escape these mountains before dying like the others. The wilderness was much more dangerous than they ever imagined.

Angry Tribes

Crow, Blackfeet, Ute, Sioux, and Apache warriors watched as the long caravan of trespassers trudged along the trail toward their homes and families. Because of the White men invading their land, a very unusual thing happened. All the tribes who were everyday enemies came together to meet and discuss a plan to push the Easterners off their land. The gathering was in the largest Blackfoot camp in Yellowstone Valley. The chiefs of the tribes held council, and many of the medicine men and spiritual advisors joined. Never had there been such a powwow in the Rockies.

Hachta arrived with Wanata by his side. The war chief had impressed him with his recent actions and decisions and Hachta promoted him to the head war chief of the Crow stronghold. The Blackfeet hosts provided translators. It was indeed a rare occasion when lifelong enemies sat across the fire from each other with no weapons in their hands. But now they had a common enemy, which could be the end of them all, so they had no choice but to join together as one to defeat the new threat to their very existence. They planned to scatter the trespassers' bodies and souls to the wind. The next day, they would take many scalps. There were to be no captives, so there would be no one to tell the story of what happened. It was imperative the White men weren't informed, or there would be repercussions.

More and more warriors poured into what was formally an enemy camp. Chiefs came with escorts, but nobody showed aggression as agreed. Their word was what they most valued, and they weren't prepared to tarnish theirs, so nobody raised a violent hand against any member of the other tribes. They all knew if they didn't unify now, they would find the mountains populated with Easterners in a few years. Nobody was welcome to visit their land whether there was gold there or not, and this unwanted immigration of White men had to stop.

All weapons were left on buffalo skins outside. This included knives, arrows, and clubs—any weapon that could be used to inflict damage at close quarters. The trust in each other only ran so far. Their host made the rules, which was considered a wise decision by all. Some of the men sitting in on the council were young, and sometimes testosterone spiked during a ridged debate, and one of the new war chiefs might act out irresponsibly. Without the weapons, the chief stopped anything from happening before there was a chance. Then again, the Blackfoot chief had more enemies than any other leader in the lodge.

Their host, Running Rabbit, entered the dwelling where all the other tribes' chiefs, war chiefs, and medicine men awaited him. He was a menacing, tall, dark figure with a large, hooked nose. Several eagle feathers hung from braided pigtails. Several scalps were sewn into his buckskin sleeves and hung from his shoulders. His icy eyes held the other chiefs' briefly, one by one, before he began to speak.

"Bring me the pipe," Running Rabbit ordered. His face was an unreadable mask. Soon, clouds of smoke billowed around his head, and he passed it to his right. "Chief Hachta," he said, nodding, his mouth no more than a gash.

This was the first time these two adversaries sat so close to each other they could reach out and touch. Hachta sniffed the air so he could memorize the smell of his lifelong enemy. When they locked eyes while exchanging the peace pipe, electricity seemed to crackle in the air between them, and the room went silent, anxious to hear what came next. They all knew of the rivalry between Running Rabbit and Hachta. It was in many of the tribal songs.

But both chiefs knew that if they didn't show an example now, the meeting would immediately fall apart and could end in violence. All it would take was for one warrior, war chief, medicine man, or brave to break the rules because his life would instantly be taken, and that would be a bell that couldn't be unrung. The peace powwow would instantaneously end.

The Crow chief was just as serious. His Blackfoot counterpart had been his most hated enemy for decades, and now, to their surprise, White men had brought them together whether they liked it or not. Hachta put his lips to his enemy's pipe and tasted the bitterness. Smoke hazed his image as he used the moment to spy on the Ute, Sioux, and Apache heads of their tribes. Their minds became fuzzy with the robust smoke. There was a faint smell of something other than tobacco, but not enough to detect its origin.

The mood seemed to change as the pipe got refilled, time and again, until it had made its way around to every Native American present. What was at first a roar of loud voices softened to a rumble and then to a murmur. Eventually, the room went silent as all eyes turned to the Blackfoot Chief Running Rabbit. They waited to hear what he had for a plan. Of course, others also had ideas of their own. Some were riskier than others, but they all ended in the demise of the trespassers in the caravan, down to the last man.

Once the formalities were completed, Running Rabbit stood and paced back and forth before the assembled heads of the different tribes. He crossed his arms and rested his chin in his hand, deep in thought. He knew that negative minds would evaluate every word he uttered, so he had to be as diplomatic as possible but still try to sway all five tribes to his idea, which he believed to be the best approach.

Now, he considered who to join together as he eyed the four other leaders. Which tribes hated one another the most, and which ones had had friendly relations in the past? It was evident that all of them had battled with each other for years at some point. Yet, some tribes were currently signing loose peace treaties with others.

There were exceptions like the Crow and Apache. They had kept the peace with each other sometimes as well, even though they, too, had killed one another. There wasn't a leader there who was not guilty of the same crime. For them, it had been a way of life for as long as they could remember. It was a natural evolution for the tribes to try to take land that wasn't theirs as their populations grew.

In a roundabout way, they were guilty of the same crime they accused the White men of committing, only it was between other Native Americans. Still, tribes often pushed others off their land, forcing them to move to new country that could support a large camp's need for wild game, water, and shelter. At times, this meant that masses of people were dislodged from their homes and pushed hundreds of miles to land that wasn't currently claimed by another tribe. That or a place where the local Indians were friendly, of which there were few in the 1840s.

The Tonkawa Tribe was pushed all the way from Texas to the Oklahoma Territories by several tribes. Those included elders, women, and even children. Their customs offended even the feared Comanche ways. Shoshone warriors ate the hearts of their victims while in battle to capture the spirit of their enemies. But the Tonkawa took it a step further and ate the whole body along with the tribe. This custom offended a half dozen leaders, and they decided to act.

After being pushed off their land and sent packing hundreds of miles, they were nearly wiped out in an act of genocide. It appeared all men could commit the same disrespectful acts. Who was right usually depended on who was looking at the situation, but at this point, no one saw the big picture. This infighting that had lasted for ten thousand years could cost them all their land and livelihoods.

"The caravan is at the edge of the valley, but maybe a hundred Easterners have slipped through our fingers," Running Rabbit said, avoiding the Crow chief's stare.

They both knew he had let them through intentionally to test their neighbor's strength. "But there are at least five hundred more, so we must stop them before they can organize themselves, or we might not be able to weed them out in time. If we linger and take too long to act, the fur trappers' meeting will be dragged into the current situation. Then, we would compound our problems. We might scare the traders off, and then we will have to send men to Fort Boise, and it is a dangerous path for us all. There we will find more tribes who are enemies."

The Blackfoot chief stopped momentarily to ensure all the leaders were giving him their undivided attention. Two were talking, and his eyes shot daggers at them until they shut their mouths and didn't dare disrespect the meeting further by speaking out of turn. This meeting was as serious as it gets.

"Who knows how long our mutual peace arrangement will continue? The future is currently held in a delicate balance, and the change in the direction of the wind might be enough to provoke a war with the bluecoats. Then again, if we kill too many White men, the army will be sent by Washington and maybe wipe us out like they are trying to do to the tribes on the Great Plains," Running Rabbit continued. "This is a double-edged sword, and we must plan carefully. How could we eliminate all the trespassers in the caravan and not leave too many bodies? That is the question we must answer. If they think it is a massacre, the white war dogs will surely retaliate."

"We can always throw the bodies into the volcano," Chief Hachta said. "All of Yellowstone is one big volcano anyway. We can take the dead near the geysers and hot springs. There are crevices where steam escapes from the molten lava beneath. All we must do is slip the bodies through the cracks, and they will disappear forever. Then Washington won't have any evidence to prove they died in Yellowstone Valley. They could have perished anywhere along the way back to Fort Boise. The only thing we must make sure gets into the Indian gossip is that there is *no* gold here."

"Maybe we can find a way to turn them back, frightening them so much that they never want to return," Running Rabbit said. "I am convinced if we murder all the men trespassing, we will awaken the beast, and there will be swift and hard retaliation."

"I am not afraid of the White men and their army," the Apache chief growled. "I say we kill them all and scatter their remains to the wind so they can't enter their spirit world. It is said if a White man is not buried, he cannot go to his Christian Heaven. We can do this to make sure they suffer for eternity."

"I don't care how we do it," the Ute chief said, "as long as it is done now and not tomorrow or after another full moon. Delays will cost us lives, and our peace treaty will only hold water with our warriors for so long. I can see that they want blood, even with the truce. They were taught all their lives that we are enemies, so it is difficult to untrain such minds."

TRESPASSERS FATE

WARRIORS FROM FIVE DIFFERENT TRIBES FOLLOWED THE long caravan of fortune seekers. They could see the White men with mules loaded down with tools. Now, they were recognized for who they were—gold prospectors. The Indians saw them as the biggest fools in all creation. The tribes also felt that they proposed an intrusion of settlers. The sought-after yellow mineral had never been seen in the mountains or the valley, but if they did find gold, they would never leave on their own. The fever would consume them and turn them into slaves to their own desires.

If somebody did strike it rich, the army would come to protect the valuable minerals. If it weren't for the newspaper in Fort Boise, none of them would have ever come. Of course, all the tribes had at least one spy in the fort, if not a dozen, coming and going or living near the vicinity. Not so close as to be accused of being a traitor by their tribe, but far enough away to live by their decade-long customs without peering eyes or snoopy noses.

That and easily communicate with the messengers that constantly moved between the valley, mountains, and the fort to keep the Crow chief up to date with any changes or unusual actions or movements. Most White men's activity came from Fort Boise before heading for the valley if they didn't come from the East and faraway Kansas. Still, Boise represented the most significant danger for settlers because it was only a two-week ride from Yellowstone Valley.

For so many men to strike out after gold that wasn't there was beyond the Indians' understanding. They knew little of the White men's newspapers, but they all had contacts, whether they were Indians friendly with the Easterners in the fort or White men who were secret friends. None of them would ever imagine it was due to Mister Weston, the journalist—a man who started it all with a small fabrication—a single untruth—eventually to be seen as an out-and-out lie.

As simple as it seemed, when Perry printed his fabricated article, no one ever imagined the actual repercussions that would follow. They would be enormous in the end. He personally would be responsible for hundreds of deaths without even knowing it or probably not caring, either. Maybe somebody should look him up and tell him all about it. More than one warrior had that very thing on their mind, but at the moment, there were more important issues to address. Their enemy was so close they could smell their soap.

The Crow and Apache were on the north side of the already-worn trail, and the Blackfeet, Ute, and Sioux were on the southern side. The trail ran through a narrow valley with steep mountains left and right. Goats could be seen jumping from ledge to ledge with incredible balance. They seemed to perch on the side of the steep cliff like birds, never slipping. They seemed oblivious to the danger and the height.

The Indians hid in the shadows made by the sun and places hard to see with the human eye. Some warriors had honed their skills for decades and were impossible to spot if they didn't want to be seen. They shadow-shifted from one hard place to another like a distant hazy smoke. By now, the gold seekers had lost all their fear of the local hostiles and had forgotten all they had read about the Indians' torturing skills and to shoot themselves before getting captured. It appeared that now they feared nothing and were more confident than ever in their venture into the valley of death.

A few hundred men in three groups began to merge and become one. The confusion was such that nobody had their exact numbers clear. The guesstimate was four hundred, but nobody knew for sure. Especially over the days, some prospectors had snuck off into the night to find a claim on their own, running before the others, hoping it was their lucky day. Others had joined the main groups from other smaller ones. So, the numbers fluctuated constantly, making anyone trying to keep track give up in frustration.

The Easterners made so much racket and left so many scars on the land, a legless, blind man could follow their slug-like trail. Their numbers were impressive, but the details were not lost on the hostile Indians. Many of the rifles were brand new, and their tools were as well. These would be greenhorns tagging along with the wiser, more experienced miners, of whom there didn't appear to be many.

The vast majority were men unskilled in this environment, so their marksmanship would also be in question. It took years to become a dead shot, and none of these weapons had enough wear and tear to be even a fair shot, not to mention an expert. The men seemed uncomfortable with their rifles, with heavy, long octagon barrels cradled in their arms.

The Crow and Blackfoot chiefs locked eyes. Hachta had crossed the road far enough ahead that the prospectors hadn't seen him. He and the other chiefs all moved to one side and observed together with the other leaders of their tribes. With one hand, Running Rabbit curled his finger to come. Hachta gave him an angry look, but he neared him just the same. The Blackfoot chief harrumphed and curled a sly grin, then motioned toward the white men with his chin.

"I only see a dozen gold seekers with used tools and equipment," Running Rabbit said with a sly grin. "I've never seen such a large group of foolish men."

"The ones with guns that look like an extension of their arms will be the men to kill first," Hachta whispered. "It is surprising how few frontiersmen there appear to be. Foolish? I believe they are more than just irrational. As far as I have seen, they are all *stupid*. I have little tolerance for dumb people, especially if they are White."

"Trespassers are all the same to me," Running Rabbit said. "At times, even the Crow." He stared deeply into his enemy's eyes. Then he smiled, and it reached his eyes, turning into a grin. "But not today. Today, we will be friends. That way, the others will be more likely to trust one another once the shooting starts—maybe even refrain from killing each other. It would be easy to murder a secret enemy after the battle begins and chaos washes over us."

"I'll keep an eye on my men," the Ute chief said. "Sometimes they are like little children but with weapons and the desire to kill."

The Apache and Sioux leaders nodded in agreement. They hadn't spoken yet, but they obviously hadn't opposed anything said. Sometimes, the wiser men were those who waited and listened silently.

"So, everybody agrees; now is the time to attack?" Running Rabbit asked, raising his eyebrows.

Hachta curled an amused smile, then bunched up his lips and shrugged. Both chiefs turned their attention to the men on the trail below, and their eyes grew wide and angry as Running Rabbit sniffed the air and nodded. A terrifying war cry followed, bringing hundreds more cries from painted warriors, as the miners below stopped suddenly and stared wide-eyed at their very demise. They never imagined there could be so many Indians in the valley and mountains. What they saw before them seemed like countless terrifying men, who were all armed and racing toward them as fast as they could, and their intentions were obvious. With each long stride, they closed the distance.

Indians with painted faces in colorful clothing appeared in the hundreds all over the mountains on both sides like ants on an anthill. They all screamed as they ran as one toward the trespassers, brandishing weapons in their waving arms. Both behind them and before them, dozens more blocked the trespassers' trajectory forward on the trail and their retreat at their backs.

They had walked into a trap, and apparently, their

belief that traveling in numbers would ward off all dangers was unfounded. Bunching together in one group made them more accessible to annihilate and simpler to manage, making sure not a single intruder survived. Rather than spreading out to make them a more challenging target to hit, they bunched up, making it impossible to miss hitting flesh and bone with bullets and arrows. After a few minutes, the ball of humanity looked like a pin cushion.

Hundreds of White men struggled to unsling their rifles or pull their pistols quickly enough. What felt like a million bullets crisscrossed between the sides and the center of the trail. The odd Indian fell with a well-placed round, but the White men tumbled over like tenpins in a bowling contest. They died by the dozens with perplexed expressions on their ghost-like faces.

The Indian chiefs present also joined the battle as they all raced down the steep mountain and onto the narrow valley floor to engage the enemy. With his heart racing, Hachta hit the ground at a full run. Warriors yearned to fight their enemy hand-to-hand because they could better show their bravery, and every important chief or warrior was present that day. All their peers would see how brave they had been. Who would be the man to ride away with the honors today?

In the center of the mayhem stood twenty haggard-looking, middle-aged men in buckskins. Unlike the others, they wore little modern clothing, preferring that of the frontiersmen. These were obviously the only ones in the group with enough experience to try to defend their position. But their situation was impossible due to the location and crossfire from both sides of the mountain.

Still, they fought with that fading glimpse of *hope* dangling in their minds like most dying men. Until that very last split second before death, they waited for the miracle that would never come. Hope was the last thing they gave up before their lights went out.

Gunfire sounded like the Fourth of July, with fireworks coming from all directions. The gun smoke was so dense it was hard to see the enemy. The White men targeted anything that moved. Still, return fire continued as a few haggard prospectors tried to take as many of the enemy with them to their graves as they could. Now, there was no question that they would all die, and everyone knew it. The only question was at what cost?

Another war chief fell dead as he ran beside Hachta. A neat round hole appeared in the center of his forehead. Still, the Crow leader continued to run screaming, with his tomahawk in one hand and his knife in the other. In seconds, he clashed with the White men, with Running Rabbit screaming at his side. It sounded like a nightmare as blood splattered their faces and buckskins.

The dun of continuous gunfire dwindled to a scatter of shots as the last of the trespassers were finished off. Warriors waded through the dead, scalping each and every one. They would wear their hair on their clothing as a warning to others with the same intentions. It would also show their bravery in battle; today, there would be plenty of scalps.

As soon as the warriors left the battlefield, the vultures that circled a mile above a moment before soared down, pulling up at the last seconds, spreading their six-foot wings with a whoosh as their talons sunk deep into the already stiffening flesh. Long beaks sought the softer part of the body to start. In seconds, dozens of buzzards pulled at red meat as they flapped, sending feathers flying. Crows perched on tree limbs, cawing in protest. They would have to wait for the scraps. Coyotes began to appear on the outskirts of the battlefield. It had turned from a market for death to a feast for the scavengers.

When the massive war party returned to the Blackfoot stronghold, hooves hammered the ground like thunder as braves called out war cries, shaking blond scalps in their fists over their heads.

"Look around you, Running Rabbit," Hachta said, grinning like a possum. "Everybody here is exactly different."

Vanquishing All Enemies

Thunderclaps rang out loud as lightning lit up the sky like day. Firey bolts struck the ground across the distance, and hailstones as big as marbles began to tumble to Earth. Hundreds of Indian braves sat mounted on ponies. The chiefs raced across the front lines. Despite the angry weather, the men sat on their horses bravely and proudly. They had defeated the White men once again and pushed them off their land. They openly bragged that the Easterners would never return, but deep down inside, they all knew it wasn't true.

Sure, today, they were victorious, but they had primarily fought unprepared men. It wouldn't be the same if the trespassers were army bluecoat soldiers. Then, even with the massive numbers of Indian braves, they knew they might not win the day. But a battle won was a good step in the right direction for the moment. That is, if the news didn't get back to Fort Boise and the military. Then, the battle could become a double-edged knife that might come back to cut them in the end. The last thing they wanted was for the army to snoop around Yellowstone Valley and the mountains just above. There would undoubtedly be violence, and that would beget even more pain and suffering. Everybody living there was caught in a whirlwind and was waiting to see where they got spat out.

No matter how many trespassers the Indians turned back, there would always be more behind them to take their places. They were like termites, gradually feeding on their surroundings as they took possession of more and more wood. Still, the Indians chose to live in the present and bask in the glory of a victory, if not a war. Today was theirs to cherish because there may be no tomorrow. Such was the life of the men and women of the Indian Nations. If they lived for the future, they would have no dreams.

"Life was good to us this winter," Running Rabbit said, eyeing his counterpart. "I suppose now we must become enemies again."

Their faces were dyed black and red, and their fists clutched shafts of spears, bows, or guns. Luckily, none of the Indians were worrying about somebody confronting them. There were over four hundred warriors. Lucky for the mountain men, too. They had an agreement with the Crow and the Apache people but not the Ute, Sioux, or Blackfeet. If caught by them, they would just be more White trespassers.

"I don't see the advantage to return to the days of rivalry," Hachta said. "Haven't we fought long enough? We're growing wiser with age. Maybe it is time to make a secret peace treaty. Of course, if I tell my warriors Blackfeet are no longer their enemies, they will rebel, and I will have to kill those who challenge me. Such are the ways of a chief. We must be crafty and not offend your men or mine."

Running Rabbit looked at his adversary with suspicion. There would always be doubt for these two men, even if they did make a secret agreement. And who was to enforce it if nobody knew what it was? A frown crossed the Blackfoot leader's face, but he caught himself and instantly changed to a mask again, but it was too late because Hachta had already seen. Then and there, they both knew there would never be a peace treaty between the two. They realized they would be enemies for life.

Unseen on a mountain across the valley, Rusty Steel watched with his spyglass. Captain Forrester lay by his side with his looking glass, memorizing faces for future reference. You just never knew who you might bump into in the wilderness, and it was always better if you knew who they were before you said the wrong thing. The person he focused most on was the Blackfoot chief, Running Rabbit. He knew one day they may cross each other's paths. A smile crept onto Will's face as he considered the mental and physical challenge if he were ever to face this man. He looked like a battle-hardened warrior.

"It looks like the tribes cleaned up that mess," Rusty said. "It's a dog-gone shame that so many men had to die. I wonder what got into those fella's heads. Why in the world would they think there was gold here when we've never come across any, and I've spent a couple of years lookin'?"

"When men get bitten by gold fever, you just never know what they're gonna do," Marshal Walker said. "From my experience, prospectors are the most unpredictable men I've ever met. And the most distrustful, to boot. It seems to come with the job. I reckon they're always worryin' about somebody jumpin' their claim."

"I'd say there's currently a shortage of miners in the Fort Boise area," Captain Forrester said. "Still, one day, White men will come this far west, and that, my friend, will be the end of our paradise."

"We've got more work to do, so let's get movin'," Rusty said. "We've still got fresh tracks to follow, and I wanna make sure every one of these rascals is run down."

"Whatcha wanna do with 'em when we find 'em?" the marshal asked. "We can't just go around shootin' people just because they're trespassin' on somebody else's land. You can't protect something that you can't claim your own. How do you think that would work out in a court of law?"

Rusty looked around and asked, "Where is that courthouse you're talkin' about, anyway? There ain't no law out here but what we make, Joseph. You know that."

"Still, as a marshal, I can't let ya go around murderin' White people," the marshal said.

"I bet you wouldn't be threatenin' me if they were Indians that were to die and not White folks, would ya?" Rusty growled. "Don't go bringin' your Kansas law up here. We don't need it. We've gotten along all these years without a lawman, and I reckon we'll survive another decade without a constable. Like I said, we follow the code of the mountain man, and I would suggest you do the same while you're visitin' my house."

"You are the orneriest man I ever met," Marshal Walker said, shaking his head. "Don't make me arrest you, you old fool. If you push me to it, I'll do it, whether you like it or not."

"Old fool, ya say?!" Rusty roared. "It'll be the day when you can take me, Mister Bigshot Marshal. Up here, a fancy shiny badge don't mean squat."

"Both of you are the most cantankerous men I've ever met, White or Black." Virgil laughed. "If I thought you were serious, I'd almost be worried."

"Stop your bickering," the captain said. "If we don't get a move on, they're going to get away. We can decide what to do with them when we find them, but if we sit here all day, we won't find anybody."

Minutes later, Joseph emptied the coffee kettle onto the fire. It hissed and steam momentarily blurred their vision. The track was clear, and they rode at a lope, hoping to catch up with the man they were chasing by the end of the day. They pressed on with only a short stop for some stale biscuits and coffee, then mounted up again and continued the tiring pace. Finally, they saw a string of black smoke in the distance.

"Will these fools ever learn?" Rusty asked. "I can't believe there's another fire marking where they camped. They should just turn themselves in to the Indians and save us all the bother of runnin' all around the countryside."

"I've seen more stupid people this week than in a year of Sundays." Joseph chuckled. "Let me have a word with him before you kill 'em, please. Maybe we can figure out the which of why of all this mess."

When they crept up on the campsite, the prospector was asleep and appeared to be all alone. A rifle leaned against a stone well out of reach. Green wood smoldered and popped steam, ushering a string of black smoke towering into the windless sky. Rusty took point, and Dahteste drag.

Dog ran out onto the trail, barking at the stranger, waking him instantly. When he opened his eyes, he was looking down several black barrels. His adrenaline kicked up a notch, and they got his full attention.

Will was riding in a daze, fueled by dread. He knew even if they did kill the thieves invading their mountain, it wouldn't save Levi's life. He blinked questioningly at the trespasser. Rusty kicked a leg over his horn and slid to the ground. He walked over to the man under the blanket.

Suddenly, the prospector pulled a knife and crouched, ready to lunge.

"Dag-nabbit. I plumb forgot to bring my knife." Rusty cackled and looked down at his gun as his lips curled. Instantly, the man turned to run, but a quick bullet in his backside stopped his flight. "Remember, boys, if they've got a knife and you're unarmed, you run away, but if they have a gun, ya rush 'em. If ya don't, you could get shot in the butt like that fella."

Rusty waved his pistol barrel, indicating to the supposed prospector to drop his gun. When the stranger complied, Steel spat a yard of brown juice inches from his feet as he drilled him hard with his eyes.

"You do know you're trespassin' on other people's property without permission, don't cha?" Rusty asked. "If the Indians catch ya, they're gonna take your scalp. Now, tell us how all this mess got started. You do know there ain't no gold up here, don't cha?"

"Why, I know just the opposite, mister," the stranger replied. "You're the one that's mistaken."

"And how is it you know this?" Rusty asked. "Are you a clairvoyant or somethin'?"

"A clear-what?" the stranger asked as he held the flesh wound on his backside with his hand. He looked at his palm, and it was bloody. "What does that mean, old man?"

Rusty immediately took offense at being called old.

"If you don't tell me how you heard there was gold in Yellowstone Valley right now, I'm gonna put the next bullet between your eyes." When Rusty drew back the hammer, the sound seemed louder than it should have.

"I read it in the newspaper," the stranger replied. "It was printed across the headlines as bold as daylight. I can read and write, too. So, what is it to you, old man? What are you doin' up here, and why is it the Indians ain't taken your scalps?"

When Rusty raised the barrel of his pistol in the air to strike him in the head, the stranger saw the light and spilled his guts.

"There's a fella that rode with three other so-called prospectors," the stranger said. "Some folks say that they were claim jumpers. Now, this fella didn't come right out and say it, but he did tell me some wild-lookin' men in bear coats killed his three pards. He was watchin' in the distance, while tendin' to his personals, which is why he got away. I reckon that be you boys, if I ain't mistaken. I still wanna know what all this is to you, old man. You sure are a nosy sort, ain't cha?"

Again, he angered the mountain man to no end. "I'll show ya what it is to me." Rusty thumped him in the nose with the butt of his rifle. It was loud when the bone cracked, and blood poured down the man's face.

"What's your name, dumbass?" Joseph asked.

"My name's Bud Gunns. I come from Kansas," he replied with one hand holding his butt and the other trying to stifle the blood pouring from his nose.

"Do you see this badge?" Marshal Walker asked. "It says I'm Kansas law, so you best mind your manners if you know what's good for ya. Now, who is this fella? Does he have a name? You know, the fourth member of the gang of thieves."

"You mean Enoch Mills?" Bud asked.

"That's the man," Will replied. "What does he look like? And I want every detail, and you better start talking faster than you have so far because I'm entirely out of patience."

"Hell, ya can't miss 'em if ya see 'em," Bud said. "His face is as white as snow, and his hair as orange as a carrot. He talks with a heavy Irish accent, but you can tell he's well-schooled and all. I know because he used a bunch of fancy, long words I didn't understand. It wasn't two hours ago he left my camp. He stole most of my coffee. He was headed down the mountain. He told me he was goin' back to Fort Boise. It seemed like he'd had enough of the wilderness."

"Tie him on his horse, and we can bring him with us," Will said. "Come on, hurry up. You heard what he said. This Enoch Mills is just a couple of hours away, and he doesn't know the lay of the land like we do. So, let's catch him while we can."

Dahteste tied Bud Gunns to his horse, and they mounted and rode pell-mell down the mountain. In one hand, they had their reins, and the other, their guns. Enoch couldn't be far away, so after an hour, they bumped their mounts down from a long lope to a trot as they examined the land in the distance. If Enoch got wind they were chasing him, he would bushwhack them, for sure.

To their surprise, Enoch Mills was riding like he hadn't a worry in the world. They heard him whistling while he rode long before they got him in sight. Still, they approached with caution. So far, more of the prospectors they found had been outlaws than honest men looking for gold.

Rusty clucked his tongue, and all four rushed the man with hair that looked like a carrot peeking out from under his hat brim. Rusty charged him with his horse, crashing his chest into the side of Enoch's mount, throwing both to the ground.

Enoch jumped to his feet, his hands bunched up in fists, and growled, "Who in the hell do you think you are?"

The Irishman looked fighting mad. He got up, wiping slushy snow from his wool coat. The men noted the rifles in sheaths by his saddle and the brace of pistols in his belt. He didn't look much like a prospector to them. He didn't even have a mule or tools.

"Where's your gold panning equipment?" Captain Forrester asked. "What are you doing out here if you aren't panning for gold?"

"And what's it matter to you?" Enoch bravely retorted. "I was just minding my own business, and I would suggest you do the same. I'm a simple prospector looking for gold like every other lost soul out here in this God-forsaken land."

"Where did you hear there was gold?" Will asked. He had his hand wrapped around the pistol grip.

"That lie was provided by the devious journalist, Perry

Weston." Enoch smiled. "He printed it as a headline in his newspaper. It was all his fault all this happened anyway. You can be satisfied now, and rest assured that falsehood has been proven. He owns the *Les Boise* newspaper."

Dahteste remained silent. They nearly forgot she was there. Of course, she was interested in seeing the fourth member of the gang of thieves hang, but now she saw who was responsible for the trespassers in the first place. Possibly, there was more revenge to be had. She was determined to ensure that not one of the people responsible got away scot-free.

"I heard you were a member of a gang of four thieves," Rusty growled. "Just in case you were wonderin', we killed the other three. Now, do you know who we are? I was told you were watchin' from the bushes the whole time when your partners shot my friend."

"How could you know that?" Enoch retorted, shocked. *How would these ruffians know who I am?* he thought.

"Mister Gunns here has told us all about ya," Marshal Walker said. His horse side-stepped and Bud was suddenly sitting a few yards away. "He said you were one of the four, and for that, you're gonna hang."

When Enoch's eyes landed on Bud's, you could see the rage. They all saw the flash of the steel dagger as it tumbled through the air, embedding to the hilt into Bud's chest. He opened his mouth to protest, but it was full of blood, and it came gushing out, covering his chest. With his feet tied together, he slid under the horse's belly, hanging upside-down. When it moved, his head hit the ground, but he was already dead. The thin throwing knife pierced Gunns' heart. Only the handle showed, protruding from his chest.

Without hesitation, a half dozen guns went off simultaneously. Enoch jumped around like a dancing monkey as the lead slugs hit his body. In two seconds, they shot him eight times. His expressionless face was the last thing they saw before he toppled forward, face down. The fourth member of the gang who shot Levi was dead. Now, they had gotten the restitution they had sought.

"We had best bed down for the night, but not here," Rusty said. "We can ride down the trail a ways. It's gonna get mighty smelly here in about an hour or three."

They left the perforated body to lie where it fell. The coyotes would have a warm dinner that night. After another hour, they stopped, unsaddled the horses, and bedded down for the night.

"I'll take the first watch," Rusty said. "Joseph, you can take the second and Will, the third."

They didn't mention Dahteste; she believed it was just as well. She silently made her bed slip under the soft buffalo blankets and feigned sleep.

Les Boise Tabloid

When the Crow woman awoke late that night and saw Joseph dozing, she took the opportunity to silently grab her bedroll and horse and duck into the bushes, making them vanish instantly. All that was heard was a slight rustling sound, but nobody awoke. Marshal Walker would be angry when he realized he had let her slip off alone, not to mention Will Forrester, her husband's best friend.

Dahteste smiled when she thought of how Rusty would hack on the marshal for dozing off while on guard. Lucky for her, they were all tired from traveling hard, with many sleepless nights and worrying about Levi all the while. Everyone shared the same question in their minds: would he be alive when they returned?

If they could have, they would have stopped the Crow warrior, but this way, she avoided all resistance and more loss of time. Now, she could get right on to what she had planned without further delays or interruptions. They would have had to have hogtied her because she would have resisted. It was much better this way because it guaranteed no violence. This was something that Dahteste was going to do no matter what anybody said, even if it was against the orders of a White people's lawman.

All colors of races walked freely into and out of Fort Boise nearly the whole day long. Guards appeared only to close the gate at night or when something presented a threat. Among those frequenting the fort were the friendly local Indians. Dahteste hid her weapons in nearby bushes and walked toward the massive double doors that stood open. She had a skinning knife blade braided into one of her pigtails. She had been sharpening it for hours.

With the flick of her wrist, the honed steel would be in her hand. She walked her horse in and turned for the trading post and the saloon beside it. After tying her mustang, she sat on the porch and waited. She knew if she watched long enough, she would see Perry Weston if he hadn't fled, but somehow, she felt he was still there.

The Crow woman believed the description of the newspaperman would make him easy enough to recognize. Mr. Weston was said to have skin was as white as snow, and he wore a bowler hat and sported a pencil mustache, unlike the bearded, hairy men in Fort Boise. That and he was no taller than five feet three. Even those with mustaches had them drooping past their chins; some looked like wild boar hairbrushes that completely covered their lips.

Dahteste couldn't imagine mistaking such a person for somebody else, at least near the wilderness where the men were nearly as wild as the animals. Now, it was just a matter of time. If he were still staying there, as

Enoch Mills claimed, it would be nearly impossible to hide, especially if he wasn't expecting anybody.

Just like she swore, Levi's wife intended to get revenge on the man responsible for the invasion of Crow land in the Rocky Mountains and Yellowstone Valley by hordes of prospectors. Above all, she wanted restitution for Levi's possible death. She wasn't new to gunshot wounds and knew the severity of her husband's. She didn't know if he would survive, but she knew his chances were slim.

He was still breathing when she left, though, so there was still a sliver of hope. Dahteste was so nervous and angry that she couldn't sit by any longer and do nothing, so she set off to take her revenge. The others were going too slowly and had different goals than the Crow war chief. At this point, she had a single mission. She would leave the rest of the trespassers to the united Indian tribes and the mountain men. She had a personal grudge to settle.

Levi would live or die whether she was there or not. That was the sad truth of the matter. Dahteste had seen plenty of death in her young life. She had even dosed it out in conflicts. She wore black scalps on her belt to prove it was true. With the Crow people, these trophies showed how brave she was, and they honored her for it. Now, she intended to strike one more time and make right one last wrong.

Dahteste knew she had to do this herself or the moment would escape her, and she wouldn't get a second chance. With the treaty, she could freely trespass on land she would usually be forbidden to cross. She had ridden like she was being chased by a thousand Comanche, making record time, not having to worry about their lifelong enemies. She pushed her mustang into a long lope as she hung on for dear life.

Everybody knew there wasn't any gold in the valley or the mountains. If there were, the Indians would have been the first to use it to buy steel tools and weapons. Everybody in the Rocky Mountains knew it was a figment of someone's imagination, but in the end, the supposed discovery had dire effects just the same. It didn't matter if it was a lie or not. People got gold fever anyway, and everybody in their paths paid.

Dahteste had ridden for days, sleeping for two or three hours before racing off again. Only after several cups of coffee could she muster the energy to continue. Her bottom and thighs hurt from so many hours on her horse's back. She pushed her mustang like she was possessed by demons and her life depended on her quick arrival. Inside, she worried Perry Weston would catch the stagecoach and be gone before she could seek revenge. This thought made her press on even harder.

If she had to, she would board the next stage and continue the chase even if it took her to the end of the world as she knew it could. She would even chase him into a city where necessary, and all wilderness Indians feared large eastern cities. It was an environment with which they couldn't cope. Finding the person ultimately responsible for this horde who had descended on the mountain, causing injury to her husband, was an obsession for her now, and she didn't intend to let anything stop her. Somehow, she felt sooner or later, she would find him. Then, she would take revenge into her own hands.

Darkness enshrouded the outside of the fort. Inside, dozens of kerosene lanterns lit up the center with circles of light, leaving long shadows in the corners and challenging places to see. Only Dahteste's eyes showed in the dark as she blinked and her teeth when a smile crept across her face. She finally was just about to find her killer. Now was the time to exact revenge.

The Crow woman had debated how to kill Perry Weston during the entire ride from Yellowstone Valley. She wanted him to suffer, but she knew in the current situation, she couldn't linger, nor would she be able to get Weston's body out of the fort without being seen. Torture was out of the question, especially if he was still breathing.

She racked her brain for the appropriate punishment. Then, it dawned on her like a new day. He would suffer for the rest of what she hoped would be a short life. Dahteste knew she would have to be quiet, or she would do more than awaken the dogs—she would awaken the soldiers as well, and then she would be the one to suffer and maybe even die.

Now she knew how it would end—in curses, confusion, and blood. A wicked grin curled on the edge of her lips, and victory flashed off and on in her eyes. She couldn't see how it *couldn't* work out. The way she saw it, the only real risk was in the escape.

The wind blew across the courtyard, and the stars that twinkled overhead before now lay low on the western horizon.

PERRY STROLLED DOWN the center of the street, heading for the saloon. More buildings appeared outside the fort, but when there was trouble, everybody sheltered inside for protection. He wanted to whistle a new song today because he had the last one stuck in his mind, and it kept involuntarily coming back, driving him crazy. He started to hum "Red River Valley," finally slipping into a whistle, drowning out the last tune.

Weston strolled toward the courthouse and along the high adobe rampart wall. He passed the gaming house and the coffee stands. Men, women, and even Indians stood in line for a hot cup of java. He walked by the harness makers, traders, cobblers, and farriers. They all had small shops in the mud that covered the courtyard. Outside, snow remained a tinged white, but inside, due to the heavy traffic after the news of the gold strike, it was ankle-deep in brown sludge.

The journalist walked through the plaza overflowing with wagons and stock. He grumbled when he looked down and saw the state of his recently polished boots. Inside the fort walls were Americans and Mexicans, and with them, slaves to do their hard work. Weston pondered his next headline. It came to him like the hot kiss of a wet fist. He whispered, "The taste of human flesh. That could be my next hit."

The newspaper owner had heard about Shoshone Indians eating the still-warm hearts of their enemies. But what if he printed that there were Indian cannibals on the loose nearby, making feasts of White men as they devoured them whole? He couldn't think of anything more terrifying. His smile grew so wide you could see his wisdom teeth.

The chapel bell rang at dusk, forcing the bats to leave their daytime home. The mass of flying mammals circled the fort as one, then swarmed quickly out of sight. They were out for their nightly hunt to fill their bellies before they returned at dawn.

The smell of charcoal fires and fresh coffee floated on puffs of air. Boys and their dogs sat on shop stoops. Chickens and roosters perched on the bed sides, jockey decks, and tongues of two busted wagons beside the bare adobe wall. They flapped their wings and protested with an occasional *cocka-doodle-doo* from the males.

The fort was teeming with people due to the crafty journalist and his secret lies. Mountains of mining equipment were sold in the trading post. As soon as the surviving prospectors returned, they bartered their equipment and, in some cases, even their horses and mules to pay their bar bills. Even the Indians got in on the sales by bringing tools left on the killing fields. But for Weston, they all meant votes, whether they were rich or as poor as church mice. It was all the same to him.

One day soon, he would put his newspaper to use and play the coming politicians against each other like puppets on strings. He may get himself voted in as mayor. All he had to do was trash the competition in his tabloid. It was a newspaper that resembled yellow journalism in nineteenth-century Britain. He owned the only one in town, so he believed his future was all sewed up.

Did people die because of him? Perry didn't think so —at least in his opinion. If they were stupid enough to abandon their lives and run off to look for some fool's gold, it was fine with him. It was their fault and not his. Yes, from what he had heard and later printed, lots of people died.

Most perished at the hands of more local Indians than anybody ever suspected lived in the Rockies. It appeared the mountains and valley below were teeming with hostiles and a few crazy White mountain men, as well. At least, that was what was rumored.

Perry wondered what White men were doing up there with the Indians. Maybe there was another headline with the frontiersmen, too. He had heard a lot about buffalo hunters and trappers. He wondered which type of mountain men these were to live in such an inhospitable place surrounded by wild animals and hostiles. It just didn't make any sense to Perry. Still, his journalistic instinct told him there was a good story there. Maybe as good as the gold strike.

Perry took a stool near the bar and rested his arm on a large barrel that served as a table. A bottle of whiskey materialized as if by magic, along with a crystal glass, which the British must have left. The journalist watched the passersby as he sipped labeled liquor. The population in the fort grew to unbearable numbers and was overflowing with people. The tavern was full every night. The soldiers were turning back many strangers at the gates. Many sought a safe place to sleep but the fort was already at capacity.

The soldiers were on alert because of the sudden rise in population. Now, it was more challenging to keep the law even though they were in a US Army fort. They found themselves falling over sleeping or drunken bodies whenever they tried to do their drills. Enough was enough, especially since they believed some visitors were men who couldn't be trusted. Petty crime was on the rise, and it didn't look like it would slow down anytime soon.

Tents littered the area immediately around the fort. Smoke squirreled from a dozen campfires as the survivors dug in. They had lost all their money chasing a dream, and now they were stuck in Fort Boise without the fare for a stagecoach to get out.

Customers stood leaning elbows on the saloon bar with their thumbs hooked into their belts as they conversed. Perry shook his rueful head and muttered as he sipped his drink. He was worried about the next tabloid article. It had to be at least as sensational as the gold strike but in a different direction. Maybe something to do with the Indians who massacred the caravan of prospectors. That might work, too, but he needed bloody details, or it wouldn't capture his lectors.

A pretty, black-haired Indian woman's face filled his field of vision. He suddenly felt she was too close, but she smiled, so Perry didn't move. He took a breath, but her kind eyes were so convincing he didn't resist. She smelled of mint and sweat. He thought it almost erotic. Every soiled dove in the saloon knew Mister Weston from his many visits to the rooms on the second floor. He was their favorite customer.

The journalist felt warm liquid running down his leg as his face filled with embarrassment. When Perry looked at the floor, the growing puddle was red—the blood drained from his face. Dahteste had silently sliced open his pants and castrated him while he sat on the stool, dreaming of having sex with a beautiful Indian woman.

Dahteste smiled, thinking, *Perry Weston won't be having sex anymore.*

When Perry realized what had been done, he screamed a silent scream. He was so horrified his voice box froze. He rolled off the stool and whimpered on the floor, gasping for air. He flapped around like a beached fish.

Suddenly, all the men in the bar were gone. The soiled doves had vanished, too. An old man swept the floor of the saloon as Dahteste stood over the whimpering body and blood pooled under Perry. She held the knife in her right hand as dark claret dripped from her other fist. Weston held his hands between his legs and rocked back and forth, crying. As soon as the Crow woman slipped out the saloon's side door, the fowls roosting began to cackle and race across the yard, and the dogs started to bark. The noise echoed within the fort's walls.

So far, nobody seemed to notice except the man sweeping the bar, who appeared disinterested, as though it happened nearly every day. Dahteste slipped out the gates at first light with a mob of people. She quickly got lost in the crowd. As soon as the gates opened, they all rushed out, pushing one another. The Crow woman ran for the bushes, where she had hidden her weapons and horse and fled into the night. She would be home in ten days. Now, she would ride hard because she hoped to arrive before her husband, Levi Johnson, died. At least in time to say goodbye one last time.

The Funeral

As Levi lay on the cot, his face changed color like a rainbow. His pulse began to slow dramatically, and his breathing patterns became more erratic than ever. Red-tainted sweat pooled under his body as his fever soared. His eyeballs frantically shifted under his eyelids. Johnson could feel his body begin to 'let go' of life.

Even then, he could still hear Dahteste as she sang a death song in his honor, though the sound seemed to fade away. He heard Virgil mutter passages from his tattered Bible, and Betty quietly wept. They all seemed distant and wavered in the light like they might be an illusion. For a second, he wondered if he was already dead.

His wife still hadn't told anybody where she had disappeared to, and they knew better than to ask if Dahteste didn't tell them willingly. Betty had told her friend that Crow warriors had come to take her back to the stronghold. Lucky for her she wasn't there, or she would have had to go.

Beaver Johnson was clear-minded enough to know

he was passing from this world to the next. He prayed he had been a good man and would be accepted into Heaven despite his wrongs to wicked men. Some things couldn't be helped, and evil men had to die. Death was one of those things that was unavoidable as well, and now he was staring it in the face.

All in all, he'd had a lucky run until then, so he couldn't complain. Every man who lived full-time in the Rocky Mountains knew that his life hung on a thread and a change in the wind could make it break—life was that fragile.

Levi knew he was dead when the second bullet hit his chest. When he prepared for the impact, hope filled his mind and heart, wishing against all odds that the bullet would miss. But they had already seen the men were accurate shots. Maybe not as good as a mountain man, but proficient enough to kill Beaver from that distance. Had it been on the other side of his chest, his death would have been instant because the bullet would have pierced his heart.

Levi regretted not dying then and there. His wife and friends had to suffer his slow and painful struggle after fighting so hard to keep him alive. He had been lucky to have killed the last prospector standing, or that man might have shot his mentor, Rusty Steel. Or were they claim jumpers and thought that the frontiersmen had gold? When people got the fever, they did crazy things that they would never imagine doing normally. Then again, a large population of wicked men lived west of Missouri. Many of them had come in the caravan, too.

Johnson happily traded his life for the men who made him what he was. He cherished what he learned from Rusty Steel and Angus McFarlin. Despite knowing he was passing, he still felt that sliver of hope. He wondered if all dying people held on to that last second, praying for a miracle to save them. Was the word *hope* their last thought?

But save me from what? Levi thought. *I have nothing to regret.*

Johnson doubted that death could be any more difficult than life. Ever since he left the forests back home on the Ohio River, life had been hit and miss, with many friends and enemies alike dying along the way. The journey west had been long and arduous, but he wouldn't have missed it for anything in the world, even if it did end like this.

Levi thought he felt Virgil breathing close to his face as he massaged his chest. He wondered what he was doing. Johnson felt it when Virgil held his ear over his heart as it did flip-flops, threatening to stop. The bleeding had slowed to nothing, but the struggle to stay alive had been too much for even the likes of Beaver Johnson.

Lovejoy knew his friend was on the verge of a cardiac arrest, and he wasn't sure if there was anything he could do. He hoped that by massaging the muscle, he could coax it into keep thumping, but it spurted blood like a broken handpump. He counted the heartbeats of his patient, but they were hardly detectable now.

As the dying man's mind became silent and thought stopped, he sighed a final long breath. For those waiting, it seemed never-ending. Finally, a chattering sound came from the once massive man. The body lying on the table was skin and bones.

Virgil put his ear to his chest to listen for a heartbeat

one last time, but there was none. He wiped his cupped hand over Levi's blindly staring eyes and closed them. Then he put two coins on the lids to keep them from opening. A shudder racked Lovejoy's shoulders as a sob escaped his lips, but he immediately regained his composure, turned his eyes heavenward, and made one last departing prayer.

They carried the body outside and laid it on the porch table as they waited for Dennis to finish putting the final touches on the coffin. Rusty had spent the night engraving a piece of timber for a grave marker. It was evident the day before when the mountain men returned that Levi was in his final hours. The pallor of disappointment crawled into Dahteste's eyes. Rusty sniffled, shook his head, and frowned. Will, his best friend, appeared lost for words. His education didn't allow him to weep in public, so he stared into the distance blindly and tried to block out sound.

All the while, Dahteste's face was a mask. She already had her pony ready, and her saddlebags hung from its back. She would return to the Crow stronghold to live with her people as soon as the funeral ended. She couldn't stay there another day and not break down like Betty, who let her feelings be known freely.

Maybe Rusty and his friend, Will, felt the worst deep down inside. In a way, every one of them lost something with Levi's death. Some, small bits, like Marshal Walker, and others, vast voids, like Rusty Steel. Levi had been like a son to him.

Will and Rusty dug the hole. They wanted to do the task personally and with nobody watching. It was an emotional chore for them both. The ground eighteen inches down was still frozen solid from the winter just past. Chips of brown ice scattered like shrapnel. They took turns using the pick as the other scraped up the dirt with a snow shovel.

Usually, they would put a poor soul in the grain shed to weather the winter. But this time of year, things warmed up, and Levi was just too important in their lives to let him lie in the dark until the ground thawed. It was a struggle to dig that deeply, but they both did it with blind dedication. Johnson was Captain Forrester's best friend, and Rusty Steel was his mentor. Together, they had learned from the master to become mountain men.

"He was a fine frontiersman, wasn't he?" Will said and sighed deeply.

Rusty didn't dare talk for fear his emotions would show and his voice would break. He simply nodded.

Back at the main cabin, Levi lay on the table dressed in his best buckskins. He looked smaller than he did before, lying there dead. Virgil walked over to the body and laid his hand on Levi's cold arm, but he still wasn't stiff. Lovejoy frowned questioningly and looked over his shoulder at the roaring fire. They had kept it chocked full of wood for days to ensure Levi didn't get a chill, but it had been for nothing in the end. When the fever set in, they knew it would drive the last nail into his coffin.

Dennis had been working all night on a pine plank box to put his friend to rest. While alone, he cried until he didn't have a tear left. They ran down his cheeks like a river, and he couldn't seem to stop, but finally, his shoulders ceased to shudder, and he wiped his sawdust-covered face, streaked by tears.

Lazarus of Bethany

The loud gasp from the porch table surprised everybody. Betty was so shocked she fainted on the spot, dropping to the floor. Suddenly, Levi's eyes spread wide as two coins clattered against the wooden deck. His heart hammered in his chest a hundred miles an hour. Sweat popped up on his brow and glistened on his face. It was a miracle, but he was breathing again. Levi sucked in a bolstering breath and gobbled air. He bolted upright, staring blankly into space like he didn't know where he was.

He tried desperately to breathe but felt like he was filling his lungs with sand. The fog behind his eyes began to lift. Little by little, he could see the hope and excitement in everyone's eyes. He blinked, opening and closing his foggy eyes. The ringing in his ears was deafening. His head pounded distantly like an echo chamber.

Dahteste's eyes grew wide, and she couldn't stifle a smile. She finally relaxed her face, allowing the mask to drop away, and she opened the dam and let the tears flow, despite her pride. She felt empowered rather than embarrassed. His wife rushed to his side and gently lay him back down. More tears splashed onto his face as she hung her head over him, making her raven black hair serve as a curtain so they felt alone for a second.

"Diiawachisshik," Dahteste whispered in her husband's ear. She could see in his eyes that he loved her, too.

Of course, none of the mountain men had ever heard the medical term "the Lazarus effect" or autoresuscitation. Although rare, in heart attack cases, it can occur once in several million. On rare occasions in the past, the dead suddenly showed signs of life after as much as seventeen hours.

"Just like Lazarus of Bethany in the Bible," Virgil whispered. "I've never seen a real miracle before."

"I swear he looked as dead as a doornail." Angus smiled, then stared googly-eyed at Rusty. For the first time in all these years, he saw his old friend weeping openly; he, too, set his pride aside just this one time.

Captain Forrester grinned from ear to ear even though he got a bad case of the shakes. He unconsciously shook his head around like a broken doll. He certainly didn't understand what was happening, but it was all good. He thought he had lost his best friend, and it looked like they all had a second chance at life. He warned himself not to be so reckless in the future, and maybe they could age like Angus and Rusty, after all. Who said miracles didn't exist? He had just seen one with his very own eyes.

"I had a distant relative who had something similar happen to him. He, too, had a heart attack," Will whispered in shock. "Back home, my relatives are wealthy, and we have a family mausoleum. He was inside and already in the coffin when they heard him cry out just before my family left and locked the gate. You must be the luckiest man in the world, Levi Johnson." The captain's empty sleeve flapped in the wind like a flag of honor.

Dahteste couldn't resist after so many days and grabbed Levi's neck and kissed him on the lips. They were dry and cracked but warm like a living body and not cold like before. Blood was pumping life through his veins, slowly but surely.

"Careful now, girl," Virgil clucked. "We may have just witnessed a miracle, but Levi ain't out of the woods yet. But I've gotta admit, God must be lookin' down on us, all right." He looked up again and said, "I'll never doubt you again, Lord." He turned to his friends and said, "Let's get him back into the cabin and next to the fire. I doubt we'll be so lucky to have two miracles in one day."

Wood Duck

"Did I tell you boys who I was huntin' before I decided to take a sabbatical on my marshal's job back in Kansas and find the pass to the Pacific?" Joseph asked. "It's been so long ago I nearly forgot. Back then, it was said he was on the run westward. Hell, this scoundrel had the law from every state between here and Indiana after him. He is, without a doubt, the meanest man I've ever met. He even scared me, and I ain't all that easy to frighten. Then again, I doubt you've heard of him way up here in the mountains. Y'all have no idea what's goin' on in the rest of the world, and ya ain't even curious. You only see a newspaper a year, and that's at the Rendezvous, and it's already a month or two old."

"We didn't always live in the mountains, ya know," Angus retorted. "Rusty used to be a river captain, for Pete's sake. We've all got a past. Just because we're mountain men now don't mean we were born to it like Levi was."

"You're just probably repeating your stories like you've been doin' all winter," Rusty growled. "I've heard enough of your fibs and tales to last me three hundred years. But I must admit, at least you have the good manners to lie and exaggerate a little every time, so at least the fib sounds a little new. So, how did ya twist this same yarn into soundin' like somethin' else?"

"Why are you so dad-gummed ornery, Rusty?" Joseph spat. "Were you born that way, or did you intentionally make yourself like that? Hell, what would you know about Wood Duck anyway?"

Angus and Rusty exchanged glances, and both froze the instant they heard the name. It was like ice was injected into their veins. They turned questioning eyes toward the marshal. Their stares suddenly became frigidly cold.

McFarlin repeated the two words, but nothing came out. He tried again and said, "W...Wood Duck, did ya say?"

Rusty's eyes narrowed, and he frowned and said, "I haven't heard that man's name mentioned for ten or twelve years. I thought that outlaw was long dead and gone. I know him, all right—personally. We had our day and danced the dance, but neither of us won. Or maybe we were both winners because we walked away alive. Wood Duck, ya say? He's the devil walkin' the earth, is what *he* is."

"He was headin' this way, last I've heard, but he could be anywhere by now," Marshal Walker said. "That was at the beginnin' of summer last. He may have run north, from Kansas to Colorado, or south to Texas. I think those are the last places he ain't wanted. He has a bounty on his head everywhere else. Then again, nobody has bounties here. We don't even have the law."

Rusty sucked his quid, suddenly grumpy, and spat a

stream off the edge of the porch. Then he looked at the marshal so strangely that Joseph got hackles on his neck.

"Well, well, it appears you two do know what's happenin' in the rest of the world after all." Joseph chuckled. "He has a two-thousand-dollar bounty on his head. Could you imagine having that much money all in one neat pile? That must be somethin' all right."

"If I remember right, he don't ride alone," Rusty said. "At least back then, he didn't."

"Last I heard, he rides with the same eight men he's been with for ten or fifteen years," Marshal Walker said. "Everyone is from a different tribe, and even a White fella is in the mix. It must be the oddest outlaw gang I've ever seen. I heard that only a few folks saw him and lived to tell the tale."

"I knew Wood Duck's mother," Rusty said. "I never met his father, but he was gettin' on in years then. He was a Comanche warrior, and that's one tribe I don't like too much. I reckon they're both dead by now since the outlaw is the same age as me. If I remember right, his father was disgraced or banned from his Comanche home or somethin' like that. He built his gang from different tribes' outcasts and rebels. It's a motley lot, that bunch. If it's the same fellas, they're just about as dangerous as they get. He's much more than an outlaw. He enjoys torturing his captives and has a wild imagination. He must spend nights awake, thinkin' of ways to kill folks. Besides that, he's dead crazy. As soon as you look into his eyes, you can tell. He's lock, stock and barrel wacko, gone to the moon on loco weed."

"Personally, I'd rather not meet the man," Marshal Walker said. "He sounds more dangerous than taking two hundred wagons across the country to the Pacific Ocean."

"I knew it," Rusty spat. "You just added somethin' to the same danged thing you've been tellin' us all winter."

"Well, maybe the last part, but what I said about Wood Duck is true, mark my words," Marshal Walker replied. "He ain't somebody I'd mess around with."

"And why would a gang of thieves come up here where there is nothing to steal?" Will asked.

Levi laughed, then winced in pain. He sat at the edge of the table in the white rocker. He pushed himself back and forth as the plank floor groaned.

"That's a good question, Will," Levi said in a weak voice, then smiled. "When you throw logic at 'em, they're suddenly lost for words."

"Yeah, I reckon you're right," the marshal said. "But it would have made a fine conversation; you've gotta give me that. He's still the evilest man I ever heard of."

"And the wickedest," Rusty added. "Like I said, the devil walks the earth."

The Recovery

Levi Beaver Johnson began to see that the road to recovery would be long and arduous. There was no easy way to regain his lost weight and muscle. He smiled when he thought about all the wood he would have to chop that summer to get back into shape. And to think he was all but dead, declaration and all. He shook his head and sighed.

I feel mighty good to have survived, he thought. *I figured I was a goner for a minute or two. I could swear I saw bright lights—maybe angels.*

Later, when Rusty shyly showed Levi the grave he and Will had chiseled out of the frozen earth, it gave his apprentice an eerie feeling and hackles on his neck. Rusty seemed almost embarrassed that he had dug a grave for what he felt was like his son. The pine box Dennis made to bury him in still stood leaning against the outside of the cabin wall. It was a deadly reminder of what happened, making him pause and consider his past actions. Still, he did it to save Rusty, so it was what it was. He would do the same again today, were the threat to reappear, and he knew for a fact Rusty would do the same for him.

When Levi and Dahteste were alone at night, she whispered something in his ear. He felt a small leather pouch inside her palm when she offered her hand. She smiled when he took it but giggled at the puzzled look on his face.

"They are Perry Weston's walnuts," Dahteste whispered, smiling. "Is that correct, or is there another name in English?"

"I understand ya well enough, so walnuts will do. I don't wanna be teachin' ya dirty language," Levi said as he fingered what felt like two small marbles in the soft goat skin pouch. "Did he survive?" he asked, now a little worried. "Nobody in the fort saw ya, did they? He could call the law on ya if he's still alive."

"White men like him can't tell one Indian from another," Dahteste explained. "To him, we all look alike. I doubt he even suspected what tribe I'm from. Maybe I should wear a dress and hide in plain sight." She laughed.

Every day that passed, Levi got stronger. As soon as he could eat solids, Dahteste put him on a diet of elk steaks and some special broth a medicine man back in the Crow stronghold made for him. It smelled terrible and tasted worse, but it made him eat like a horse and numbed the pain.

His chest was going to hurt for a few months at least. The boys did a great job but were more like bulls in a glass shop than professional surgeons. Just the same, Virgil saved his life, even if he didn't have fancy letters after his name. Rusty and Will nearly pulled his ribcage apart. But he knew they were scared to death and had the best intentions.

As the afternoons warmed, they returned to the porch full-time. Since Levi got shot, they had breakfast, lunch, and dinner together. Only when the day was done did they each retire to their beds. With the help of canes, Levi managed to walk to the other end of the compound after a couple of weeks. He was on the road to recovery.

In the distance, the sun appeared to hang from a string as it slowly lowered to the horizon. As the orange globe touched the snow-white covered earth on the towering peaks, it cast long shadows on the land before it. Now, it began to disappear faster until a sliver of fire was all that was left. A prism of colors shot off into the sky, swallowed by cloud cover stretching from the eastern side of the world.

Levi sat in his rocker wrapped in soft buffalo blankets the following day. He rocked to and fro as he watched the others shoveling food into their mouths like there was no tomorrow. He made a tired smile when his wife Dahteste brought him a plate. He picked at the diced meat like a little bird. Sure, he had survived, and it had taken a miracle to do so. Now, it would be a complex recovery, but in a couple of months, they hoped he was back to his usual vital self.

"I'm going to sit here and make sure you eat every scrap on your plate, Snowflake," Dahteste said. "This picking at your steaks like a chicken won't do. You need to eat all you can to get your strength back, and I'm here to make sure you do it. I'm not going to lose you after all we've been through, and I don't want a skinny husband."

Levi smiled despite his cracked and bleeding lips. His eyes said everything, though. He wondered if any others suspected what Dahteste had done when she disappeared from the tracking party. They may suspect a dozen reasons, but they would never imagine the truth. He picked up the book from his lap with trembling hands. The cover was so worn that the words outside were no longer legible. It wasn't until he opened the binding that he could read the title. It said Snowflake and Mister Perry Weston signed it as a gift to his dear wife. Dark red stained the first pages.

This gift to Johnson proved his wife's undying love. She had taken revenge on the last man living implicated in her husband's near murder. Still, just because Perry was laid up or dead didn't mean the paper wouldn't continue to publish trash. But, then again, it was a tabloid, after all. They should not expect any less.

None of their friends knew why she picked such a strange endearment for such a big man, but they all believed it had some secret meaning. When Levi and his wife were out of hearing distance, they wagered on what provoked her to give such a rugged frontiersman a moniker so sweet and innocent. Nobody had a clue why, at the moment, but they continued to guess just the same.

Levi was recuperating as quickly as could be expected—especially for a dead man. At first, everybody babied him like an injured child, but Johnson soon stopped that. He didn't want any preferred treatment and refused to slow down the rhythm of his friends. He didn't want them to waste any more time looking after him. He was tired of all the fuss and pampering, if the truth be known. He wanted to face his recovery square in the face and go at it like a rabid dog. He promised himself to make the speediest rehabilitation ever.

"Ain't cha ever seen a man shot before?" Levi growled. "Stop pawin' on me like I was dyin'. I just want y'all to go back to treatin' me normal. I can take care of myself now. I've got two feet, and I can walk on my own."

Rusty sat and watched his apprentice as the edges of his lips curled. His eyes danced with delight to see Beaver was alive and maybe not kicking yet, but he was young and strong, so he didn't doubt he would beat all records in recovery, just like he beat every other record in the mountains and plains below.

Birds chirped in the trees, and a family of raccoons trundled across the back of the compound yard. A doe peered over the split-rail corral fence, blinking at a mule. The first hint of spring was fresh in the air, and the temperatures rose daily. Rain came and went with regularity, making things grow and turn lush and green.

Betty sat beside the captain and rubbed her fingers over his scarred hand. Today was warmer, and he let his empty, unpinned sleeve flap in the wind. Betty curled his hair with her finger and whispered something into Will's ear. They used fresh-baked cornbread to wipe the plates clean. Angus passed whiskey-spiked coffee all around. Steam disappeared inches from the cups.

Rusty Steel kicked the marshal's chair and asked, "Do you feel anything when you shoot bad people like these?"

"Of course, I feel somethin'. I'm only human," Marshal Walker replied. "I feel the recoil."

A Look at Book Nine:
Wood Duck: A Western Double

In a land where justice fades, blood fills the void.

Wood Duck

A ruthless killer is tearing a bloody path through the Rockies—and his name is whispered with fear from Fort Boise to Yellowstone. Half-Comanche, half outcast, Wood Duck hates every race equally, leaving slaughter and ruin wherever he rides. When the bodies start piling up, Marshal Walker and Captain Will Forrester take the fight to him.

Levi Johnson joins his friend, despite Dahteste's pleas to stay behind. Some battles can't be avoided—and some enemies aren't just dangerous, they're evil.

The Last Rendezvous

The fur trade is dying. Once-packed Rendezvous grounds now sit nearly empty, and the market for beaver has dried up. Levi, Rusty Steel, and their friends face a hard truth: trapping days are over. The only way forward is buffalo—but hunting them may pit the mountain men against the tribes they've long called neighbors.

On the ride to Fort Boise, old tensions catch fire. Dahteste is recognized by a bitter enemy and falsely imprisoned. Her hanging is set for noon. With time running out, Levi and the others must risk everything to save the woman who once saved them.

AVAILABLE MARCH 2026

ABOUT THE AUTHOR

Ash Lingam was born and raised in Southern Ohio, not far from the mighty Ohio River. He had somewhat of an isolated upbringing on a family farm with his sisters. His best friends were his horse, Sugar, and his grandfather.

Born in 1886, the family patriarch grew crops, raised cattle, and doted on the young boy. At his grandfather's side, Ash learned about livestock and firearms at an early age. His grandad carried an old Colt with him at all times. It helped spawn a young boy's dreams of yesteryear.

Ash was only eight years old when his grandad taught him how to trap muskrats to prevent them from draining the farm's ponds. He gave him a double-barreled shotgun at twelve and taught him how to hunt to put food on the table.

It wasn't long before Ash was breaking horses. His spirited Tennessee Walker never allowed any other rider on her back. Together, they searched through the plowed fields in the spring, looking for Miami Indian arrowheads to add to his grandfather's ample collection.

Ash's family was among the early settlers in pre-

Revolutionary America. He has traced his lineage back to around 1746 when his ancestors immigrated from Europe to the aspiring American Colonies.

A retired marketing executive, Ash devotes his spare time to training police dogs and writing novels. He has found his niche in the Western, historical fiction, and adventure genres. With his vast vault of experience, he never runs out of sources for new stories. He has lived in eleven different countries and worked in a total of forty-six to date, Ash has written approximately 130 novels, short stories, and poems. More than one hundred of his eclectic titles help the American frontier come alive for his readers.

https://www.ashlingam.com/

Join the Lawless Waters Western Readers & Writers Facebook Group

www.ingramcontent.com/pod-product-compliance
Lightning Source LLC
LaVergne TN
LVHW040216110826
845146LV00005B/1305

* 9 7 9 8 8 9 5 6 7 5 7 1 7 *